MURDER AT THE MINYAN

SHULAMIT E. KUSTANOWITZ

ISBN 0-7414-3382-6

Published by:

INFIN∞ITY
PUBLISHING.COM

1094 New DeHaven Street, Suite 100
West Conshohocken, PA 19428-2713
Info@buybooksontheweb.com
www.buybooksontheweb.com
Toll-free (877) BUY BOOK
Local Phone (610) 941-9999
Fax (610) 941-9959

Printed in the United States of America

Printed on Recycled Paper

Published November 2006

Dedication

To my parents, Deborah W. and Rabbi Benjamin H. Englander,
whose devotion to a Conservative pulpit made their home
such an interesting one to grow up in,
and
To my husband Al, who wasn't afraid to meet me
on the common ground between
the Orthodox and the Conservative worlds.

Acknowledgments

I am deeply grateful to my husband, Al, for keeping me motivated and on track. I also want to thank Rabbi Gary Listokin, who read an early version of this book and offered many valuable comments.

The best help came from my children: Esther, an experienced editor and a published author; Jack, a careful reader with profound Jewish insights, and Simmy, a professional writer and actor. My daughters-in-law Penina and Ilana were very enthusiastic in their support, too. They all have been a great source of encouragement for this project, and I am very grateful.

And to my readers, I offer a Glossary and thanks.

MURDER AT THE MINYAN

A Novel

SHULAMIT E. KUSTANOWITZ
www.MurderAtTheMinyan.com

Prologue

By nine, even the mourners had left. Avi stayed because he had an appointment.

"My family will be here soon, Rabbi London," Bill Fernberg said to him. "If you don't mind waiting, I'd like to face these decisions together with them."

"That would be fine," Avi replied with a smile. He wasn't yet finished putting away the religious accessories that he used at the morning service, so he didn't mind the wait. If the family was late, the meeting could probably be condensed to under an hour anyway. And even if they weren't finished, he could always depend on his wife, who was one of the Hebrew School teachers, to supervise the children's ten o'clock Sunday morning arrival.

He zipped closed the two velvet bags in which he stored his gear for daily morning prayers and stashed them in the desk drawer in his office. He checked his phone and computer for messages, but his mind was still on the strange behavior he had observed that morning.

Morty Fenn had been unusually sociable at the minyan and, if Avi overheard correctly, he was asking Bill his opinion on women's roles in the synagogue. The rabbi was astonished at Morty's recent interest in coming to the daily service at all, and it was a further surprise that this subject in particular interested him.

Dennis Shine, on the other hand, nearly always voiced strong opinions, but this morning was strangely pensive. His wife Reeva was doing better, so that was probably not what was on the man's mind. Perhaps he was thinking about his mother's sudden decline. Or maybe his mood had something to do with the argument the night before in the parking lot. Avi had heard both Dennis and Phil Schwartz shout the word "wrong" but did not know what had ticked the two mourners off. The rabbi decided he should speak to both men that day and not let a sore spot fester.

Now, however, would not be the right time. The last few men were leaving the Shul, and Avi had to wait for the Fernbergs.

The rabbi checked with custodian Joe Kripski to make sure everything was ready in the kitchen for that evening's Sisterhood Chanukah party. He also asked Joe to set out donuts for the children who would arrive soon for Hebrew School. In two weeks, the children would be off for their December vacation, so the classes during Chanukah had to provide an anchor for their Jewish identity that could withstand the undercurrents of the Yule tide. Donuts would help.

"Okay," said the always cooperative, but never talkative, synagogue employee. Avi learned a long time ago that Joe always did what he was asked to do, but volunteered nothing about what he was thinking.

Joe returned to his chore of taking out the garbage and Avi walked back toward his office. He found Bill there waiting for him.

Rabbi London had just begun explaining to Bill the agenda for this family meeting when a gunshot stopped him in mid sentence.

The two men ran to the back door and stopped short when they got to the parking lot. Avi took a few more steps, and then held his breath as he surveyed the scene.

Joe was standing at the trash bin, acting as if nothing were wrong.

Bill's wife stood next to her SUV, parked in the space next to her husband's car. She and their kids appeared to be all right, but they were frozen in mid movement as they were getting out of their vehicle. They stared in the direction of another car, but did not seem to know the woman and teenagers standing next to it.

Avi looked toward the part of the lot nearest the building, next to the parking space he usually used, and saw other people he knew at their cars. From inside one luxury automobile, eyes facing mortality stared lifelessly through the windshield. The murderer's target dripped, soaking the asphalt with blood.

Then Rabbi London saw the gun on the ground.

How could this be? the horrified rabbi wondered. *Just a few minutes ago, I shared lofty prayers with these people. Now we are lost in a haze of violence and death.*

How could this have happened? He could not even have imagined such a scene a few minutes earlier.

But maybe he should have seen it coming, his conscience accused him. There might have been signs a long time ago that he ignored. At the very least, he should have detected something was wrong in October, when the deaths began.

But he didn't.

Chapter 1

Making the Minyan

Avi sat alone where he always did, on the right end of the third row of seats, as the group waited to begin the weekday evening service. There was almost always a minyan, but sometimes they had to wait a while to begin davening until a tenth man showed up.

Getting the minimum would be easier if the congregation's officers came, he thought. But as devoted as they were to philanthropic projects in general and fundraising for the congregation in particular, the president and Board members could not be persuaded to participate in most religious activities. Avi, on the other hand, as an observant Jew and the spiritual leader of the synagogue, was usually there and on time.

"Good evening, Rabbi London," each arriving man said to him before heading to a seat. Even the mourners with conflicted emotions were polite.

Congregation Tefillah drew a respectable crowd on Shabbat and holidays but struggled to get the minimum for daily services. As a Conservative synagogue, though, it was committed to trying, and October's pleasant weather – with the warm High Holiday season over and winter's cold not yet a hardship – should have meant it would be easier for members to come.

The daily daveners met in the downstairs room, where small high windows barely cleared the outside ground level at the front of the sloping property. On the eastern wall of that utilitarian gray, all-purpose room, a plain wood closet with a small light above it held a single Torah scroll.

The worshippers' metal chairs all faced toward the Torah and Jerusalem, as was the custom. The tinny feet of the folding seats scraped the commercial tile floors every time a man arrived and took his place, and the chairs never stayed in the perfect rows they were placed in.

The nicer prayer hall with permanent seats was upstairs and had seen heavy use during the fall festivals, but that main sanctuary was reserved for weekend and holiday services or for special occasions, not for the daily minyan.

Relieved to be finished leading all the fall holiday worship was Cantor Neal Goldberg, a part-time insurance representative and the Shul's chazzan. He was ready to lead these services, too, but was always glad to relinquish his regular duty to any layman who wanted the honor.

The cantor sat at the left end of the front row with his ten-year-old son by his side. Eitan was impressed by the knowledge his father had of both the liturgy and the melodies that the others found a struggle. The tall, slim, handsome father smiled. Neal appreciated the adoring looks he got from his son and hoped the boy's voice, too, would mature into that of a chazzan, with the control, range and mellifluous tones that daveners found so inspiring.

Phil and Matt Schwartz, however, were not inspired by any of it. The two middle-aged brothers chose the back row instead of the front, where their father Mendy always sat. Colon cancer had claimed him in his old age, and now the sons were at the minyan as mourners to say Kaddish. They hadn't taken on the obligation for their mother when she died three years earlier, and Mendy had been distraught about it, so the sons promised to do their duty when his time came. Accordingly, there they were, present but still reluctant to be seen observing any Jewish customs at all. To ensure that very few people would know about their participation, they chose to attend weekday evenings, when the service was short and the crowd was small.

As mourners, it was Phil's or Matt's right to lead the service, but they always refused the honor. They couldn't do it even if they wanted to. Neither of them knew how.

In front of Avi sat four of the five men who did know how and could always be counted on as minyan regulars and to lead the service. They were retired, and some of them remembered the European "old country" that determined their accents. They might not understand everything in the Hebrew and Aramaic prayers they recited, but they knew all the words because they had davened every day since they were young boys. They were at this minyan simply because they always came. It was habit, a cornerstone of their lifestyle, and they looked forward to the chance to share a Yiddish joke with each other in Shul, their synagogue.

The fifth of the regulars stood at the lectern in front of the room, facing the Torah and waiting. In the absence of a mourner who wanted it, Mr. Day usually claimed the privilege of leading the fifteen-minute Maariv evening service, and he was impatient to begin. His slight frame draped over the lectern, which he called a "shtender" in his native Yiddish, and he waited. He pushed his gray fedora back on his head and rested his glasses on the large-print prayer book before him. An arthritic finger tapped the open page, and he waited some more.

Although he was a long-time regular at the minyan, no one knew Mr. Day's first name or how old the ancient-looking man really was. Well, his wife – whom he had married while they were still in pre-World War II Poland – probably remembered. His children – who were born in New York after the war – didn't know if their father even had a first name, aside from the Hebrew one that identified him for a religious honor. Nor did anyone know his real last name or who else might have shared it with him but was lost in the Holocaust. Even his friends didn't know what he did in the war, whether he hid from the Nazis, cooperated with them or killed them. He preferred it that way. He seemed to gain comfort from putting the past behind him.

At exactly eight o'clock, Mr. Day heard the back door open. He straightened up, put on his glasses and leaned on the shtender with both hands. He knew to the second how long it would take for Bill Fernberg to take off his coat, and before the garment hit the chair, the old man called out the opening phrase to the Maariv service, "Vhu rachum yichaper avon vlo yashchis."

As the rest of the men stood and responded, the rabbi's thoughts went to Phil and Matt.

That initial call has got to sound like a mouthful to anyone who doesn't know Hebrew well, Avi reflected. He glanced back at the two mourners. As their father's rabbi, Avi had officiated at Mendy's funeral two weeks before, and he knew how unfamiliar all this was to the two sons. A few pre-Bar Mitzvah years in an afternoon Hebrew school, followed by a hostile adolescence and a few college years filled with contempt for all religion, certainly was not going to prepare them to be comfortable as adults with Jewish ritual or routine.

At the cemetery, Rabbi London had vocalized the words of the Kaddish with the two men so they could say it there. Avi reminded them that the mourner's prayer was a public proclamation of faith rather than a tribute to the dead or a consolation to the mourners, but they were concerned only with the mechanics of getting it said. Luckily, they remembered from their youth how to enunciate the holy language's sounds, so Avi transliterated the Hebrew and Aramaic for them, using "ch" for the same guttural sound that starts the word Chanukah. No, pronouncing unfamiliar words was not the worst of their religious problems.

Worse was their disdain for organized religion in general. For both Phil, a businessman, and Matt, a teacher, healthy skepticism meant a total intellectual turnoff to anything they saw as antiquated custom. That went double for all things Jewish and certainly made the rabbi suspect. They made it clear to their clergyman that they would come to the minyan only to discharge a deathbed promise. Rabbi London had to admit it was doubtful their Kaddish commitment would last even the customary eleven months.

Avi turned his attention to Maariv. He opened his prayer book, bowed at the waist, and read the words of awe at the orbiting of heavenly bodies that determined the earth's days. He covered his eyes as he pronounced the core statement of Jewish monotheism, "Shma Yisrael," "Hear, O Israel, the Lord our God the Lord is One." He stood as he recited the eighteen blessings of the silent devotion and again when the congregation said Aleinu, acceptance of the yoke of faith.

In response to that proclamation of acceptance, mourners stood to say their Kaddish. "Yitgadal v'yitkadash ...," "Magnified and sanctified be God's great name," they began, reciting the public proclamation of faith in its traditional phrases. When the service was over, Rabbi London turned around to put on his trench coat and saw that the Schwartz brothers were already gone and that Bill was halfway out the door.

Mr. Day, having discharged his duties, was right behind them. He was quickly followed by others of his generation who, having fulfilled their responsibilities, were in a rush to get home for an evening of prerecorded programs on their televisions. The cantor and his son left next, but waited for the rabbi outside. Joe Kripski had already finished his custodial duties and had left for the day, so on Avi's way out the door, the rabbi locked up. There was only one door to be concerned about, anyway. The front remained bolted all week, and anyone wanting to enter the building during that time knew to come in the back door from the parking lot.

The Goldbergs waited for Avi near the vacant parking spaces. They lived just a block farther from the Shul than the Londons and, like Avi, had walked over, so they expected to escort the rabbi home after the minyan. But the big playoff game had already started, and the baseball coverage was drawing both Neal and Eitan to their TV. Avi recognized that their legs were longer and their calling more urgent, so he suggested they go on ahead.

As the chazzan and his son said "good night" and marched off, Avi looked around at the deserted lot. Tucked in behind the building, it was surrounded by a tall picket fence and shaded by oak, maple and pine trees, and no one passing in a car could see what might be going on there, even in the daytime. Of course, it wasn't likely that a stranger to the town would be walking or driving by: The immediate area was a few blocks away from a through street, so traffic was very light and primarily local. Even so, Rabbi London had asked the East Belleridge police to check the building on their rounds and they promised they would, but the officers assured him that crime in this town was rare. This was suburbia, after all.

So he felt safe. Avi buttoned up his light coat and strolled, alone, through the falling leaves, the one long, level block to his house. The peaceful side street was well-lit and lined with trees, and the cool weather was pleasant. He didn't mind the refreshing walk at all.

He rounded the curve and saw his house on the far corner. The white colonial was on a slight rise, which made a hill of the driveway and required a flight of steps between the sidewalk and the front door. Avi decided to take advantage of the arrangement by walking home from the synagogue, starting to run when he could cross the avenue and bounding up the steps. He considered the total effort his exercise for the day.

"How was Maariv, Avi?" asked Emma as he opened the door. She was in the next room at the kitchen table, writing lesson plans for the opening session of the Hebrew School.

"It was fine. We didn't have to wait too long until we had a minyan," he called back to her as he closed the door.

"Maybe if you would count women, you would reach ten quicker," his wife's voice wafted from the kitchen, with an I-told-you-so lilt.

Avi knew this was a favorite subject of his wife's, but he told her the quick truth. "Emma, even if we counted women, we would have had to wait. There were no ladies there." Sometimes women came to the service, but not often. Furthermore, other Conservative congregations that did count women to the minyan did not report having any easier a time getting the minimum of ten daveners for a service. He was glad this synagogue chose the traditional rule of counting only men, but, knowing his wife had mixed feelings on the subject, he chose not to prolong the discussion.

"Where are the kids?" he asked as he went into the kitchen, as much to change the subject as to know the answer.

"Ahuva is upstairs on my computer Googling for research on a paper she has to write about the American Revolution, and Josh is watching the game on TV," she said.

He paused. This was an opportunity to confer with his wife on a subject that he had been avoiding. Well, better get on with it. He walked over to the dinette alcove to face his wife.

"I can't go to Kevin's Bar Mitzvah party," he said. Kevin was Emma's cousin's son, and the event was less than three weeks away. Josh and Ahuva were not invited, so the commitment had presented Emma with a chance to plan a rare entire day with just her husband. Moreover, she wasn't often able to share occasions with her extended family because her husband's rabbinical duties kept them so busy. This time, she was determined to go, and she was sure Avi had already cleared his calendar for the event.

"Don't tell me that you're choosing the Shul over me again," she pouted. This would be the latest in a long list of instances where last-minute Shul business took precedence. There was the family vacation that began with a U-turn home when a message, waiting at their destination, said a prominent member had died. Avi had missed the graduation ceremony at which Emma got her math teaching certification because a member's wife suddenly took sick. He had skipped an endless number of their children's birthday parties and forfeited several theater tickets because of one congregational emergency or another. She was tired of it and tried to stand her ground, but she knew she would eventually lose to his sense of duty.

"Sol and Sylvia Cohen's daughter Sophie wants to get married that day because it's the only time in the next few weeks that she and her fiancé can both find room on their calendars," Avi explained. "She's forty-seven and it's her second marriage, so they want it quick, small and soon. They don't want the ceremony at the Shul at all and don't even like the idea of having it at my office there, but they did like the image of getting married in our house. I had no choice but to say OK."

He looked at his disappointed wife.

"Ahuva and Josh can help me set it up that day," he continued, "and we already arranged for a substitute teacher for your Hebrew School class, so you can go to the Bar Mitzvah without worrying about your students or our kids or the details of this wedding." He hoped the proposed solutions and long explanations would soften her displeasure.

Emma considered her forty-eight-year-old balding but still-slim life partner. Avi's hair had been full and dark when they first met at his New York rabbinical school and then married. It was thinner but still dark when he introduced himself to the neonatal intensive care nurses as a clergyman and, because of his credentials, got to hold their newborn Josh before anyone else in the family could. By the time Ahuva arrived, Avi's hair had just enough gray to make him look distinguished. He was always a doting father and a devoted husband, but Avi also made room on his calendar every time a remote family member needed a rabbi for a wedding, funeral, unveiling or counseling. And he either traveled the distance to meet with them personally or spoke to them at length on the phone. A very loving family man as well as a distinguished professional, Avi was an unusual man – both a source of strength and a scholar. How lucky she was, she concluded, that he was hers.

Emma reluctantly accepted the compromise. She would miss the hours she might have had alone with her husband, but at least she would get to visit with relatives she had not seen in a long time.

"Can we have a date soon, just the two of us?" she asked.

Avi grinned and looked at his forty-six-year-old bride of nineteen years. She had just a touch of gray in her wavy brown hair and a couple of extra pounds around her waist. By the way his wife gave him a coy smile, Avi knew she would be okay despite the disappointing news. Emma was great that way, very supportive of his commitments to his profession. She shared his values and faced every chore with a noble attitude. Her students loved her, whether she taught them math during the school day or Jewish subjects in extended hours. She brought out the best in her own children, and in their father, as well, he thought to himself. Well-educated and intellectual, she provided a wonderful sounding board for his ideas. What a gem. How lucky he was, he concluded, that she was his.

"Ahuva knows where the chuppah and poles are, and Josh can be a witness, if he's needed," Emma said, showing that she was trying to be a team player. "It might actually be a memorable experience. After all, how many teenagers get to run a wedding?"

And so it was settled. Emma would go to the family gathering without him.

Once again, she resented the intrusions Avi's profession made on their private life, but once again, she did her part, and this evening her role included giving him a telephone message. "Dennis Shine called," she told her husband as she returned to her paperwork. "He said he would stop by this evening to talk about his wife."

The call itself was not unusual, Avi thought, but consultations with Dennis about his wife were becoming more frequent. And when the president of the congregation – and one of its main financial supporters – wanted to talk, the rabbi had to listen.

The doorbell rang. Avi smiled knowingly at his wife, tossed his coat (which he hadn't had time to hang up yet) on a kitchen chair (which he hadn't had time to sit on yet) and answered the door.

"Hello, Dennis. Emma told me you called." Avi had deduced from the message that the man wanted privacy. "Let's go to the study where we can talk."

Avi walked Dennis through the picture-perfect living room, thanking his wife silently for her devotion to neatness.

Emma understood their lives included unexpected arrivals like this one, so the rabbi's house was always ready. She insisted that family members keep the entrance hallway, coat closet, dining room and living room areas uncluttered. The parents had to confine the daily *Record* and *The New York Times* as well as current issues of *Newsweek* and the *Jerusalem Post* to the kitchen table or bedroom night stands, and the kids had to keep their copies of *Sports Illustrated* and *YM* upstairs in their rooms. Cable program schedules belonged with the TV in the family room up there, too.

Visitors did not have to know that clothes and papers littered the upstairs and that half-finished projects cluttered the basement. They did not have to open the kitchen door on the main level and see unread magazines or dirty dishes. But they might see everything else, so a large part of the house had to look pristine.

In the living room, vases held artificial or long-lasting live plants, end tables were empty of everything but the simplest candy dish, and attractive volumes that didn't fit in the library neatly filled bookshelves along the walls. The piano in the corner was tidy, with sheet music carefully stored in the bench. Dining room chairs lined up straight around the polished table, and its silk centerpiece reflected the home's colors. Muted golds, browns and shades of green on the furniture, floors and walls gave the house an atmosphere of silent dignity and neutral mood.

Strangers arriving for rabbinical consultations over crises, Emma had decided, should feel they've entered a soothing setting.

Avi escorted Dennis through this serene ambience into the study, a library room added to the house on the main level. Some books on the tall shelves were in English but most were in Hebrew and Aramaic, some were in sets and others stood alone, some volumes were recent publications and others family heirlooms. Avi closed the study's glass doors and sat in the swivel chair behind the desk in the middle of the room. Dennis took the chair opposite him, facing the sheer white curtains that covered windows above the short bookcases.

Dennis looked at the curtains but couldn't see the intersection outside. The side street led to the Shul in one direction and the town's hospital in the other. The main avenue linked several New Jersey suburbs, and occasional buses provided public transportation between the quiet town of East Belleridge and malls along the nearby highway. But now it was dark outside and there were very few cars passing by, so the two men felt they were alone.

"I thought you'd be home watching the game when I called earlier," the president said, turning his attention to Rabbi London. "I was wondering where you were. Maybe there was a congregational emergency I didn't know about." The short, stout, bald man glared at his spiritual leader as if he had caught him playing hooky.

"I was at Shul. The tenth man was slow to arrive to make the minyan, and I was glad I was there to be counted. Besides, I enjoy davening," Avi said, using the Yiddishism for praying because, although Dennis rarely did it, he knew what it meant, "and I usually go."

This veiled criticism was lost on the Shul president, who should have felt a similar obligation but didn't. Dennis never came to daily services and had no concept of the schedule. He was unaware, for instance, that evening davening couldn't even start until sundown. Furthermore, Dennis saw the rabbi as no more than an employee of the congregation, which he himself headed, and the Londons' home as simply an extension of the synagogue. Dennis felt free to pop in at the rabbi's house any time and to boss Avi around whenever he thought the clergyman could be helpful.

"What can I do for you this evening?" the rabbi asked.

"Well," said Dennis, "It's my wife again. Reeva refuses to go back to the doctor, even though the medicine he gave her seemed to help her focus on reality. Without it, she yells at me and accuses me of loving my mother more, just because we pay for her assisted-living apartment. Reeva says awful things to our daughter, like when she accused Pamela of hating her and wanting to abandon her. And sometimes she tells Brendan someone's out to get her and that, as our son, he should be her protector.

"You should talk to her as a rabbi. Calm her down and help her make sense. And convince her to see her doctor, while you're at it. Can you come to see her tomorrow?"

Avi was embarrassed to realize that it had been at least a few months since he last saw Reeva. He remembered what people said, that when she was younger, she had been a skilled accountant and had loved the transition to computers as they came onto the scene. But she stopped working a long time ago, and whenever Avi had seen her in the last few years, Reeva seemed dazed and dull. She rarely came to synagogue events and never attended services. Northwood was nearly an hour's drive from East Belleridge, but Avi knew the distance shouldn't have kept her away from the synagogue or him away from his congregant. He really should have gotten to know her better.

"Sure," Avi said, not sure at all how he could really help her but trying to show he cared. "Suppose I come to your house at about two and I visit with her for a while."

"Thanks, Rabbi. It's Columbus Day and the schools are closed, so we'll all be home. Come earlier and bring the whole family so we can have lunch together."

Here Avi hesitated. He didn't know how strict the Shine home was on the rules of kashrut. Kosher meat was one thing, but there were other issues. Did they have separate dishes and the right ingredients for meat and dairy meals? Did they buy only groceries that had kosher symbols on them? Did they avoid bringing home leftovers from their frequent non-kosher meals out? These were some of the finer points that might not matter to the Shines but did matter to the Londons. On the other hand, it was important for the rabbi not to offend a man who could influence his future employment as the spiritual leader of the congregation.

"I promised the kids we would do something together in the morning, so I'd better take a pass on your kind invitation for lunch," Avi wound up saying, thinking he'd better come up with a plan so that what he said would not be a lie. "Thanks anyway. I'll be there at two, and if they're available, I'll bring the kids."

After Dennis left, Avi asked Emma if the children were doing anything on their day off from school.

"No, they have nothing planned besides catching up on homework," she said. "After that, Josh will be glued to the TV for programs about baseball. Ahuva has to straighten her room but she has nothing in particular scheduled for the afternoon."

"Maybe I'll take her with me to the Shines'," he said. "Ahuva and their daughter Pamela are close in age. Maybe they can visit together so I can have a long talk with Reeva."

Right after lunch the next day, Avi and Ahuva drove up the steep slopes into the forested hills that cradle the more expensive neighborhoods of northern New Jersey. The route took them into mountainous areas, part of the Appalachian chain that parallels the northeastern coast of the United States.

When Ahuva and Josh were younger, Emma and Avi would take them, and any relatives who came to visit in the fall or winter, to the deer reserves in those hills. The stately animals were nearly the size of horses, and the children would bring bread and feed the deer through the wire fence of the sprawling pen. An assortment of bucks and does spent the cold seasons there protected from hunters, and the fence kept people safe from the animals' growing antlers. In the spring, the deer were released into the woods and mountains of the Garden State.

Among the trees, near the deer reserves, visitors could stop at lookout points on mountain trails to see the view that George Washington had of the area's battles during the American Revolution. Now, on a clear day, that same view was of highways that defined residential suburbs and directed traffic flow east toward the modern skyscrapers of New York City, visible only fifteen miles away.

The Londons enjoyed their journey into nature and always felt that they had gone far away for the day, even though the ride there was well under an hour.

The remote area was certainly not walking distance to the Shul, but this was not a factor for the Shines. They drove to the synagogue even on the holiest days of the Jewish year, convinced – as were Reform Jews in general, most Conservative Jews and a few affiliated with Orthodox shuls – that the rules against traveling at those times were antiquated. These Jews felt the restrictions couldn't possibly apply to automobiles and certainly not to them, people who provided the financial backbone of many religious institutions.

"It's so totally pretty and quiet in these mountains," observed Ahuva. "I wish we could like live here instead in that old house in East Belleridge. It's so noisy on that corner. I hate the buses.

When they come by I can't hear my music, even when I use headphones. And I can't stand the ambulance sirens coming from the hospital down the street day and night. Can't you get a regular job in a quieter neighborhood? One like this?"

"I don't know of any Conservative synagogue around here that is looking for a rabbi," Avi answered his daughter, "but I'll keep my ears open for other opportunities."

Ahuva returned to her music and the car went on with its climb. At the top of the mountain, it made one more turn, passed through a gate, followed a circular driveway and entered the parking area. Avi turned off the motor and announced that they had arrived. "You remember Pamela, don't you?" The Shines' fifteen-year-old daughter shuffled out from the lavish apartment complex to show them in.

The girls did not have a lot to say to each other. Ahuva was two years younger, a couple of pounds heavier and several inches shorter than Pamela. As young teens, all that made a big difference.

They attended different schools, too. Pamela was a junior at Northern Public High School, where she was friendly with Jews and Christians, whites, Asians and blacks, all on her socio-economic level. Ahuva was in the ninth grade at Yeshiva Beinoni, a Jewish middle day school that drew from several towns and income brackets and where most of her friends were white, all of the students were Jewish and some of the classes were separate for girls and boys. Social occasions and sports events were not the same, each having different dress codes and schedules. The two teenagers' social circles never overlapped.

Moreover, Avi noticed for the first time that although the girls both wore their long brown, wavy hair tied back and were dressed alike in jeans and T-shirts, they had very different temperaments. He wondered if bringing his daughter had been a mistake. Considering Ahuva's liveliness and Pamela's withdrawn demeanor, Avi gave up any illusions of a possible friendship and only hoped the girls could manage to be cordial while he spoke to the adults.

As the three ascended in the elevator to the fifth floor, the rabbi recalled that Dennis had invited the whole London family on the promise that the day off would find all of the Shines home. "Is Brendan home, too?" Avi asked when they entered the spacious apartment.

"No. He just got his driver's license and I bought him a car, so he went out with friends," Dennis said without guilt. "I'm glad you brought Ahuva to keep Pamela busy. I'll take them down the hall and they can visit a neighbor there."

As the girls left, Avi glanced out the sweeping picture window and saw the same view toward New York that the Londons treasured on their rare trips up these mountains. He also saw the swimming pool, tennis courts and gym that made living in this development so glorious.

Avi turned around when he heard Dennis's voice.

"I'm glad the girls left. The kids should not see her like this. Reeva is …"

The rabbi followed Dennis, but did not find what he expected when he entered the large rec room. Reeva – her highlighted, red hair in cascading curls – was sitting on a chair, facing the turned-off large-screen entertainment system, rocking and muttering. Dennis stopped near the door, but Avi went closer to her, trying to hear what she was saying.

"He's trying to finish it. I won't let him. I'll find a way. I'll get help. I don't know who he thinks he is, telling us what to do all the time, but I'm sure I'm right. We won't let him. We can't let him. I know what to do if he tries. I remember how. I know where to look. I'll do it. But I don't want to. I'll get help. We won't let him win. But what if he tries to kill me? I'll get help, that's what I'll do. We won't let him. We can't let him," she repeated frantically to herself. The rabbi could see her wringing her hands and he could hear what she was saying, but he couldn't understand what she was talking about.

"Reeva? It's Rabbi London. Remember me? Can you look at me?"

She looked right at him, but he didn't see any recognition in her eyes.

"You believe me, don't you?" she asked him. "We've got to stop him!" she pleaded. "Help me!"

Over Avi's shoulder, Reeva peeked across the hall to Dennis's home office. She could see the phone, computer and printer on the desk, and her eyes dropped to the locked drawers below them. Then she realized that Dennis had stepped into her line of vision and was standing at the door to the rec room. She stared at him, and slowly returned her gaze to her now tightly clasped hands, sat still and stopped talking.

Rabbi London didn't know what to make of it. He looked at Dennis. "How long has she been like this?"

"For about a week, but it gets worse every day. Today, she wouldn't eat anything."

"Bring some food she likes, like ice cream, and I'll try to get something into her," said the rabbi. But she would not eat when he or the housekeeper tried giving it to her, and when Dennis offered to feed her, Reeva started screaming.

Rabbi London knew this was more than he could handle, so he suggested Dennis call her doctor, who told them to take her to the hospital right away. "I'll drive," the rabbi said.

They left Pamela, who looked pale and too scared to move, at home. Dennis sat in the back on the passenger side. Reeva, behind the driver, sat perfectly still. Ahuva sat in front, wondering what the hell was going on and knowing beyond a doubt that she should not be there.

By the time the rabbi and his daughter got home, they were worn out. They had stopped at Northwood Hills Hospital, where Dr. Obes checked in the sick woman as a patient. Dennis reached his son on his cellphone, and Brendan said he would drive over and take his father home.

Avi promised to call Dennis later, but first he went home to decompress. He couldn't tell Emma the details of Reeva's bizarre behavior because it was the private information of his congregants. She would understand that. But he worried about his daughter. It wasn't that Ahuva wouldn't respect confidentiality (he knew she wouldn't talk about what she had seen), but as she headed to her room, Avi wondered how badly a young teen could be wounded by witnessing a crisis like this. He was sorry he had taken her along.

Supper time would be a return to normalcy for the London family, and they were all looking forward to it. The four sat down in the dinette alcove and started to eat the stew Emma knew they all loved. Avi piled chunks of meat, carrots, onions and potatoes on his plate next to some broccoli and passed the rest around. He poured some soda for the kids and himself, and was all set to dig in when the doorbell rang.

"I'll get it," said Josh. He was sixteen and sensitive enough to know that his father and sister had had a rough day and that his mother had worked hard on dinner while he watched sports on TV.

A young woman stood at the door, crying. "I have to talk to the rabbi," she blubbered. Avi went to the door and sent Josh back to the kitchen. Somebody might as well eat while dinner was hot.

"My father said he would kill me," the woman cried as Avi escorted her through the peaceful ambiance of the living room into his study and closed the door.

The remaining Londons sat down to eat, but the doorbell rang again a few minutes later. This time Emma got it. It was the woman's father.

"Where is she? I'm gonna kill her!" he screamed, waving his fist in the air.

Rabbi London came back to the front door and took the angry father into the study. There, the father and daughter could hash out their problem verbally in a soothing setting under the calm, wise guidance of their spiritual leader.

Emma returned to the kitchen. She and the children looked at each other and at Avi's cooling dinner and flattening soda. They all knew that the stranger's threat to kill his daughter was probably just angry rhetoric, not to be taken literally. And the children wouldn't be surprised if they or their father never saw the distressed family again, so their problem was not likely to interfere with the Londons' lives. But eruptions like this one intruded on what should have been a quiet family dinner at the end of a grueling day.

Ahuva rolled her eyes and Josh slumped in his seat. Emma shrugged, knowing they had discussed this kind of situation before. Soon they each picked up a fork and ate. They pretended that they could not hear the shouting between the furious father and the distraught daughter in the study. They also hoped that the unhappy family there would not listen in to the Londons' dinner conversation in the kitchen. Such intrusions, pretenses and hopes were standard procedure, for such was life with a pulpit rabbi.

Chapter 2

Conflicts With Congregants

Getting the required ten men to show up for a daily minyan was a measure of a rabbi's success, and on that count, Avi was not doing very well.

Tuesday morning, only a few arrived on time for the forty-minute Shacharit service. Of course, the rabbi and cantor made it a point to be there every day unless something urgent called them away. Mr. Day and three of his four senior friends were there, as usual, but Harvey Stein stayed home because he wasn't feeling well. Evening regulars Bill Fernberg and the Schwartz mourners never came weekday mornings, claiming it was too hard for them to get to the minyan at seven and still be on time at their jobs. No one else in the community was a mourner looking for an early service, so the group was short four men, and the hour was getting late.

Sol Cohen looked at his watch and then at his Yiddish-speaking buddies. "Emek Emet is scheduled to start soon and they will probably hev a minyan," he said, with only a trace of an old-country accent, and he put on his coat. Isaac Iskilovetzky and Greg Greene knew Sol was leaving for the Orthodox shul because that's where they went whenever their favorite synagogue couldn't meet their religious needs. The two men looked at each other and knew that today was going to be one of those times. Then they glanced at Mr. Day, knowing he would join them, aimed an apologetic shrug at the rabbi and followed Sol out the door.

Avi and the cantor reluctantly agreed that joining the Orthodox was the best idea and they prepared to follow. On the way out, Rabbi London put a note on the door saying where they had gone, in case anyone else showed up, and waved to Joe Kripski, who was just arriving to start his custodial work day.

When Avi got home just after eight, Emma was leaving for her morning teaching job as a corrective math teacher and computer consultant in a nearby elementary school. The kids were almost ready to leave, and Avi wondered if he had time to grab a cup of coffee. When the kids were young, Avi and Emma had agreed that one of them should be at home to help their own kids start the day, and that habit hadn't changed just because both children were now teenagers. Today it was Avi's turn.

"I'm almost ready," Josh yelled as he flew down the stairs. He had begun Drivers Ed in school, but until the summer, when he would turn seventeen and get a license, the morning routine was not going to change. The kids would eat breakfast at school, but to please their mother they had orange juice at home before they left. If they missed the bus, as was usually the case, Avi would drive them to their yeshivas, which were in different parts of a neighboring town. Neither school was far from home – he could get to both and be back in about forty minutes – so Avi accepted the fact that everyone was running late. His own breakfast would have to wait until both kids were where they should be.

The educational institution was for Jewish children in grades pre-K through 12 and taught with traditional attitudes toward religious practices. The school was spread out over three buildings in two towns to accommodate more than a thousand children. The record-high enrollment was a recent phenomenon, representing an influx of Jewishly interested (although not necessarily Orthodox) families into northern New Jersey.

The growth was part of a population shift to the area from the crowded boroughs of New York City and the sparsely populated suburbs of New Jersey and New York State. The surge of interest in Jewish day school education seemed to be in response to a rise in anti-Semitism around the world. Whether the increase of incidents was a reaction to events in the Middle East or to the world's growing religious fundamentalism was the subject of endless debate among the adults of the community. Students, on the other hand, argued about more pressing matters.

"You had enough, Blimp," Josh hollered at his sister as she finished her juice. He pulled on a sweater and put his books in his backpack. "Hurry up. I'm late."

"You forgot your lunch, Stupid," Ahuva responded as she threw him his sandwich and put on her jacket.

Emma had taken the five-year-old blue Toyota minivan, so Avi and the kids squeezed into the newer black Honda compact that he used on his clerical rounds.

With Josh in the front passenger seat and Ahuva in the back, the car headed to Yeshiva Gavoha first. Josh was scheduled to lead the opening prayers of its Shacharit minyan, so he was supposed to be there and be ready a few minutes ahead of the other students. He didn't arrive on time, but luckily the other kids were even later.

Josh jumped out of the car and ran to the school's shul. Like the other boys, Josh already had a kippah on his head, and tzitzit fringes were hanging out his shirttails. He would get to his place just as the other boys were finding their seats. They were all post-Bar Mitzvah, so they would put tfillin straps and boxes on their heads and arms, completing at lightning speed their usual uniform for the morning service. The girls would arrive soon, too, wearing modest tops and skirts. But, because they did not have to don religious garb, they would chat quietly at seats on their side of the sexual divide, study the male student assortment and wait to begin the service.

Ahuva's pattern was similar. So, after dropping Josh off, Avi drove to her junior high school. Like the upper school branch, Yeshiva Beinoni was co-ed and its separated-by-sex Shacharit would be followed by a quick, cold-cereal breakfast in the cafeteria before classes began.

When Avi got back from his chauffeur duties, he settled down in the quiet of an empty house to enjoy a bowl of microwaved oatmeal, a cup of freshly brewed coffee and the morning newspaper. The cereal began to absorb the milk, the raisins were softening, the sliced banana on top was starting to turn brown around the edges and the coffee was still steaming when, as the rabbi could have predicted, the phone rang.

It was Sol Cohen, whose daughter, Avi noted sarcastically to himself, was an adult who didn't need a ride to school. Sol had certainly had breakfast already, Avi was thinking, but then he heard, "Rabbi, Harvey Stein's vife told me he just vent to the hospital. I knew it had to be serious for him to miss the morning minyan."

Avi assured the caller that he would get right over there. Sol and Harvey were both Holocaust survivors, but Harvey was very special in one particular way. He was one of those rare nice guys who preferred to see someone laugh than to get pity for himself for what he had been through. He supported philanthropies and Shul activities with every resource he had. Avi wanted to see the old man as soon as possible to make sure he was okay. He ate breakfast quickly and left.

By the time Rabbi London got to the hospital, Sol was already there, and so were Isaac and Greg. The rabbi was painfully aware that this made him look late, and he hoped it wasn't too obvious to Harvey's wife. Ida was very worried. She had already called their three adult children, and they were on their way.

"It looks like a heart attack, Rabbi," Dr. Heller said. He wouldn't ordinarily have discussed the case so casually with anyone outside the family, but he knew he was talking to their clergyman and had met Avi before under similar circumstances. "Harvey has a history of heart problems. It's really amazing that he made it this far. This was his first full-fledged heart attack, and he's lucky it wasn't worse."

Harvey looked bad enough, thought Avi, as he returned to the patient. The sick man was gray and sluggish, and his humor was gone.

Avi leaned forward to have a personal moment closer to his weak friend when Harvey whispered, "Look out for the laymen."

What Harvey meant was a mystery to the rabbi. Sure, Avi knew that "laymen" referred to the non-clergy members of the congregation, but what was Avi to do to "look out" for them? When he heard Harvey's next statement, Avi thought he understood because he assumed it was in the same spirit as the first, that Harvey believed he might not be around to do the jobs he saw as his.

"Take care af my femily, Rabbi."

"Of course I'll help you take care of them," Avi replied with a big grin, acting surer than he felt of Harvey's complete recovery.

Rabbi London gave encouraging comments to the Stein family and in front of them reminded Ida how to contact him and the doctors if she had any further questions. The clergyman made sure the patient's records specified a kosher diet and left the group with an optimistic smile. Convinced he had done what he could to reassure Harvey and his family, the rabbi continued with his day's schedule.

It was mid-afternoon already, so he grabbed coffee and a corn muffin for lunch at home and headed to the Shul. Avi supervised the afternoon religious instruction and he had to make sure everything was in order for the beginning of the program's short year.

The Hebrew School was only in session for eight months, from October through May, in order to clear Jewish holidays in the fall and achievement tests in the public institutions in the spring. The program was designed for children ages six through thirteen who lived in the area and were enrolled in neighborhood public education, and the curriculum was intended to fortify their Jewish identity. They learned the basics of Hebrew language, the turning points of Jewish history, important holiday customs and some stories from the Bible, but never really got past a surface treatment of those subjects. And that was okay with their parents, who often knew no more than their children.

The Jewish education of students in a private day school was different. The local style was for youngsters to begin yeshiva in pre-K at the age of three and to continue through high school. The scholastic year was mandated by law, so it was the same ten months on the calendar as the public schools, but each day was longer by as much as three hours. The program was designed for students to get a deeper understanding of their lifestyle, so Hebrew literature, the flow of Jewish history, the rules governing observance of the holidays, the meaning of prayer and the interpretation of holy texts were taught as normal subjects, as much a part of the curriculum as the government-required English, world history, science, math and gym.

But in Congregation Tefillah's Hebrew School program, the pace was slower. Small groups met in four classrooms off the downstairs all-purpose room during the hours of four to six, either on Mondays and Wednesdays or on Tuesdays and Thursdays, in addition to the ten-to-twelve time slot on Sunday mornings. Students also were expected to attend Junior Congregation services from ten to noon on Saturdays.

After the kids spent six or seven years following that grueling schedule and feeling free to be absent when something better came up, they would finally celebrate their Bar or Bat Mitzvah (boys at age thirteen and girls at twelve). With that, they and their parents assumed their Judaic responsibilities had been met.

Emma did what she could, but knew that the Hebrew School population's priorities ranked Little League or mall shopping way above afternoon religious training. In that resentful atmosphere, she successfully taught two Hebrew School classes, which meant that she worked hard with reluctant students six days a week. As soft-spoken and gentle a person as she was, she was a firm disciplinarian and a fine educator and was usually assigned the oldest students. She had their respect and affection, but as hard as she tried to convince her charges otherwise, most refused to accept the notion that adolescence marked the beginning, not the conclusion, of their religious education.

Rabbi London, who served as principal, chief authority figure and always-available substitute teacher for the sixty-student program, had no better luck persuading the pre-teens to continue their studies than his wife did.

The school year's opening session required extra time after dismissal for the rabbi to discuss curriculum objectives for the year with the education staff, review particular student challenges and make Thanksgiving and Chanukah plans with individual teachers. The details were wrapped up quickly, but it all took time. It was after seven, an hour later than usual, when the rabbi and rebbetzin headed home.

Avi and Emma were tired and needed the evening off to unwind, and they were delighted to find that a good meal was nearly ready when they got to the house. The children had arrived home earlier, and their hunger motivated them to start cooking. Meatballs were a specialty of Ahuva's and Josh liked making spaghetti, so they cooked before bickering about who had worked harder and who should set the table. When the parents got home, Emma added salad and Avi got soda and put ice in four glasses, so everybody could soon sit down to a good dinner.

The parents were loading the used utensils into the dishwasher when Avi got the sad call. Eighty-eight-year-old Harvey Stein was gone. His son and two daughters had arrived during the day to visit a strong man who they believed had triumphed over a manageable health crisis. That evening, however, Harvey suffered a massive heart attack and died within an hour.

Rabbi London met the family at the hospital as soon as he could, offering them words of comfort while they waited together for the Jewish Funeral Home staff to arrive and take over. Ida was quiet and seemed to have a strong hold of the situation, but Avi let the adult children review the details of their father's passing, knowing that letting them talk would make them feel better and would help them accept the reality they had to face. When they seemed spent, he took over, easing them into the next steps.

The rabbi explained that Jewish law required the burial to be as soon as possible, certainly within three days of death. The widow knew that and made the decision. The funeral would be Thursday.

In the meantime, Avi continued, a group of Jewish volunteers called a Chevra Kadisha would cleanse the body and wrap it in a shroud. One of the men would stay with the deceased so that the body would not be left unattended until it was buried.

Avi reminded them that customs popular in America – such as embalming and viewing the deceased, dressing the dead in fancy clothing and jewelry, burying the body with keepsakes and flowers, using a metal or a fancy wood casket, choosing above-ground burial or opting for cremation – were not permitted by traditional Jewish law. The shell that held the soul in this life would return simply to the ground from which it came, based on the way creation was described in Genesis, that God formed humans from the earth. The material goods that had adorned Harvey in this life would remain with the people he left behind in this existence.

The widow decided that for the unassuming man her husband had been, a simple graveside service was the most appropriate. A minyan was ensured by Harvey's friends, so by the time they and the family arrived at the Beit Chayim Cemetery for the funeral, everyone knew what to do and what to expect.

Ida stood trembling in the bright sunlight with her brood: three kids, their spouses and two grandchildren, the only ones of the six tots deemed old enough to attend. The widow and her offspring tore a corner of their clothing as a sign of loss, and Avi gave a short eulogy. Employees of the funeral home lowered the casket into the grave while the rabbi recited Psalms, and then Avi helped the mourners recite the Kaddish. Family members or friends who wanted to participate in the mitzvah of burying the dead took a shovel and helped to fill the grave with soil. When they were finished, they formed two lines, through which the Stein family left, and everyone went to their cars.

The family returned to the Stein home to "sit Shiva" and allow a week there for grieving. By the time they got there, the synagogue's Sisterhood committee had done what was necessary to ready the house. The women left the Steins something to eat and covered the home's mirrors, a custom meant to ease mourners' concerns over their appearance during that time. Low chairs were in place to be used by family members. To start the first Shiva meal, the rabbi gave each of the mourners a hard-boiled egg, which he described as a symbol of the cycle of life.

This was all routine for Avi in his rabbinic career. As he had done many times before, he now launched into his explanation of customary details for the grieving family. During the week of Shiva, friends and relatives would visit, not to party and distract mourners from their grief but to offer condolences. The surviving Steins, for their part, would tell stories about Harvey, of blessed memory, and his life. They might also talk about his passing, if they were comfortable discussing it.

Rabbi London told them that the Shul would provide a minyan at their home morning and evening, so the relatives could daven and say Kaddish. Shiva would be suspended for the Sabbath, during which the family could attend regular synagogue services at the Shul.

If they wanted books on Jewish bereavement practices, he could lend them a few, the rabbi continued. For the time being, he gave them guidelines. At the end of Shiva, the mourners would start resuming regular activities through the first month and then approach normal behavior in the first year. That would give them an introduction to how annual occasions without the dearly departed would feel from then on. Saying the mourner's Kaddish at services would be appropriate whenever they attended during that year. Every year after that, they should light a twenty-four-hour Yahrtzeit candle at home and say Kaddish at Shul on the Hebrew anniversary of Harvey's death. On holidays, they should mention him during the Yizkor memorial service recited in Shul. Finally, sometime during the first year, a tombstone would be placed to mark the plot and the rabbi could help them plan an unveiling.

"Thank you for seeing us through this," said Ida. She, like her husband, was always ready with a smile, and for now she was having trouble imagining herself a widow. "Harvey knew you would help us do this right."

Among the visitors who came to the house soon after the funeral was Dennis Shine. As president of Congregation Tefillah, he always paid an official condolence call at a Shiva house as soon as possible, but tried to time his visit so he wouldn't have to be part of the minyan. He came to the Steins' that afternoon to pay his respects, but left quickly when he saw the rabbi going out to his car. Dennis had something to say.

"Rabbi, how could you permit someone so important to the congregation not to have a *real* funeral?"

"This was a real funeral, Dennis. Jewish law was followed in every detail."

"But there was no ceremony at a funeral parlor at all. And because the whole service was at the cemetery, there was no sign-in book, no chairs for a large crowd and no long eulogies by the family. I'm a good Jew and have been to lots of memorial services, so I know the difference. How can you call this a real funeral?"

"Because none of those things are required by Jewish law," explained the rabbi. "They're nice extras, but this family felt a modest, traditional end suited Harvey better. And their decision was the one that mattered."

Dennis did not seem satisfied, and Avi realized how much needed to be explained to laymen, no matter how Jewishly observant they were in their private lives or how broadly involved they were in public Jewish life. Even Dennis, who called himself a "good Jew" required instruction on how to separate Judaism's basic precepts from the fluff. He certainly did not understand that what people perceive as traditional practice can be colored by what they see on TV.

Avi questioned, though, how he could teach deeper insights when he couldn't even get members of his flock to a daily minyan. Dennis, for example, instead of criticizing what he found wrong about the funeral, could be more helpful just by showing up at the synagogue to be counted at a service. He must know, thought Avi as he drove home, that it will be harder than usual to get the minimum at the Shul while a Shiva is being observed in the community. A few of the regulars will go to the Steins' house, where they can catch a minyan earlier, and the reduced numbers at the Shul will give up and go to Emek Emet.

Resorting to Orthodox resources became a regular bone of contention at the monthly meeting of the Congregation Tefillah Board of Directors.

The regular date in the all-purpose room was considered a way for laymen to address the business aspects of running a congregation, so the rabbi was not expected to attend. But for some reason, the relationship between the two shuls was considered appropriate at this non-religious venue, so, as usual, members would discuss any tensions between them at length that night in the absence of their spiritual leader.

"That the congregation was not invited to Harvey Stein's funeral was only the beginning of the problem," said Stu Eisen. He was on the Board because he was a past president of the Shul and, as such, he felt free to complain. Stu based his opinion on the common misconception that people should be invited to a funeral. Any rabbi could have explained to him that the tradition expects people to come just because it is a mitzvah and they were informed of the schedule.

"That would have been bad enough," Stu said, "but having services a half hour earlier during Shiva at the Stein home means that there may be no minyan at the usual hour at the synagogue. The people who need the minyan in order to say Kaddish will have to go to the Orthodox shul! That's a black mark on our reputation," he concluded. Stu, like Dennis, came often on Saturday mornings but, despite talking about how hard it was to sustain the daily service, never came during the week. And, like Dennis, he was convinced people only came to the minyan if they were in mourning.

Dave Smith and Sig Fleishhocker, two men who had a more religious bent and attended the minyan occasionally, were new to the Board. They quietly agreed that Stu could relieve the minyan shortage by making an appearance in one of those places with one or both of his teenage sons. After all, they agreed, you don't have to be a mourner to be counted as one of the daveners, just be Bar Mitzvah age or older. Then, aware of what they were implying, they agreed that maybe they themselves should go to the daily minyan more often than the once a month they were averaging.

And then Dave had another thought. In a louder voice, he asked, "Does it spoil our image because a shul with two hundred member families can't get twenty men to sustain two services, or is it because our members dare to mix with the Orthodox?" It was a hypothetical question, meant only to elicit discussion regarding the tensions between the denominations, but the question went unanswered.

Recording secretary Florence Fischman, who frequently appeared Saturday mornings but was the lone woman at the meeting, reprised her regular litany on the numerical advantages of counting women at religious events. She noted that adding the women to the total at a service made it sound larger, but no one responded to that, either.

"It goes beyond that," said treasurer Larry Lansken, who occasionally attended Saturday mornings but never came to the daily service. He always watched expenses and wanted to get to what he considered the heart of the matter. "Because our folks didn't feel they were an important part of the ritual, they will avoid making the donations they might have considered otherwise. I figure our Shul lost hundreds of dollars because of some of the decisions made today."

"I agree," said Dennis, who never started the blame game but was always happy to fan the flame and identify a target. "We probably won't get the books that are donated 'In Memory Of,' or the brass memorial plaque with Harvey's name and dates on it. Those donations could have underwritten the cost of a computer-connected fax/copier/scanner answering machine that the Shul office needs. It's another bad call by the rabbi."

"Didn't the rabbi fight you on buying that machine?" asked Morty Fenn. His family name had been Fenstermacher before he became a lawyer and changed it. Morty was a frequent davener on Saturday mornings and upon very rare occasion came weekday evenings but never to the daily morning minyan. He was at the Board meeting representing the Employment Review committee. "As I recall, Rabbi London wanted more prayer books and said we could live without the fax machine! Rabbis must live with their heads in the sand. They just don't understand how businesses run and how important hi-tech is these days."

"And don't forget how he wanted to send the proceeds from the Shul's Yom Kippur appeal to some hospital in Israel," added (his Shul friends called him "ledger") Larry. "As if we don't have hospitals here! It reminds me of the time he suggested we raise money for Jews in Russia instead of the homeless in New Jersey."

This recollection evoked some discussion of the purpose of fundraising, where dollars were needed most and what a Jewish organization's priorities should be. A large portion of the funds the Shul raised went to congregational necessities, such as upkeep of the building, salaries of the employees and equipment for the Hebrew School. Emergency money was available for members' crises. The board earmarked a portion to go to the local OJO (Organization of Jewish Organizations), which would funnel needed support to both Jewish and non-Jewish projects, including hospitals, yeshivas, kosher old-age homes, food pantries, aid for people in dire straits around the world and support for Israel's needy. All of these categories were reviewed by board members and had a slot in the budget.

Beyond that, individual congregants sustained national projects ranging from housing the homeless to supporting medical research. The members were an active group when it came to social causes, and they struggled to prioritize needs.

But the consensus at this point in the Board meeting was to move on beyond budgetary matters because something more pressing had come up.

"Under new business," said the Board's chairman Harold Harrison, "let's spend a few minutes discussing this year's interfaith Thanksgiving event." He had no trouble praying with Gentiles. It was his coreligionists that made him uncomfortable. He attended

Shul services only for holidays and the rare special event that he could see no way to avoid. For him, all prayer rang hollow and the most religious Jews and their ways left him cold. He was proud to say his synagogue involvement rested on a foundation of philanthropic projects and social activities. "Last year, we had a joint service with two of the churches in town and it went very well. I say we do it again."

"That was a great day," said Stu. "The service was at the biggest church in town, so if it were held here this year, our synagogue would be thought of as the largest or most important Jewish congregation. Last year, the Orthodox didn't come at all, but we'll invite them this year anyway and maybe a few will show up. More important, though, is that it will show we are more significant than the Reform. And, having it here would be great for our reputation when we advertise for more members!"

"Could we do it?" Harold asked the Board. "I think we have the room but we would need more seats. Dennis, ask the rabbi if he knows where we can borrow some folding chairs."

If he had been there, Rabbi London would have smirked. Finally, regardless of other subjects the Board agenda covered – the traditions of a funeral, maintaining a minyan, the woman's role in religious life, the purpose of charity, relations among synagogues, interfaith dialogue – finally, its members agreed they had come upon an issue for which they needed a rabbi. Chairs.

"More to the point," said Florence, "is whether Christians will enter a synagogue at all, let alone pray in one." She reminded them that, only a few years earlier, local Christians protested when a law was passed requiring that government events open with a nonsectarian prayer instead of one invoking Jesus Christ.

"What about the propriety of having non-Jews at a synagogue service at all?" asked Dave. He had had business dealings with a wide variety of people, and because Smith was so neutral a name, he had overheard conversations and putdowns that were not meant for Jewish ears.

He remembered one man who claimed that God did not listen to the prayers of Jews, and a woman who was convinced all Jews were suspect because they secretly ruled the world. Another time, his boss had explained in a casual conversation over lunch that the only reason Israelis won their 1948 War of Independence against the Arabs was because of the financial support they had gotten from Jews in the United States. Dave felt like he was ready to kill somebody that time, but put his job on the line instead. He calmly countered that although there was some money donated by Jews here, the war had actually been won by Holocaust survivors who had already lived through hell and fought as if they had nothing left to lose. Discussions like these had taught Dave caution in, and a basic distrust of, the Gentile world.

"The Thanksgiving event isn't a religious service anyway," Dave's friend Sig assured them all. He shared Dave's distrust of Christians because of his own experience with his wife's Christian family. And to show his friend some camaraderie, he added, "God doesn't listen to idol worshippers, and Christianity is in that category, with their crosses and saints and all."

Several people at that meeting winced when they heard that. Sig himself realized that what he had said sounded harsher than what he had intended, and he wanted to return the discussion to the spirit of friendly coexistence that the occasion symbolized. He decided to put his next thought into the context of a patriotic gesture and said, "This get-together is only a made-up gathering for the American holiday. We shouldn't think of it as spiritual at all."

Thanksgiving is spiritual, Florence thought. She knew for sure that America was a Christian country and felt comfortable ridiculing that religion. "Imagine, the whole basis of a religion is that a woman gets pregnant and says God did it! It's amazing that so many people believe it."

Stu and Harold reacted angrily to what she and the two men had said, accusing such attitudes of undermining interfaith harmony and those who have them of being insincere when they talked of American tolerance. Just as the discussion was heating up to reveal some ignorance and prejudices that were anathema to ecumenism, a cellphone rang. Dennis's mother had fallen and was being rushed to the hospital. As he ran out, Dennis asked that somebody please call the rabbi and tell him to go see his mother. "And ask him about the chairs!"

Avi arrived at East Belleridge General Hospital soon after Dennis got there. Poor Dennis, the rabbi thought, first Reeva and now his mother.

The doctors were gone for the day and Dennis could not get straight answers from the staff on duty, so the rabbi pulled rank. He called the primary physician's service and introduced himself as a clergyman. He was put through immediately.

"Yes, Rabbi," said Dr. Frank. "We were worried that Hannah Shine had broken her hip, but X-rays, CT scans and MRIs are not bearing that out. It looks like she escaped the worst. We'll keep her a couple of days – because after all, she is ninety-two – and then she should be able to go home."

Avi explained all that to Dennis, who was grateful that the rabbi's clerical clearance had been able to cut through the red tape, reach the physician in charge and get some straight answers quickly. Yes, Dennis had to admit, sometimes there were advantages to being a man of the cloth. It was even better not to be encumbered by religious restrictions but to have, like he did, a rabbi to call on when you needed one.

"By the way, Rabbi," Dennis said to his clergyman later, on their way out of the hospital after visiting the old woman, "do you know where we can borrow some extra folding chairs? At the Board meeting, we were talking about having the annual interfaith Thanksgiving service at our Shul."

"Harold mentioned that when he called about your mother. Was it the consensus of the Board that we host a community event this year?" Avi asked.

"I left before it came to a vote, but Harold and I think it's a good idea," Dennis answered.

If you men both agree, Avi thought, then it's all settled, even if a majority of the rest of the members disagree. He understood that these were two of the most powerful voices in his congregation. Strange, though, that no one had considered asking the rabbi for his opinion.

Avi remembered last year's first-ever community-wide interfaith service at East Belleridge's Our Mother of Mercy Church. Going there was not Avi's maiden voyage to a Catholic house of worship, but it was his first time in that particular one, and he was amazed at how much it resembled an expansive European cathedral. The church's outer facade was made of dark gray, rough-hewn stone, which supported a roof topped by a square bell tower. On one side, in matching stone, was the rectory, where clergy resided who were associated with the diocese. On the other, built of more modern brown brick, was a Catholic parochial school that sorted nearly five hundred of the area's children into grades K-8.

Inside the church, the stone walls, vaulted ceilings and stained glass windows made the shadowy, cavernous space seem larger than it really was. Votive candles flickered in nooks anchored by statues of saints along the left wall. Three confessional booths lined the right side. The altar, which displayed the incense and communion accoutrements, was located at a wider area near the front, giving the building the overall shape of a cross. An elaborate and detailed crucifix focused attention on the front wall. In the pews, burgundy cushions were hinged and so were the matching padded stools worshippers kneeled on to say private prayers.

The religious behaviors of the varied crowd had showed when the Thanksgiving assemblage arrived. The nearly two hundred Catholic faithful followed their routine, stopping at a basin of holy water at the foot of the center aisle and genuflecting before marching down the gray-carpeted center aisle and sitting down.

The three dozen Jews who attended that event had been cautious. They dressed the way they did when they went to synagogue Saturday mornings, but they sat together and didn't talk. They looked wide-eyed every time a Catholic made the personal sign of the cross. They stared at the artful depiction of the painful crucifixion every time a speaker approached the podium at the front of the room. Some Jews found this excursion into another religious setting enlightening. Others found it disturbing.

The hundred or so other Christians who came that day took their seats and reached for hymnals. Avi had been at the Protestant East Belleridge Community Church once for a town meeting and remembered it as dignified but not imposing. Its white steeple-topped building stood catty-corner on its lot at a main intersection. The bright room had brown cushioned pews for more than four hundred, which made it as large as the Catholic church but more modest in appearance. The ceilings were not as high, the brown carpet matched the seats, the walls were eggshell white, the room was an unassuming rectangle and the religious symbols were simple. The large cross at the front, for example, did not explicitly depict the suffering Nazarene.

That a crucifix, which was an ancient instrument of torture, should become the symbol of a peace-loving religion always baffled Rabbi London. Regardless of this gut reaction, however, he had visited several houses of worship in the U.S., Israel, Europe and the Far East and respected the idea that people reach out to their Maker in their own ways. But he always wondered if the rest of his congregation saw it from the same viewpoint.

Avi tried to imagine what Christians would think if they visited Congregation Tefillah. They would enter the light-brown brick, two level, simple building by going up a half-dozen steps and going through large glass doors under the peak of the slanted roof. A flight of stairs on the left led to the downstairs, but from the foyer ahead, wooden doors opened to an unpretentious and well-lit sanctuary. The high-ceilings and wood trim of its modern decor, plus restful shades of blue fabrics on the seats and floor, gave the room a dignified look.

Pews, with seats on both sides of a center aisle, faced the Holy Ark, over which an eternal light hung and inside of which Torah scrolls were stored upright. On the right side of the Ark was a pole holding the blue and white Jewish flag, and on the left the red, white and blue American banner. Along the same wall, four high-backed armchairs provided imposing places for the rabbi, cantor and officers of the congregation. A large table in front of the Ark was covered with a blue velvet cloth, but was usually empty because the surface was used during only those parts of the service when an open Torah was placed on it and read to the congregation.

There were a few chandeliers for decor, some stained-glass windows with biblical quotes for mood, and book shelves and racks for storing prayer books and Bibles. The only other decorative element was the sentence in raised gold letters above the Ark that said, in Hebrew, "Know before Whom you stand." All together, it was a simple setting more suitable to Jews, who came to participate in a familiar group activity, than to Christians, who came to witness ritual and repeat words of inspiration.

Aside from the venue where last year's gathering had taken place, the event itself had drawn mixed reactions.

Most of the Christians liked the Thanksgiving ecumenical spirit and some had brought the gathering to the attention of the local newspaper.

The Jews were split. Emek Emet's Orthodox members were inclined to boycott the occasion, saying Jews should not ever enter a church. The Conservative Jews were cautiously optimistic, saying they thought having interfaith contact was the right thing to do. Most of the Reform members of Temple Tikvah insisted that the intermingling was long overdue and that having the joint service would encourage mutual respect.

Members of the town's small mosque didn't come at all. The Muslims thought the whole idea was awful, calling Thanksgiving a national holiday that should be free of religious or political overtones.

Considering the culture shock of the location and the range of reactions to the event, Avi wondered what the whole effort achieved.

"Do you think the town's religious leaders will go for it?" Avi asked the Shul president.

"I'm sure they'll love it," Dennis said, dismissing the subject as unimportant compared to the feeling of relief that came over him that his mother was going to be all right.

"Funny," Avi told Emma later that night, "leaders of our congregation are sure to come out for an annual ceremony with Gentiles, but they wouldn't come anywhere near a daily Jewish service even if their lives depended on it."

Chapter 3

Background for Brotherhood

Maybe going once a year on Thanksgiving was easy but supporting a daily minyan was just too much to ask, thought Avi that night as he locked the door, checked the windows, turned off the lights and went upstairs.

As a practicing Jew, he chose to daven like he chose to eat, setting aside a few minutes for prayer three times a day. He started a typical day with the Shacharit service, ended it with Maariv and squeezed in a Mincha sometime in the afternoon.

As part of a group, though, the commitment was harder. Accomplishing group prayer depended on finding nine other men who wanted to follow the same discipline on the same schedule. Thank goodness for mourners, he found himself thinking as he climbed the stairs. If it weren't for them wanting to say Kaddish ... but then Avi felt ashamed. Even though the time for saying Kaddish arrives in every life, mourning is not something he'd wish on anyone.

"Good night, kids," he called in the direction of his children's rooms, where the lights were still on. "Go to sleep soon." No, mourning is not something he'd wish on anyone sooner than necessary.

There were some people who were not mourners but supported the minyan, he admitted to himself on his way to the master bedroom. The regulars, for instance, were driven by religious devotion. Then there's Bill Fernberg, who came as often as he could because he wanted to learn more about tradition. Morty Fenn (I'll always think of him as Fenstermacher, Avi thought) seemed to sense his responsibility, too. But Harold Harrison, Stu Eisen and Dennis

Shine, despite their dedication to the Shul and other Jewish causes, felt no obligation at all.

"When other people are depending on you to make a minyan, it should make you feel valuable, so why doesn't feeling important make you want to be there?" Avi reasoned aloud to his sounding board as he and Emma got ready for bed that night.

"You." Emma stopped folding the extra blanket. He didn't mean her, that was for sure. Her husband put his thoughts that way all the time and, although she always protested, he continued thinking in terms of the men's role and ignoring the fact that women were different. She had reminded him in previous discussions that the minyan was not dependent on the women at all. For centuries, she said, women were home setting living standards and preparing for holidays. But even now, when they were also out in the working world, the female role in public religious life was limited.

Their contribution to Jewish survival was crucial, he always agreed, but Jewish tradition put women in charge of transmitting Jewish values to future generations and maintaining the dignity of the Jewish people. That task was not strictly time-dependent, whereas the clock determined much of the men's role. Making a minyan, for example, was outside the sphere of women's responsibility because time determined when prayers were appropriate. Therefore, when davening required the minimum number of participants, women were welcome but were not counted even if they were present. Women could be there, but it wasn't their job.

Emma never went. But in discussing the subject, she always told Avi that she felt looked down upon by men who thought that women were not important enough to be counted or to receive public religious honors. The disdain in the men's eyes hurt, she said. It was the same pain women suffered when they were under the thumb of domineering husbands. They felt powerless, devalued and robbed of their dignity.

But Emma chose not to bring up that topic again now. She knew Avi was trying to work through a line of logic and she wanted to be helpful and stay on point.

"On the other hand," she said out loud, "there are lots of things you do as an individual that wind up determining your identity." Emma sat down, took off her shoes and rubbed her feet while she mentioned some of the things Jews did, whether they were men or women. "You eat kosher, observe Shabbat, circumcise your sons, come of age to observe mitzvot and marry under a chuppah regardless of whether or not there is a congregation of Jews in the vicinity."

"What you do by yourself ensures your own Jewishness but not that of the People," Avi responded. "It would not have given us cohesiveness through the generations." The rabbi folded his pants. "Sure, as one person, you can commune as a Jew directly with God, but the language of prayer is usually plural. 'Forgive us.' 'Heal us.' 'Bless us with peace.' We approach God as a People, and it is as a People, not as individuals, that our identity has endured for three thousand years while other cultures have changed and disappeared."

Emma understood what he was saying and that the discussion still didn't address what he was really struggling with, that men, who are critical to the count, don't feel it's important enough to show up.

She turned down the bedding and gave in to her first reaction. "The need to daven as part of the group goes for women, too, right?" She put her pants and sweater into a drawer. "So by the same logic, they're integral parts of the People you refer to. That's why women expect to be counted to a minyan. Being eligible for the count would validate their role and might make sustaining the community seem more important." She fluffed the pillows and felt she had made a good point.

"Of course women daven and have as valid a relationship with God as men do, you know that," Avi said. "But the purpose of their roles in the Jewish community is different. Women bring sanctity and insight to daily life. It's private, personal stuff, and women tend to be much more sensitive in that way."

Emma accepted that as true, knowing how essential she and other women in the Shul were when it came to things like planning a celebration, visiting the sick or taking care of mourners. But she suspected that feminine "sensitivity" was also used by many religious authorities as a convenient answer for why they exclude women from the public arena.

"But in the communal sphere," the man continued, "here is the given: Having a working definition for a congregation gives the concept legal parameters. Once there is an official congregation, certain liturgical phrases make more sense. Kaddish, for example, either as a link between sections of a service or as a proclamation of faith by a mourner, is not directed at God. It is only said in the presence of others who can witness the pronouncement and respond 'Amen.' It makes no sense for someone to say it if nobody's listening."

Avi surveyed his closet and considered his wardrobe options for the next day. "Sure, individuals can operate in a vacuum, but when they want strength in times of weakness and celebration in times of joy, both the men and the women want friends, and they'll find them in their group."

Emma yawned and yielded.

"So," he continued, "Jewish law makes some rules and defines a prayer group as a minimum of ten men. *Men.* By insisting on a quorum of males for public worship, a congregation is larger because women and children are also likely to be part of the package. If you count both, five couples could meet the minimum requirement but ten people would not be a critical mass for a viable congregation. The math would work just as well if a minyan were defined as ten females, but women's lives are sometimes unpredictable." He paused. "What would happen to a congregation of ten if one of them unexpectedly broke her water and went into labor?"

Avi looked deep into his wife's eyes and Emma had to smile, remembering how suddenly labor had started with both of their own children and how it began frighteningly early the first time.

He thinks he's so smart, she thought. Avi might be right about our personal history, but what about women who are not married or pregnant? Why isn't there some public celebration, different from when a boy approaches manhood, that celebrates a woman's ability to conceive, give birth and nurse? Why isn't she at least mentioned when her son gets called up to the Torah for the first time, when in fact she should be praised for preparing him to be part of the Jewish People?

"Enough philosophy for one night. It's late," she said, knowing they would return to this subject many times in the future. They kissed good night and turned off the light.

But as Avi's head found its favorite spot on the pillow, he added one fact to his mental exegesis. Counting women along with the men doesn't work. He saw no evidence that there is more regular minyan support when the basic count is for ten people. When men think the women will go, the men stay home.

Avi rolled over into his most comfortable sleeping position while he wondered if Jewish identity could be secure without the group. Perhaps the habit of kashrut, davening, studying and observing Shabbat by just a small percentage of Jews really was enough to secure the survival of the People. Surely, the role of Jews – and most of the time not observant ones – has been prominent in world history.

And in his own congregation, one of the nicest guys and staunchest supporters was Ray Fisch, who simply was not observant at all.

But Jewish thought raises living to a higher level, he told himself. Humans, like animals, lived, ate, procreated and died. The gift of our religion was to impose rules and invest sanctity in those activities so that humans could be different from the rest of the animal world. That sanctity makes us responsible for each other and respectful of the life we find around us in both animals and people.

Yes, that's it. Jewish logic added quality to living.

Avi personally felt duty-bound to explain that principle to whoever would listen, and he fell asleep cozy with that calling.

As he brushed his teeth the next morning, Avi was relishing the memory of the discussion with his wife the night before. Intellectual exchanges like that were integral to their decision-making process. A conversation like that one had led them to consider a move to East Belleridge three years earlier.

At that time, he already had fifteen years' experience in the pulpit rabbinate. He and his new wife had launched his career by serving a congregation in Tokyo for two years. The young couple spent the next three years in Portland, Oregon, where he was as an assistant rabbi and where they started a family. Then, after a decade in a Detroit suburb where he was as an associate rabbi in a large shul, Avi looked for a position where he could be the sole spiritual leader of an established congregation.

Avi was thinking about the start of his career as he came downstairs and put on his fall jacket. Emma was already in the kitchen and, as he left for Shul, she hollered, "Have a good day, and don't forget to put out the garbage before breakfast." It was Emma's turn to see the kids off and would leave for her morning job before Avi got back. She knew that sometimes he was distracted by lofty logic and forgot necessary chores, so she often reminded her esoteric husband to focus on mundane matters.

That morning, as Emma suspected, Avi's mind was some-where else. While he walked to Shul in the cool morning air, he reviewed the details of this synagogue's original job proposal. The contract had a decent employment package, with an adequate salary and benefits. In addition, the Shul had a "parish house," a residence that it owned and maintained for its spiritual leader. The Londons still lived there, one easy block from the Shul, in a four-bedroom house maintained by the congregation. Even though Emma and Avi always wanted to have their own home and to build up equity for their retirement, this arrangement meant a lot of money saved on rent and repairs, and the location couldn't have been more convenient.

The rabbi rounded the last corner and entered the Shul building from the parking lot while he was thinking about East Belleridge. When they first saw it, they already knew the large town was not what Emma or Avi would have called affluent, but it was pleasant enough. Most residents owned the fifty-year-old Dutch colonial, Tudor-style ranch house or duplex condo they lived in, but there was a smattering of rented garden apartments, as well. Small office complexes and industrial zones cushioned the business presence better than the tall corporate buildings did in neighboring communities, and local parks and tree-lined streets added to the suburban feel. Trains and buses to several malls and into New York fought any feeling of isolation, and plentiful parking made commuting easy to most area destinations. The town's population had a majority of whites and Christians, and the rest was a mix.

Only a small number of Shul families lived in town, and the Londons understood the reality of life at a Conservative congregation: A lot of members drove to Shul on Shabbat and holidays even when, by traditional Jewish custom, they shouldn't. But both Emma's and Avi's families had an assortment of Orthodox and non-observant relatives, and this kept them tolerant, and even respectful, of striations of beliefs.

Avi had realized that his attitude of treasuring diversity would be an advantage in this new position. Congregation Tefillah comprised professionals as well as business people, those who were comfortable with religious observance as well as those who found it strange. This assortment would challenge him on Jewish legal issues and keep him sharp with incisive questions.

Arriving at Shul at ten minutes before seven on this fall morning, the rabbi was pleased to see that Mr. Day had already used his key to open the doors. Avi was further delighted that there were nearly enough men for the service already in the all-purpose room. Avi always wore a kippah, so he quickly took off his jacket and retrieved from his office the velvet pouches that held what he needed for the morning service. He unzipped the pouches, took out his tallit and draped it over his shoulders. Then he unpacked the tfillin and wrapped the straps that held Scripture-filled cubes on his head and arm. With that done, he was ready to daven with the rest of the minyan.

He looked around the room and observed that only about half of the men used tfillin. Putting on those straps and boxes in the right positions and in the correct order and with the appropriate blessings was much more complicated than popping on a yarmulke or draping a tallit. Avi knew that most of his laymen did not know how to do it right and didn't want to learn.

From the beginning of his tenure at Congregation Tefillah, he had understood that the majority of its members were traditional less by routine than by opinion. They wanted a rabbi who knew Jewish law – and a rabbinical family that lived accordingly – so they wouldn't have to spend much time on those details in their own lives. They had classic views on subjects most people in the Conservative movement were willing to consider with progressive eyes, such as women's participation at services and homosexuality in religious life. Maintaining a traditional stance on those issues meshed well with his own views, so staying that course was fine with him. It had seemed like a workable match.

After the service, Avi packed up his pouches, stashed them in the desk in his office, checked his computer and phone and peeked into the Shul's kitchen. "Did the caterer drop off the cake and fruit yet?" he asked.

Joe Kripski was just completing a mop-up of the cooking area and had already made space in the refrigerator for the refreshments. "No, but I'll wait for 'em," the custodian said.

Nodding his thanks, the rabbi headed home. As he approached his corner, he recalled Emma's reminder and put the London family trash at the curb. He looked down the quiet street in both directions, noticing that the neighbors had already put their garbage out but that the efficient town's hauler hadn't collected it yet.

East Belleridge, he had told Emma long ago, was not only well-run but also well-located, and the second fact made the New Jersey suburb increasingly popular with Jews in general. It was close enough to vibrant Jewish population centers to offer a variety of kosher food venues for socializing and shopping and to provide sources of religious supplies for congregational and personal needs.

For the Londons, being near New York offered both the parents and the children a wide circle of acquaintances who were like-minded and well-informed, some of them – like the Londons – connected to the rabbinate or to Jewish education.

The bonus was the area's assortment of educational institutions of every degree of religious strictness, especially on the high school level. This variety gave their children a choice of friends beyond any they might find locally. And, on the northeastern grid between Boston and Washington, there was a plethora of secular colleges with a large number of Jewish students, something Emma and Avi would have to consider for their children very soon.

Another factor was that the Londons always longed to be closer to where both their families' roots were so they could see relatives more often.

Emma's childhood in Atlantic City gave special nostalgic weight to being near the Jersey shore's crashing waves in general and to the cemetery inland from that town in particular. She also yearned for proximity to her sister in Baltimore and her brother in Philadelphia that would make a visit easier.

Most of Avi's American relatives also lived in Philadelphia and were more likely to get to New York for special occasions. Some also might stop to see the Londons on trips up or down the east coast or en route to visit kin in Israel.

Israel. Avi ruminated as he stirred his breakfast coffee. The Jewish State had special meaning for him, both as a rabbi and as the direct descendent of some of its pioneers. But the subject had also turned out to be the first sticking point between the new spiritual leader and his congregation. During his first Rosh Hashanah at Congregation Tefillah, Avi gave a sermon on the historical relationship between the Promised Land and the Chosen People. How was he to know that his laymen would perceive the love of Israel to be in conflict with Jews' loyalty to America?

He tried to explain to them that there was indeed no conflict. If there was any distinction, it was based on the two ways to look at history. First, Jews were Jews because they became a People in the Land of Israel and lived there as a nation for more than a thousand years. After Jerusalem was destroyed, most Jews were exiled for nearly two thousand years, wandering the globe and longing to go home. But the second view focused on recent centuries and on a new world that welcomed this ancient People. Here, in America, the two vistas of history converged.

The emphasis of Avi's talk that day years ago had been on long-range world history, but the dissonance that surfaced shed light on his new situation. He would have to remember their reactions and to word future presentations carefully.

The long-ago morning of dissonance was when he first met Dave Smith and Sig Fleishhocker. Both men liked what they heard Rabbi London say about Israel but had other religious problems that came from family power struggles.

Dave was from a very Orthodox New York family that all but disowned him for marrying the girl he fell in love with in college. She was smart and sincere, and Dave's relatives didn't mind at all that she was black because she was Jewish from birth. But along with her Jewish mother came a Conservative rabbi for a grandfather, and Dave's parents couldn't abide moderately observant Jews on their meticulously religious family tree.

Sig was from a non-observant family in the rural Midwest, where public school education was substandard. Instead of risking academic disappointment, his parents looked for the best private school around, and that happened to be a Jewish day school. He liked what he learned there, and after a summer trip to Israel, decided he wanted a ritually full life. He married a woman raised in a fundamentalist Christian home, and when she converted to Judaism, her family gave her an earful of anti-Semitic vitriol and shunned her.

Dave and Sig found each other and discovered they saw the importance of Jewish tradition the same way. They agreed that keeping Judaism in their lives on a toned-down level was their key to a peaceful reality. Israel was part of their tradition, and they accepted it as such.

On the other side of the issue was Stu (who was then president), Harold (who was then and still was chairman of the Board) and Dennis. Avi had met them in the hiring process and found out then about their lack of love for religious ritual. They were, however, devoted to the community and to the good that could come from their hours, energy and money. Until the day of the controversial sermon, though, Avi never realized that, in their minds, Israel ranked way below America and lifestyle in significance. He would have to remember in future lectures that many congregants rated America as most important, then local community, next family, and then maybe religion and Israel.

After understanding congregants' priorities better, the rabbi was more careful about the tone of his talks, trying to strike the tolerant note that was his true pitch. By the second year of High Holidays, he had focused on personal improvement, both as Jews and as individuals. This year, he worked hard to bring his congregation in closer touch with other synagogues in town and to thaw relations among their members.

Avi remembered that rough beginning and, as the steam rose from his now-clean breakfast dishes, decided it was time to warm up community relations. If it was important to bring Jews of varying inclinations together, it was also valuable to honor the relationships among fellow Americans. Thanksgiving was a perfect opportunity to combine the religious essence of each element in town with the pride of being an integral part of the American dynamic, the rabbi proudly opined. If the other clergymen in town had a similarly positive attitude, a brotherhood service could be a wonderful way of encouraging mutual respect.

Avi's mind was racing with excitement over the bonding that could be achieved by a well-done ecumenical event as he picked up challah at the bakery, clothes at the dry cleaners and a bouquet at the florist. By the time he got home, Emma was back from work, too. They put the flowers in water, lunched together on coffee and grilled cheese and then turned to their respective tasks.

Emma got to work cooking for Shabbat. As she told Avi again and again, arrival of the day of rest might seem an effortless progression of the calendar to men, but to women, who bore most of the responsibility for making sure everything got done on time – stocking the pantry, cleaning the house, doing the laundry, cooking the meals, providing for sick neighbors, making sure appropriate clothes were ready, tying up the kids' loose ends, assigning jobs to the men and staying cheerful – it was a lot of work.

The comforting smells of Emma's Friday afternoon cooking drifted from the kitchen while Avi organized his source books in the study. He had decided to lay the groundwork for brotherhood in this week's sermon. The preacher scanned the Torah portion, Bresheet, which told the story of Creation and the beginning of mankind. He checked Jewish commentaries on the inspirations of the portion. He researched English poetry that would evoke tenderness between people. He pored over headlines in the week's newspapers for instances of kindness or inhumanity, with which he could drive certain points home. Avi wrote out his ideas, revised them, rewrote them, then called in the expert.

"Emma, can you give me your opinion?"

She knew he was working hard and expected him to inter-rupt her cooking. She checked the stove, washed her hands and took a break in the study.

Avi sat in his swivel chair and his wife sat opposite him, preparing to perform the familiar sounding-board ritual. Whenever a talk had to be just right, he delivered it to her across that desk, and the process always began the same way. Emma would glance at her watch and he would begin. The cadence of his voice would rise and fall with each point he made. His volume would increase as he came to the high point of his talk. Then, his tone would grow warm as he reached out to cloak his listeners in his conclusions.

When he was finished, he would look at the expert and Emma would give him an honest reaction.

This time, she began her reactions with the fact that the sermon was ten minutes too long. "At rabbinical school," she reminded him, "your homily class taught that, if you haven't struck oil in twenty minutes, you should stop boring." Avi smiled. He knew he had a tendency to go on and on and to use too many complicated words. Emma was good at stopping his verbal excesses.

Then she told him where he had veered off the mark. She cited his English translation of a critical phrase from the Hebrew that was slightly off and suggested how he could make it more faithful to the original. Additional commentaries might add another view, she said, and she suggested a few options. The poetry was ambiguous enough to be understood in different ways so it needed more context. The pace, on the whole, could be quicker.

Finally, she told him what she usually did, that it was wonderful. Her smile at the end assured him that he would do well.

And with that ritual done, they could finish the rest of their work in time for Shabbat. Soon they would relax over a delicious Friday night family dinner and conversation and know that they didn't have to spend any more time worrying about the rabbi's sermon.

Shabbat morning, there were more than the usual eighty people at services. Many were the parents of children who were required to help lead the Hebrew School's Junior Congregation as part of their pre-Bar/Bat Mitzvah training. Emma ran that show downstairs in the all-purpose room, where teachers and students sat on the same noisy folding chairs used for the daily minyan.

When the youngsters' session ended, everyone went upstairs for the conclusion of the regular service in the main sanctuary. There, acoustically designed walls enhanced the cantor's chanting, and upholstery and carpet muffled the noises of late arrivals and ongoing conversations. The few minutes between the end of one service and the closing hymns of the other gave the custodian time to reset the downstairs and put out the wine, cake and fruit for post-prayer Kiddush and mingling.

Basic to the group of Saturday morning upstairs worshippers, of course, were the daily minyan regulars, many of whom brought family members. Greg Greene always came with his wife, but they were joined lately by their granddaughter Melissa, who saw her Bat Mitzvah on the horizon. In two weeks, Sol and Sylvia Cohen's daughter would be married, and they were getting mentally prepared for that step. Isaac Iskilovetzky, who otherwise would have been alone because his wife Rebecca resided in the nearby nursing home, sat with Mr. Day, who was also there alone.

Harvey Stein (of blessed memory) used to come with Ida Saturday mornings, so she was in the habit of attending. Now, however, she was escorted by her children, who were staying with her for Shiva. Mendy Schwartz (may he rest in peace) had been a familiar face, too, but that didn't get his sons there either before or after his passing. Phil and Matt might say Kaddish in his memory because they had promised to, but not at the main weekend service, where they might be seen.

Avi knew that Shabbat morning drew others for a variety of reasons. Sisterhood ladies caught up on the latest fashions. Men's Club members talked sports. Kids exchanged celebrity stories. Businessmen shared stock tips. Doctors practiced a pose of humility. Educators weighed challenges. Parents pleaded for matches for their children. Young adults networked for jobs, and singles sought dates. And some people stayed quiet and kept their prayers private.

Visitors came once or twice out of curiosity. Sometimes they came back. That's how Ledger Larry Lansken got involved. He was an acceptable accountant but, although he tried, he wasn't particularly talented at Saturday socializing. Larry was eager to find something for himself because otherwise he would be alone all day. His wife reserved the day for shopping, so she headed to the stores. His teenage kids lived on music and phone calls while the sun was up and spent evenings at the mall. Larry needed a social group to which he'd be important. He found it at Shul.

This week, Harold brought his wife Jane and Stu came with Mona. Dennis convinced his daughter Pamela to accompany him, although she didn't look too happy about it. They sat with other Board members, most of them with their spouses, there because they heard that the rabbi would promote the Thanksgiving project in his sermon.

Rabbi London, like the Torah, started his presentation with the creation of the world. He noted that the order of events in Genesis bore a striking resemblance to the sequence as proposed by the theory of evolution. "And after fashioning every element of the world in that order – celestial bodies, water and dry land, vegetation and animal life – God assessed what was created and said it was 'good.' Only after bringing mankind into the picture, did God say it was 'very good.' "

On that basis, the verbose speaker concluded, "We must realize that all of mankind – all religions, races, nations and creeds – come from Adam and Eve and that we are all brothers and sisters. Furthermore," he intellectualized, "the invention of democracy vastly enhanced the development of mankind because it meant everyone could live free. Therefore, it behooves us as a Jewish congregation to welcome the American fusion into our home for a Thanksgiving brotherhood service, to unify us and to move us forward together that we may participate in the creation of our future in this great land."

Avi knew his talk had been a bit long-winded, but hoped it would be received well. He returned to his seat and Cantor Goldberg finished the service.

The usually critical congregants found fault with his reasoning, but the increased attendance amplified the general excitement. The idea of hosting non-Jewish neighbors was gaining momentum, and this pleased Harold and Dennis tremendously.

"It was a good talk," Emma reflected over lunch at home. The children seemed somewhat interested, but Josh was more concerned with baseball scores reported in the paper from the World Series game he had missed the night before, and Ahuva complained about friends she had invited but who backed out at the last minute.

The family finished the Birkat Hamazon, the prayer they always sang together after a meal on Shabbat, and the kids ran off to their rooms. They got into comfortable clothes and – with no television, telephone, radio, computer, travel or money because those options were not Shabbat-appropriate – they settled in for a quiet afternoon of reading and napping.

For the two teenagers, who always spent Shabbat morning at services with their parents, the day of rest could be a burden. Unless they needed sleep or took the trouble to make firm plans with friends, afternoons were likely to be boring. They couldn't wing it and take the chance of walking several miles to a friend's home only to find the family sleeping or, even worse, away. When plans didn't work out, staying home meant a kind of sensory deprivation that was only relieved as the sun set.

At this time of year, it wasn't too bad, since the day was over at supper time. In the spring and summer, on the other hand, Daylight Savings Time meant that it wouldn't get dark until eight or nine at night. Waiting until then on a Saturday night to make a phone call to friends was near torture for teens.

The worst was when two-day holidays adjoined Shabbat, as they did when Rosh Hashanah or some other festivals fell out on Sunday-Monday or Thursday-Friday. Holiday restrictions were almost the same as those that applied to Shabbat, and observing it all meant three seemingly-endless days of isolation until the holy time ran its course. Yes, planning ahead was vital.

But for their parents, Shabbat brought welcome relief from the daily grind and a few treasured moments of family conversation that there was no time for during the rest of the week. A day off gave the family a chance to catch up on thoughts that had troubled them and challenges they had faced all week, plus time to plan for what lay ahead. The occasional holiday stretched the period out, but the basic rhythm of observing one Sabbath day every week made time more precious, even holy.

Emma and Avi appreciated the holiness and peace of the day, but living in the suburbs exaggerated both Shabbat's minuses and pluses. They knew for a fact that few of the Londons' neighbors observed Jewish special days the way they did. People who lived nearby were busy Saturdays with shopping, traveling or entertainment. If the Londons wanted guests with whom they could enjoy Shabbat, the family had to invite them from far away, expect them to sleep over, and have their company for at least two major meals. Holidays meant longer stays, and there were few people who would be welcome for that length of time.

On the other hand, living a distance from a community of strict Jews meant unexpected visitors were unlikely to walk in just because they assumed the Londons were home. The distance also enabled the family to tailor some behaviors within their cocoon that observant Jewish neighbors might not approve. Changing into comfortable clothes and playing basketball in the back yard might not be as acceptable to others as they were to the Londons.

Isolation had its advantages, but to both internal emotions and external enjoyment, planning ahead was vital.

This Shabbat, as usual, Emma and Avi finished cleaning up lunch and headed to their favorite chairs to catch up on their reading. The phone rang, but they could hear from the message that it was not important enough for them to pick up the receiver on Shabbat, so they let the answering machine do its job. Minutes later, they were both snoring. Avi woke up in time to do his weekly hour of Talmud study before leaving for the afternoon-evening Mincha-Maariv minyan at Shul. Emma stirred as he was getting ready to go.

"If no one kills anyone tonight because they're late for the minyan and if the kids make plans to see their friends later," he said to her, "how about the two of us having a quiet evening at home and watching a movie?"

A date? Could it be that their hectic lives will let them have an evening alone together? "I'd be delighted," said the sleepy sermon expert, chief cook and bottle washer.

That night, Josh went to Shul with his father. There were enough men to start the minyan on time and there were no Shul problems that couldn't wait. As soon as Shabbat was over, Josh and Ahuva made calls and arranged overnight invitations to friends' homes and rides to their destinations.

Avi checked the answering machine and, as soon as the kids left, Emma heated up some nachos in the microwave. They inserted "Ocean's Eleven" into the DVD player, put up their feet on the ottoman in front of the couch and had a date.

Chapter 4

Commitments and Contentions

Avi was starting the week on a high and he had every reason to feel optimistic.

On Sunday, the eight o'clock minyan started on time, allowing a full hour for Avi to get home for breakfast before he and Emma had to get back to Shul.

The Shul's morning Hebrew School session started on time at ten o'clock and went well, too. Avi observed the two new teachers in action and he was satisfied that they had what it took to manage both the school's curriculum goals and its disciplinary challenges. After all, most congregants perceived Hebrew School as an imposition: It added hours to the children's school day and deprived their families of precious free time on weekends. The principal knew that all had to go well if it was to be a good year.

Avi and Emma were finished at Shul by twelve-fifteen. Once they got home, they would have time to settle details for the following week as they set up lunch for themselves, breakfast for the kids. Ahuva and Josh came downstairs still in pajamas and considered what they wanted to eat. Emma grabbed a cup of coffee and plunked egg salad on greens for herself while she explained to them her plan to go to Atlantic City for Kevin's Bar Mitzvah party the next Sunday.

"I don't mind the three-hour drive at all," she told them, "and once I get near the shore and get a whiff of sea air, it will all seem worth it. On the way down, I plan to take the exit after the Expressway interchange so I can visit Sof Maarav before the party."

Emma's visits to that small Jewish cemetery were infrequent, but she remembered a lot of the people for whom it was a final resting place. Her parents, one set of grandparents, two uncles and several more remote relatives all had their names on tombstones there. Following Jewish custom, she would always leave rocks on those headstones to show that someone had visited.

Before she left, she would also glance in reverence at Yad L'Banim, the section set aside for survivors of the Nazi Holocaust. Most of those who were bound for that area of the cemetery had left their families' ashes in Europe's death camps. They chose to be buried next to others who, like themselves, lived out the balance of their lives along the Jersey shore. Sand mixed with earth to keep the grass sparse even in that well-sprinkled section.

In case the spigots were already turned off for the winter, Emma would bring water and paper towels with her so she could wash her hands, as Jewish custom demanded, before leaving in the car.

"I'm really looking forward to getting to the hotel, though, so I can catch up a bit with my cousins. I especially want to talk to the ones who recently moved farther away." Gee, she reflected, the family is really spread out now – Boston, Tucson, Miami – and then there are relatives who live closer but are getting older, so it's important that I see them. "So you don't mind if I go, do you?"

Josh and Ahuva said it would be "no big deal" if she were away for the day. They certainly had no regrets about not being invited to that party. They hardly knew that branch of the family anyway, and although they would have to spend a few hours helping their father, they would have most of the day left to do something with their friends.

Ahuva squeezed into the seat next to her mother's place and, like her brother, wondered how they could explain to their contemporaries why they had to stay home for a wedding when they hardly knew the people.

"Why do the Cohens wanna have the wedding in our house?" Ahuva asked her father over her breakfast orange juice.

"Sophie is a forty-seven-year-old, second-time bride," Avi explained as he put tuna salad into a pita for his lunch. "She's too self-conscious at her age to have a big wedding with a flowing veil and bridesmaids. And besides, she had all that the first time – a fancy caterer, a band, lavish flowers, the works – but the marriage didn't last. Besides that, she's worried about her father's health, so she wants to be married soon. Her parents are thrilled that she's getting a second chance at happiness, and they want the wedding to be just right for her. And they trust me to make it meaningful and appropriate."

"But why in our house?" she persisted as she spread cream cheese on a cut raisin bagel.

"Sophie's daughter Soni will be here," said the rabbi. "At twenty-five, it's hard for her to adjust to the idea that her own mother is getting married a second time before she does it even once. Plus, Soni is not comfortable in synagogues at all, so where to have it was a big question. The sanctuary is out, and my Shul office is not big enough even for the small group of people Sophie wants to invite. On the other hand, our house is seen as neutral territory, a location that is not threatening to anybody in the family. And its nice and ... homey." Avi grinned at his own quip.

As he took another bite of his sandwich, though, he looked at both kids. He saw they had not smiled at his joke and in fact stared at him and looked annoyed. Avi understood that they were looking for more of an explanation, and although he could not give details, he could share some insight. He swallowed what he had chewed and wiped his mouth and hands with a napkin.

"Sometimes," Avi said, "it takes a family a while to get used to new circumstances, like a marriage," – the kids rolled their eyes, recalling the young woman who came to the door recently because her father was threatening to kill her – "and the situation can be better tolerated if it just becomes fact rather than being discussed and evaluated. That need for readjustment happens more often with an older pair or a second marriage, but sometimes a small wedding is a good idea even for a young couple if their parents are giving them grief. Anyway, it's better for everyone if this particular ceremony will be subdued and intimate, and then they all can get on with their lives. So it'll be here, where the wedding can be quiet, comfortable and quick." He looked into his daughter's eyes and hugged her, knowing from her half-smile that she understood.

Josh was more resistant to the whole idea, especially because he knew he had to be part of it. He ran his fingers through his blonde curly hair and rubbed his eyes. "Do I have to be a witness if I don't want to be?" he asked after he finished his cereal and started searching for something else to eat. Emma pointed him to a cut bagel and Josh heaped tuna and egg salad on it. He poured a large glass full of milk and continued, "I don't know these people at all. Why would they want me there?"

"You know Sol Cohen from the minyan," answered Avi from across the table as he sipped his coffee, but then he realized what his son was really asking and put his mug down. "Sol is one of the few members of his family who understands the requirements of Jewish law. I'm signing as the marriage authority and Sol's closest minyan buddy will sign as one witness, but we need one more, and Sol knows it. That's where you come in. We need a post-Bar Mitzvah-age Jewish male who's not a relative, who observes Shabbat and who can sign his name in Hebrew on the marriage contract. You're handy, so you're it." The two looked at each other, then grinned.

The hug Avi shared with his daughter and the smile he exchanged with his son had each lasted only a few seconds before the kids ran off to call friends. They had to get dressed and arrange rides to the Yeshiva Gavoha's boys' basketball game later that afternoon. But the pleasure Avi got from that moment with his children would linger, and it would last longer because Emma had witnessed it. Cherishing that vision would help him face the week ahead and the stress those days were likely to bring him.

The coming week would be heavy with the mitzvah of visiting the sick. Even though a committee of the Shul's women made regular rounds, Rabbi London planned to see two members who were at East Belleridge General Hospital. Jane Harrison, wife of the Shul's Board chairman, was going to be there for a few days for a scheduled hysterectomy. Past president Stu Eisen was also due to be a patient and might stay all week to enable his doctor to determine the reason for recent blood pressure episodes. While the rabbi was at the hospital, he would offer to visit any other patients who expressed an interest in seeing a Jewish clergyman.

Rabbi London also scheduled his regular journey to East Belleridge's Jewish Senior Home and Rehabilitation Center, where he knew some permanent and temporary residents.

Isaac Iskilovetzky's wife, Rebecca, was in the kosher facility to stay, and that visit was hard. She rarely remembered anyone, even the women who visited her who used to sit with her every Saturday morning at Shul and play Mah Jongg with her every Monday night at her home. Her day consisted of being fed mounds of unrecognizable chopped food at one meal and then waiting for the next. Between meals, diaper changes and showers were scheduled events. The nurses brought her transporter chair into the group activities room whenever something special was scheduled, but Rebecca never seemed to notice. Her occasional shrieks were unnerving to all those around her, even when the nurses explained that the sounds were involuntary and without medical cause. And although Avi was sure the staff did their best to keep the facility sparkling and its residents clean, it smelled.

While Rabbi London was there, he always made sure the on-premises synagogue was in good order, stacking the prayer books where residents could reach them easily, lining up electric Shabbat and Chanukah candelabras on a ledge and arranging the few chairs so that wheelchairs could extend the rows. The end of life could be difficult, indeed, but it should be dignified, he thought.

On his way home, the rabbi planned to stop at the nearby assisted-living apartments, to which Hannah Shine had returned with a health aide after a brief stay at the hospital. Tests indicated that nothing specific was wrong with her and that, with time, she would feel like herself again.

But first, Avi had to visit Reeva. She had been transferred from Northwood Hills Hospital near her home to its temporary-stay wing, called a Rehabilitation Center, and was put on a new medication that seemed to make a lot of difference. She slept a lot, but the nurses said she was much calmer and even ate when she thought no one was watching. Dr. Obes told Avi that she could go home soon, provided she stayed on the pills.

Poor Dennis, thought the rabbi, between his mother and his wife, he's got his hands full. It was obvious that Dennis felt better knowing his rabbi was involved, so Avi planned to see both women often and report back.

Rabbi London would get another chance to talk about the importance of visiting the sick on Friday night. He would explain it as a mitzvah to the post-Bar/Bat Mitzvah-age kids invited to the Teen Dessert program, which the Londons were initiating at their home.

Four such evenings were planned for the year for the Shul's teenagers, and Emma and Avi hoped the program would become popular as a way of reaching out Jewishly to adolescents during what is often a rebellious time of their lives. Also, it would do teens some good to shift the focus off themselves and onto others, and for that Avi would propose a plan to visit confined patients. By seeing people with major problems, the kids would understand how meaningful doing a mitzvah can be for others as well as for themselves. And although all the congregation's teens were welcome, Avi saw the experience as more important for the public school kids, who might be unaware that a mitzvah could be part of their everyday lives.

At Yeshiva Gavoha, Rabbi London had a regular chance to talk to teens, which he loved to do. There, he taught a Wednesday morning class, which he started two years ago and would begin for the year this week. The course was called "Jewish Diversity – Past and Present," and Avi spoke to a group of seniors who would face the challenges of university campus life next year, or the year after if they spent the intervening time in Israel. Because of day school students' limited exposure, they knew little about non-Jewish values or popular views on world events.

The discussion format gave the young adults a chance to ask the difficult questions they might face in the outside world. They would discuss European attitudes toward Jews after the Holocaust, or Christian passion plays, or Jewish views on same-sex marriages. Teaching every week gave Avi a reason to stay current on colleges and well-informed about his topic so he could prepare his students for a world where not everyone was pro-Israel, pro-Jewish or even pro-traditional values. It was probably the most demanding and rewarding hour of his week.

Of course, he was always available to his students or congregants – in person, on the phone or by e-mail – for a question on Jewish law or tradition. The previous week, for example, a member of the congregation had a niece who was in a long-term, committed relationship with another woman. The niece used donated sperm from a fertility clinic and bore a son, and the congregant asked if it was appropriate to say "Mazal tov" and to bring a gift to the Bris.

Rabbi London had answered "Of course," but in his mind he followed the logic further. He wondered how the Jewish child of an unknown father and a single mother or a lesbian couple should be named. By tradition, a male is called by his Hebrew name, son-of-his-father's-name. Would a case like this follow the convention used in the situation of a convert? In that case, the baby would receive a Hebrew name and be called the child of Abraham and Sarah, names that are used because those biblical characters were the first Jews.

The circumstances would require a study of Talmudic texts and other reference books Avi had in his study library. He'd also have to check current opinion essays by Orthodox, Conservative and Reform authorities in this country as well as by the rabbinate in Israel.

He really enjoyed a good question, and intellectual challenges were an important part of his profession. That's probably why he liked developing sermons so much. This week's Torah portion was Noah, and it was rich with themes. One was preparing for the future even though its events were not foreseeable, as when Noah built the Ark for the flood long before the rain started. Maybe the rabbi would mention that the Ark saved two of every animal in general but seven pairs of the kosher ones.

Or, considering that the Thanksgiving event was looming, it might be important to explain the Seven Noahide Commandments – such as the need for justice and the prohibition of incest – which apply to non-Jews as well as to Jews. The week's portion also described the Tower of Babel, a structure built to demonstrate man's delusions of grandeur but destroyed by the real greatness of God. Yes, there were several good choices for this week's sermon.

Avi looked forward to Shabbat all week. The day of rest packed his mind with lofty thoughts whereas the week leading up to it was dominated by mundane demands. Shabbat provided a break that was much needed in today's exhausting world.

But rest was a long way off. This week was just beginning and Avi had to work first.

He started with reactions to the previous day's brotherhood sermon. The talk was getting good reactions from the members of the congregation and was motivating usual sideliners to participate in the community event.

"This is the first time that I've seen a true spirit of inclusion by our synagogue," Florence Fischman announced to the rabbi in a late Sunday afternoon phone call. Avi welcomed the happy tone of her voice because she usually conveyed only caustic remarks about the absence of a role in Jewish life for widows like her. "I would be happy to work with women from the other houses of worship to arrange a collation after the service," she volunteered.

Rabbi London hesitated. He didn't remember any refreshments at the event the year before, and it would be better for all future gatherings if food were not involved at all. That would eliminate Jews' problems regarding kosher choices and the complications for Muslims if Thanksgiving fell out during Ramadan, when they might be observing a daytime fast. But Florence wanted to make it "nice" and he hated dampening her enthusiasm.

"How about flowers instead of food?" he suggested.

"Maybe seasonal decorations, like multicolored leaves and pumpkins," she agreed, still happy to be crucial to the occasion.

"Okay, but no jack-o-lanterns or other Halloween influences," he cautioned. "Maybe Emma could give you some guidance on that." He was sure Florence would take direction better from his wife than from him, and he suggested that the two women talk the next evening.

Monday, he got more encouraging calls, including some from of the town's other clergy.

"I heard you preached a great sermon Saturday morning," effused Father Dom Dehaney, who was proud his cathedral-like church hosted last year's first-ever local ecumenical service, "and I understand your congregation wants to host the event this year. Sounds great! I'll alert our choir, if you like, and they can zero in on some religiously neutral hymns to sing as part of the program. Do you have an organ?"

"Uh, no, we don't," said Rabbi London. Jewish law did not allow the use of musical instruments at all on Shabbat or holidays, so traditional congregations did not have any. Furthermore, many Jews felt that using an organ, of all instruments, would make a shul feel like a church. "I'll let you know about the program," Avi added, wondering in any case just how neutral Catholic hymns could be.

"A Brotherhood Thanksgiving service is a very American thing to do," said the always proper Paul Thorn, Minister of the picturesque Protestant church. His congregation was growing, and it was faithful to its leader. At least thirty of its members could be expected to show up, he proudly said.

"News has come to me that you're planning to do an inter-denominational Thanksgiving prayer gathering," said Omar Shukran, the imam of a new Muslim group in town. "I'll have to let you know how we can participate."

Does he mean how or if? wondered the rabbi. And if they say they're coming, do we need extra security because they support Arab causes in the Middle East? Oy, this is getting complicated, thought Avi.

On Tuesday, he got calls about the brotherhood service from the Jewish leaders in town.

"I wish the date had been cleared first by our local office," said Y. M. Pines, the local representative of the Organization of Jewish Organizations, which coordinated local Jewish philanthropic agencies. Avi had a special warm spot in his heart for the man because, like him, Pines came from a Zionistic family whose members were pioneers in pre-state Israel.

"I'm sorry," the rabbi said. "Is there a scheduling conflict?"

"No," the OJO rep continued, "but procedures have to be followed."

"What time did you have in mind for this shindig?" asked Bert Maher, the president of Emek Emet. The Modern Orthodox Congregation had outgrown the converted house in which they held a daily minyan and housed their leader. Rabbi Zvi Melamed was having his fourth child, so the shul was constructing a new building for services and classes. "Our members have a lot on for that day. After morning minyan and a meeting about raising funds for our new shul, most people will have a big dinner and watch the football game before Mincha and Maariv. I can't promise you a big showing from us."

The Reform were the last to call but were the most ready to help. Their spiritual leader, Rabbi Dana Lee, offered to bring enough folding chairs for half the fifty people she predicted would come from Temple Tikvah.

Chairs, always the rabbi's job, laughed Avi to himself.

The large Reform temple had a lot of movable seats because the room devoted to services also served as the social hall and had to be rearranged for different events. A third of the members were recent or potential converts to Judaism, too, as was the rabbi's husband, so that congregation would be especially supportive of any occasion that brought different religions together.

It looked like the total attending that day might be about three hundred ten, calculated Avi. If the Reform brought some chairs to supplement the two hundred fifty already in the Conservative sanctuary, Congregation Tefillah might have enough places to comfortably seat everyone. Just in case, he made a mental note to ask the nonsectarian funeral home next door for some extras. It seemed to be his job, he snickered.

So Avi spent Monday on the phone, Tuesday visiting the sick and Wednesday trying to locate the director of the funeral home next door and making a list of To-Dos for the Thanksgiving event. Every afternoon, he supervised the Hebrew School and, morning and evening, he went to the minyan. The rabbi was so busy that he almost forgot the semi-annual Employment Review Committee meeting, which was scheduled for Wednesday night at Shul after the minyan.

He only remembered about the meeting when he saw that the twelfth man to walk in for the minyan was Ray Fisch, who was on the committee. Luckily, Avi always looked presentable because his daily uniform was a sport jacket and an open-collar shirt plus a matching knitted kippah. For Shabbat and holidays, he had brown and dark blue suits, and when he was officiating at a funeral or wedding, he wore black. For all of them, he had an array of conservative ties and kippot. What he wore every day would be fine for this evening.

Rabbi London called home quickly to say why he'd be late, and he went into the classroom, where the eight people were gathering. As usual, he took a seat in the back.

For the meeting, three men sat next to Ray on one side of the room and the four women chose places on the other side. The seating was random, but the committee was structured deliberately, half women and half men, on the theory that they should have an equal say on what the professionals of the Shul should be expected to do for the congregants. The group met at other times regarding the chazzan and custodian, but tonight the focus was on the rabbi.

Avi was invited to witness an honest assessment of his achievements, but he wondered if the professionals of any other industry faced this. He found it absolutely unnerving to be at this meeting but he always went because he couldn't conceive of a graceful way to get out of it. He sat quietly, wearing his best poker face, and they talked about him as if he weren't there.

"Deh rabbi should get points for vot he's doing for deh community for Denksgiving," Helen Levine said in her German accented English. She had survived the Holocaust only because, as a child, she was given a different identity and sheltered by non-Jewish neighbors. The rest of her family didn't make it. She was forever grateful to pious Christians and felt deep affection for them. Now a retired secretary, a wife and a grandmother, Helen also was a fan of Rabbi London's and was always ready with a flattering remark. "He's reaching out to both deh Jews and deh goyim of our community," she said.

"Yeah, but did you hear how he vetoed a kiddush for that day?" asked Morty Fenn. He remembered the dissatisfaction with the rabbi's performance expressed at the Board meeting and wanted to see what more he could ferret out. And even though he was a grandparent like Helen, his stark opinion could usually be counted on to counterbalance her gentle words.

"It's not a kiddush. That's only on Shabbos," said Mel Rubin, who felt better educated because he attended the Shul's adult education classes. Morty meant a collation, thought the rabbi. Sure, the refreshments after Shabbat or holiday morning services were called "a kiddush," but that's because the Kiddush blessing is said over the wine. A simple Kiddush blessing is said whenever wine is used, such as at a wedding, or at home ... or at a wedding at our home, Rabbi London cocked his head and smiled to himself. But he resisted the urge to make the correction out loud. He had enjoyed years of banter with Mel and respected his analytical mind, and didn't want to nitpick with Morty. Avi was sure others in the room had noticed the mistake, too, but the rabbi felt it was an unnecessary criticism at this time.

"But I heard that Rabbi told Florence we couldn't have any food after the service," continued Mel, using Avi's title as his name. "Everybody knows that food will make it special. It'll make the difference between really mixing and just sharing the space."

Yes, exactly, thought the rabbi. That's why we Jews are supposed to eat only kosher food and drink only kosher wine. It's not that it's better or that we're better, it's just that staying kosher defines us and keeps our separate identities intact. If Mel understood that better, perhaps his kids would have married Jews, Avi concluded.

"Well, he's allowing some decorations, right Rabbi?" said Suzette Z. Siegel, a bubbly young lawyer who was new to the Shul. She was the first committee member to acknowledge the elephant in the room.

"Yes, of course, as long as the decorations reflect the season and the American experience of pilgrims and turkeys, not the Halloween images of witches and ghosts," said Rabbi London.

"That's a very fine difference, don't you think, Rabbi?" challenged Celia Dubinsky in her usual defiant manner. Her husband, having had enough of that tone, had sued for divorce last year.

"Perhaps defining that difference is a good subject for a class, Celia. Let's put that on the education agenda," suggested the rabbi, trying not to prolong the evening more than necessary. The adult education program needed something to spice it up anyway.

"The scuttlebutt is that the brotherhood sermon was very good," noted Zev Wolfson, the father of three preteen girls. "I wasn't there to hear it myself," – he made it a point never to stay in the synagogue while the rabbi was preaching – "but a lot of folks said it was right on the mark." He had been downstairs when parents, who were in the upstairs service only because it was a convenient place to wait, came down to pick up their kids after Junior Congregation. He agreed with those parents that they were better off meeting their offspring downstairs than remaining in the sanctuary and having the children join them there. They didn't want too much religion, after all. But the parents said they had heard, and liked, the sermon.

"I heard something else less flattering," said Celia in her huffiest voice, "and I heard the same thing about two different events, so it must be true. One was about Harvey Stein's funeral last week and the other was about Sophie Cohen's wedding this coming Sunday. Both were arranged bare-bones, without anything memorable about them, and I'm wondering how a rabbi can call them Jewish events when Jews won't remember them that way! It doesn't do our Shul's reputation any good at all."

There were apparently two approaches here, thought Avi. Celia, obviously, was more of the Dennis-Shine-Outward-Signs school of thought than the rabbi's Discipline-Of-Deeper-Personal-Meaning-By-Practicing-The-Ritual educational thrust, he said sardonically to himself. He snapped out of his reverie of private sarcasm and looked around the room to see if he should answer or not. It seemed not. These folks were just venting. But it would be wise for him to remember that his flock had a variety of views.

"Are the rabbi's accomplishments commensurate with his salary?" asked Phyllis Kimmel, who had been quiet until now. She was the dominant figure in her marriage as well as here. Her two boys never won an argument with her in the past and, like her husband, they no longer tried. She looked around the room at the other committee members who were staring at her and, not getting any signals that they understood her question, she rephrased it. "Are we getting enough bang for the buck?"

Silence.

Avi expected someone to say something in his defense, but no one said a word. Many of the people sitting there had seen him rush off to visit sick congregants. Some of them could verify from personal experience that Rabbi London was available for emergencies at any hour of the day or night. Several in the room had benefited when he took care of families at their moments of greatest joys and deepest sorrows.

No one remarked how he always tried to give people a spiritual word that would help them cope with challenges or a joke to put problems in perspective. Or that he never refused to prepare remarks for a special occasion. Or that he could always be depended upon to lead a service or to teach a class if no one else was available.

He knew he wasn't perfect, but he tried hard. He was ready to organize large events and to raise funds for the Shul. He could explain Jewish tradition to anyone and could discuss contemporary American subjects, as well. He got along with Jewish and other religious leaders and was getting to know the area politicians.

Moreover, Rabbi London always had a good word to say to and about every congregant and he was happy to put it in writing any time it might help.

His wife was a doll. His kids were well-behaved. He was not hard to look at or to listen to. Was that enough bang for the buck?

"The Hebrew School is growing, so the rabbi-rebbetzin team must be doing something right," said Ray. He was a doctor and a good man, and his wife and three kids seemed to appreciate Avi's finer points. Ray smiled in Rabbi London's direction, as if he knew this had been an undeservedly rough night for the spiritual leader. Avi appreciated the friendly gesture and smiled back, and that one moment got him through the ordeal.

"How was Shul?" Emma asked her husband when he finally got home. It was her usual question and, like when someone asks "How are you?" but really doesn't want to know, he gave his perfunctory answer. "Fine."

The week had started out well. This was just a bump in the road, Avi said to himself as he hung up his jacket. I'd better focus on the good stuff – the wonderful wedding scheduled for Sunday in the house, plans for the brotherhood event, the love of my wife, the glow of our great children, the success of the Hebrew School, the impact of a good sermon ...

"You're muttering," said Emma. She had stopped writing her math lesson plan and was looking at him. She could see he was tense, but didn't know why.

"Sorry," he said, not realizing that his grumbling was audible. He tried to keep his problems to himself. His wife carried the lion's share of running the house, child rearing and keeping the family together in general. She took charge of staying in touch with her relatives as well as with his and attended to family health issues that surfaced from time to time. Besides that, she taught in schools morning and evening, pitched in when he needed her help on a Shul problem and kept up with current events in the community. Emma had enough to do. "Sorry," he repeated.

She worried about him. Avi worked so hard, taking everybody else's problems to heart and helping in any way he could. He kept the Hebrew School running and was an engrossing preacher and teacher. And he was such a dedicated family man! She wished she could do more to lighten his load. Avi had so much to do. "I'm sorry, too," she said.

The next morning, Avi got back to his routine, finishing his list of visitations, calls and study that had to get done. Slowly, the sting of Wednesday night's meeting faded, and the memory of it captured it for what it was, a small meeting in which there were a few narrow minds. He knew he was managing a multifaceted job that affected many people in profound ways. Besides, Shabbat was coming.

When Friday night finally arrived, the peacefulness that settled on them as Emma lit candles soothed both the adults and the children. Avi got back from the evening minyan at Shul, and the family of four sat down to Shabbat supper. Avi started the meal with Kiddush over the wine and Motzi over the challah, and the tensions of the week melted into the vegetable soup. The Londons reviewed the success of the yeshiva's basketball team as they passed the chicken, and complained about the quality of Drivers Ed classes as they cut up pieces of noodle kugel and salad on their plates. By the time they started compote and sang the Birkat Hamazon, Avi had put the past week behind him and was ready for guests to arrive for the first Teen Dessert evening.

This informal gathering was intended as a way Emma and Avi could keep in touch with kids during the formative years between Bar Mitzvah and college. They enlisted the help of their own children, who understood that the program was meant for Congregation Tefillah families, and although they didn't want to be there, Josh and Ahuva did the best they could to be polite. It was part of the job.

The cantor's son Eitan lived down the block and, although he was only ten and too young to be there at all, he was the first to arrive. Mark and Jeff Eisen were next, followed by four of the Fenn kids. Brendan and Pamela Shine made it a total of seven boys and two girls, in addition to the Londons.

Emma was sure to put out desserts kids would like. The girls demurely munched grapes and cookies as they stood around the dining room table and seemed happy, but hardly spoke. The boys dived into the brownies and non-dairy ice cream and sat in two groups in the living room, wolfing down their portions. Between gulps of soda, one group of boys talked sports and the other griped about their parents.

Rabbi London brought the girls into the living room just as Brendan was complaining about the car his father had bought him, calling it "Dennis's symbol of control." Pamela shot her brother an angry look and he stopped his tirade.

The rabbi dismissed what he observed as adolescent angst, wished them all a "Shabbat shalom" and welcomed them to the

London home. From that point on, Avi followed his agenda. He made sure the kids understood they could contact him at any time. Then, he broached the subject of a group mitzvah, such as a weekly schedule to visit the sick. Finally, he said he hoped they would come to the next Teen Dessert and bring their friends. Perhaps then they could discuss other topics on their minds, such as college, Israel, interfaith dating, or even abortion. They chatted a bit longer, and by ten the evening was over. Whether the program was a success or not was anybody's guess.

Shabbat morning, Avi thought his sermon went well, although he didn't think most of the congregation appreciated the Seven Noahide Laws any more than they accepted the authenticity of the Ten Commandments. Both called for justice, but the modern mind dismissed them both as ancient folklore, not to be taken seriously.

But for Avi and his wife, and for their children, the wisdom of the ancients and the Shabbat respite it demanded was restorative and fortified them for what might lie ahead.

Chapter 5

Life Cycle Complications

Barring Saturday-night celebrations or emergencies, Avi's regular work week began at Shul early Sunday morning. Most people were not working on the weekend, so the Shacharit minyan was scheduled to begin at eight, an hour later than the weekday starting time.

This morning followed the usual schedule, with the Hebrew School convening at ten, but this time Avi substituted as the teacher in his wife's class.

Emma had left home early for her trip, but before she pulled out of the driveway, she made sure that the house was ready. She put a vinyl cover on the dining room table, onto which the caterer's staff would put a disposable white tablecloth, blue plastic utensils and platters of food. The workers also would set up folding chairs in the living room. After the wedding, the same staff would clean up.

As soon as Avi arrived home, he got the particulars ready for the two o'clock nuptials. He arranged the documents on the desk, made sure he had two pens that worked and put two chairs where he usually sat.

While Avi worked in the study, Josh got himself out of bed, clipped a kippah on his unruly short locks, dressed in a nice shirt and pants and came downstairs. He stopped in the kitchen to grab a bagel and headed to the study. As he munched, he reached up to a top shelf. Enjoying the nearly six-foot height that he recently accomplished, he easily took down the folded chuppah from where Emma had stored it in a plastic bag.

The wedding canopy was just a lined and finished square of maroon velvet with brass rings attached to the corners, but Avi's mother had sewn on it a gold-colored band of trim in the shape of a Jewish star. The project was a gift from her in Israel to him in New York on the occasion of Avi's being the third consecutive generation in that family line to become a rabbi. The decorated fabric had tremendous sentimental value to the rabbi's family and was just right for occasions like these.

By itself, the chuppah was not free-standing. Four seven-foot, dark wood poles – designed to support the fabric's corners from nails at their tops – were stored behind a tall bookcase in the study. Josh held the rest of his bagel between his teeth as he fished the poles out and stood them up in a corner near the fireplace at the end of the living room. He unwrapped the velvet canopy and put it on the coffee table, then popped the rest of the bagel into his mouth.

As soon as Ahuva finished putting on clogs, a blue dress and a matching hair barrette, she headed down the stairs.

"You sound like a herd of elephants," Josh remarked, starting the day as usual, with a sibling jibe.

"You look like more of a dork than usual," Ahuva replied in kind as she headed toward the kitchen for some juice.

Soon, Ahuva began her work. She put a small table in front of the living room fireplace and covered it with a white lace cloth. On it, she arranged a Kiddush cup, a bottle of wine, the rabbi's manual and a small, stapled, paper bag in which there was a burned-out light bulb. The chuppah, which would stand over the table, would be set up later when guests were available to hold the poles.

The fifty-year-old groom and his family were the first to arrive. For Cliff Rosen, this was a long-awaited first marriage, and his elderly mother was happy she had lived to see the day. She finally had a grandchild, too, although a new adult in the family was not what she had envisioned. Not important, she thought; her deceased husband would have been happy to see his only child finally find a life partner.

The bride's family arrived next, Sylvia and Sol bursting with pride. Sophie wore an off-white suit and carried a fifteen-inch-long bridal veil that would meet traditional requirements and then be easily removed. She and the groom joined Sol and his best friend, Isaac Iskilovetzky, in the study. Josh was already there, standing next to his father.

In the living room, four men from among the two dozen guests moved to the front to take direction from Ahuva. She made sure the chuppah's corner brass rings were attached to the nails on top of the poles and positioned the men supporting them so the cloth above stretched out as straight as possible and formed a canopy.

Meanwhile, guests sat quietly and discreetly listened to what was going on in the study. Its glass doors, which were slightly ajar, enabled guests to see the witnesses sit at the desk to sign the contractual agreements that legalized the union for both God (a Ketubah) and country (a New Jersey marriage license). Sophie and Cliff were told what the ceremony would entail but, more importantly, what their coming together would mean for their family as well as for the Jewish people.

Sophie put her head piece on and got ready for the attached veil to be flipped down, but Cliff hesitated and asked if was appropriate for them both to be there. "I thought it was bad luck for the groom to see the bride right before the ceremony."

"It may be bad luck in the Christian world, but among us Jews it's considered the groom's obligation," Rabbi London explained. "The Torah says that, when Jacob wanted to marry Rachel, he had to work seven years for his future father-in-law as a dowry. The night of the wedding, though, after Jacob had bedded his veiled bride, he discovered a switch had been made: The father-in-law had substituted the older sister Leah. Of course, there was nothing wrong then with a man having two wives, and Jacob still wanted Rachel, but the old man made Jacob promise to work another seven years for the bride he first wanted. From then on, to avoid the extra work, we men lower the veil ourselves to make sure we are marrying the right girl!"

The story always made a jittery couple laugh, and the fact that it was a serious part of the tradition focused everyone's thoughts. The wedding was not only important to the potential of these two individuals and the nation they were building, but the couple was an extension into the future of everything that has happened to the Jewish people in the past.

It was time to link the past to the future. Cliff lowered the sheer material over Sophie's face in the study and Isaac opened the glass doors to the living room. Josh and Ahuva stepped into the background as Avi walked to the front.

Rabbi London, now under the chuppah, sang out a blessing of greeting, and the groom approached from the study.

The veiled bride came next and stood under the wedding canopy with the groom. The rabbi explained that the chuppah defined their unique entity, a new Jewish family. The open canopy symbolized Abraham's tent in the desert, with its four sides open in every direction in a gesture of hospitality. Cliff recited the "Harei At" formula and placed the solid gold band on the bride's right index finger. Sophie moved it to her left ring finger while the rabbi read the Ketubah. Avi said blessings, and Cliff and Sophie tasted the wine.

Finally, the rabbi spoke of the destruction of the Temple in ancient Jerusalem and explained that it is remembered at all happy occasions. At a wedding, a broken glass is the symbol of the devastation, so Cliff stomped on the bag that held the glass, and its contents made a loud crunch.

"Mazal tov!" everyone shouted, especially joyful that the ceremony was warm and brief. The groom kissed the bride, who was happy to be free of her veil at last, and everybody was ready to eat. Sophie's daughter Soni made a toast to the new couple that started off hesitantly but ended with an enthusiastic wish that they find happiness together. She drank her Champagne, arranged a plateful of whitefish salad and cake and sat down in a corner to get acquainted with her new grandmother.

Ahuva and Josh watched the scene, recognizing life's joy when they saw it. They each helped themselves to some pastries they were eyeing and then put away the ceremonial props that were no longer needed. An hour later, the house was empty of wedding guests, refreshments and extra chairs, and the rabbi's two kids were on the phone making plans with friends.

The teenagers were still at the movies when Emma got home from the Bar Mitzvah party. Avi had a lot to tell her about the wedding, but he wanted to let her talk first, while scenes from her day were still vivid.

"It took less than three hours to get to Atlantic City, and the weather was so good that the drive was a pleasure. I took one break, at the pish-and-switch rest stop we usually use," – her husband smiled when she referred to the highway eatery where they usually changed drivers – "made a quick stop at the cemetery and then went to the hotel near Uncle Sholom's house in Ventnor."

Until he died three years ago, Uncle Sholom had made Atlantic City, and then Ventnor, his home, but most other Jews from that beachfront community had moved to newer towns along the New Jersey shore. The Beach Ball Hotel housed one of only three kosher places still existing in the immediate vicinity. The beach-block property provided parking, rooms for out-of-town guests and a large ballroom that held the party of a hundred very well.

"The three course, sit-down dinner was delicious, and thankfully the acoustic tile kept the music volume short of deafening," she said. A small band provided Jewish circle dances during dinner and a DJ played popular tunes familiar to the kids during dessert, which they ate between dance sets.

Kalman Bavli, the Ventnor congregation's rabbi, greeted the locals, who knew Kevin from their Conservative shul or the nearby day school. He also welcomed family members who had traveled a distance to get there. The boy's parents said how proud they were of all three of their children, and then the 13-year-old gave his speech.

"Kevin could have given the same talk at the party that he had given at his Bar Mitzvah in shul the day before, when he spoke about Noah and Flood," Emma said, "but to his credit, he chose to deal with another story in the same portion, the Tower of Babel." Kevin had said the structure was intended to be so tall that it would reach heaven and prove that people were as good as God. When God made them speak different languages, he said, they were confused, and the resulting chaos put an end to the project. "Kevin's conclusion was that we can build peace among nations only when we can understand each other. The idea was really very insightful," she said.

"The best part of the day, though, was seeing my brother and sister and getting reacquainted with their kids." Jerry's family lived in Philadelphia and Belle's settled in Baltimore, so it was an occasion whenever the three of them got together. "Their businesses suffered when the economy was bad, but they seem to be recovering. They're both very lucky that they married great people. Without their encouragement, these last few years would have been tough."

In final updates, Avi learned from his wife that some of the relatives from Arizona and Massachusetts didn't come. "Still, it was nice to see distant cousins who came in from Canada and Mexico. Some elderly aunts and uncles were showing their ages, and it's important to enjoy a simcha with them while we can." Her first cousins seemed to be all right, but the oldest of the more remote relatives was talking divorce. "I hope they can work it out," Emma said. The update was important beyond a regular devotion to family. Whenever her relatives needed a rabbi, they called Avi.

"It was the middle of the afternoon when the party ended, so there was still time to go for a walk on the boards," Emma continued. As a group gathered to discuss who wanted to go, Kevin's rabbi approached her and asked if she was from East Belleridge.

"He told me he remembered Dennis Shine!" Emma said to her husband. "About five years ago, there was a meeting about fundraising for the day school in that area. Dennis is one of their main supporters!"

She didn't know it, but hotel manager Marvin Kent overheard the conversation and remembered the man and his redheaded wife, too. Dennis had checked in for that gathering and, despite the beautiful weather, left his wife in the room for several days while he was at meetings. He called the room often to make sure she was there and ordered food to be sent up for her. Marv was on the Food and Beverage staff then, and he delivered several orders.

"My husband wants to get rid of me," Reeva had whispered in Marv's ear the last time he was there. "He might have brought the gun. It used to be mine. Shooting was just a hobby, but I was good at it. But then he took it away from me. He said it wasn't safe. Or maybe he said I wasn't safe." She paused, and then looked directly at the waiter. "He keeps it locked in his desk, you know."

Marv pretended he didn't hear her, positioned the food cart near a chair and left, but he couldn't forget what she had said. He told Rabbi Bavli, who was organizing that fundraising meeting, but the rabbi shrugged it off. "It's very sad. Such a mentsch, he is. Dennis gives so much money and time to our school and to so many other causes. He told me she's 'a little off,' and now I know what he means. God bless him, he doesn't deserve to be burdened with a woman who talks about him that way."

Rabbi Bavli glanced at Marv, now behind the reception desk, and remembered the long-ago incident, too. The clergyman turned to Emma and asked her as casually as he could, "So how are the Shines?" He hoped the phrasing was general enough that it would elicit any news important enough for him to know.

Emma knew that Dennis had spoken to her husband several times about Reeva and that she had been in and out of hospitals recently, but didn't know the details. Even if Emma had known, she would have respected congregants' confidentiality and kept her response general. When she answered simply that Dennis and Reeva were fine, Rabbi Bavli said his usual "Thank God" and dropped the whole subject. He turned back to the crowd and got busy saying goodbye to the rest of the people he knew.

About thirty of Emma's relatives put on warm hats and coats and headed for the herringbone-patterned boardwalk with her. They paused at the rail and inspected the scene, acting as if they were in charge of the size of the waves and the condition of the beach at the start of winter. They breathed deeply, enjoying the crisp wind that carried the smell of the surf.

The tide was coming in on fine sand strewn with broken shells. Cackling sea gulls, as if to demonstrate how they had created the scene, swooped overhead and checked to see if they had missed anything. One gull found a promising tidbit near the surf and perched near it to get a closer look. Convinced it was worth a try, the bird took the clam shell in its beak and soared almost straight up, then dropped it. The gull landed quickly next to the broken shell to see if there was anything edible inside. There wasn't, but the bird caught up with a small crab that raced by and feasted on that instead.

More gulls patrolled the beach and hovered mid-air along the walkway to see if snacking humans might drop a few morsels. Cooing pigeons strutted along the boards, inspecting the cracks for crumbs they might eat, and escorted the party guests as they strolled "uptown."

Setting out from Ventnor toward Atlantic City was to walk northeast on the compass, but it was thought of as heading due north because the ocean was on the right. Ahead, the uptown boardwalk widened to make room for Atlantic City's rolling chairs. Pedestrian traffic was bustling, as casino hotels outdid each other's gaudiness to entice gamblers. Souvenir shops, fortune teller niches, saltwater taffy stores and pinball arcades along the boardwalk and on the piers were busy, and bargain hunters – eager to spend their winnings – gravitated to fashion boutiques in hotels.

Beyond the uptown end of the boardwalk and past the lighthouse at the curve of the shore, yachts docked at the marina and upscale hotels lined the inlet. The marina was not far away but the whole inlet was out of sight of the boardwalk. Between the two bustling areas were the city's poorer avenues, whose residents hoped the gaming industry that employed them would someday fulfill the promise to share their wealth.

It was a changing town. When Emma grew up here, Atlantic City's hotels were in decline but its beach remained pristine. Summer brought hordes of city dwellers to join locals sprawled on the shore's fine sand or bobbing in the breaking waves. In the cold weather of past winters, small numbers of hearty visitors would take their daily constitutionals on the boards or ride ponies along the water's edge.

Now, cars, buses, trains and planes every day, year round, ferried thousands to casinos, which had no appeal at all to Emma or her family. The beach and ocean, however, which they loved, looked abandoned. Its view was hidden behind a mound of sand that was

held in place by wild grasses and was meant to control erosion. But
the dunes ruined the treasured glimpse of the sea from the
boardwalk, one of the main attractions of this seaside resort.

Emma and her relatives turned around to go back to the
"downtown" residential end of the boardwalk. There, the off-season
was quiet. Storefronts sold books, T-shirts and antiques. Hotels and
motels on every block fronted the walkway to offer a view of the sea,
but there were few takers.

As it got dark, Emma said her goodbyes and headed home.
"Everyone asked for you," Emma told her husband. Her family
understood that the Londons' plans were always subject to the
congregation's needs. "Our relatives send their love," she said.

Avi told his wife how sorry he was that he couldn't go to the
party, but that the Cohen wedding was important. "It went
beautifully, thanks to your planning and the children's help," he said,
skipping the part about the insults that were typical of the kids'
interaction. He explained how Ahuva and Josh had worked as a team,
getting the details set up and respecting the significance of the
occasion. "They were dignified and delightful. You can be proud of
them."

When the teens got home that night, Emma gave them a
short version of her report and Avi repeated his praise. It had been a
good day.

Avi was looking forward to the next day, not knowing how
hard it might be.

"I have a meeting this afternoon with the Fernbergs," he told Emma
during the Monday morning routine. "We're in the final stages of
planning their son's Bar Mitzvah, and I want to get some details on
their family background."

It was Rabbi London's practice to meet with the parents of
the celebrant a few weeks before the event so they would have time
to find the answers to his questions about family history. Usually, the
interview revealed a grandfather who studied with a famous rabbi in
Europe or a great aunt who married an immigrant and became a
driving force behind a major philanthropy. The stories were always
interesting and encouraged conversations with relatives that might
otherwise never happen. This time, the meeting would be more than
a pleasure, Avi thought. These people were straightforward and
genuine, always a delight.

Carey and Bill Fernberg were both in medicine, she a nurse
and he an X-Ray technician, and they had a well-behaved boy in the

Hebrew School. The family attended Shabbat morning services regularly and Bill sometimes came during the week, too, especially now that his son was planning his Bar Mitzvah. In their home, they were as careful as their logic would let them be to use only kosher products and observe the Jewish holidays.

And when the rabbi spoke about applying Jewish values to current events, these people really listened. For instance, when Avi cited Saddam Hussein's conduct of wars in Iraq – where soldiers fought to win no matter the cost to the public or the environment – and compared it to the rules of battle given in the Bible – which forbid rape or the destruction of trees because they were important for rebuilding societies – Carey and Bill both listened closely and had good questions. Rabbi London was sure their son would grow up to be a pillar of the American and Jewish communities.

The Fernbergs entered Rabbi London's office in the Shul while the Hebrew School classes were in session. Andrew came along with his parents, as expected, but before they started discussing the Bar Mitzvah, the family had something to say. They had reviewed the issue at length at home and now were telling the rabbi. The Bar Mitzvah boy, explained Carey and Bill, was not their first child. Andrew has an older sister.

"Bill and I were young when we got married, but we wanted to have kids immediately," she said, trying to control her emotions. "I conceived right away, but Laura was a difficult child. We tried everything we could with her, even medication, but nothing seemed to work. Maybe now they would call her problem Attention Deficit Disorder, but then, who knew?" Carey stopped to dab her eyes.

"We did our best with her, but nothing worked. Laura was almost ten when Andrew was born, and by then she was already talking about leaving home." As far as Carey and Bill knew, they told their rabbi, Laura's been living on a commune in southern Israel since she was fifteen.

Rabbi London was sad to hear that the picture was not as rosy as he thought. It happens in so many families, he started to say, that friction wore away family ties.

"We haven't talked to her in years, so I'm pretty sure Laura won't want to come to the Bar Mitzvah, but we wanted to tell you anyway. We were talking about it last night, and Andrew doesn't want her to even be mentioned," Carey said. She and Bill were relieved that this shocking piece of information was finally out in the open.

"It's just as well, since Carey's parents won't be there, either," said Bill. "They don't accept us at all."

"Why is that?" asked the rabbi. It was hard enough to understand that these kind people had a child who didn't get along with them. He couldn't imagine a good reason for Carey's estrangement from her parents, as well.

"They never really felt she was their daughter," Bill explained. "Can you imagine, such an intelligent person, so pretty, so honest, so giving." Bill smiled at the woman he loved.

But something bothered the rabbi. He wondered if more was to come that might be a problem. "Why didn't they accept her as their daughter?"

"They never quite got over the fact that they had to adopt instead of having children naturally."

Adopt? Carey was adopted? "And from where did they get a baby?" the rabbi had to know.

"From a family in the Midwest somewhere," Carey said. But that's all she knew. The birth parents wanted all the records to be sealed.

"Did you undergo any sort of conversion?" Avi asked Carey.

"Of course not! I was a newborn!" she exclaimed. No, she was sure her parents would never have been concerned with that detail. "We weren't religious or anything but we always knew we were Jewish. There was a tree at home in December, but we called it a Chanukah bush. And there were candlesticks on the shelf that my grandmother brought from Europe. Many of her relatives were killed in the Holocaust, you know. No, there was no need to remind us that we were Jewish." She sat deep into her chair and crossed her arms, as if she had settled the matter.

"You don't know anything about your birth mother? There was never a conversion?"

"No," Carey said, looking at her husband and wondering what the rabbi was getting at.

"Where did you get married?" Rabbi London asked. They thought he was changing the subject, but he was gathering facts.

"Bill was in the service and I was traveling, and we met in France," she continued. "We decided to get married in Prague because the Czech Republic is so pretty and we both lost so much family there in the Holocaust. A part-time Reform rabbi there performed the wedding. Of course, we didn't know much then, so we didn't have a Ketubah or anything religious, but there was a chuppah and it was very meaningful. We have a document from the U.S. Army verifying the marriage, if you need to see it."

Oy, thought Avi. "And where were the children born?"

"Well, when Laura was born, we were living near Indianapolis on a farm. By the time Andrew was born, we saw from Laura's twisted view of things that we needed help raising children in a meaningful way. We moved east to be closer to other Jews, but Laura left our lives when Andrew was still tiny. He doesn't remember her at all.

"Our family of three landed here, and the community has been great. Andrew got a lot of inspiration at the Hebrew School, especially from your wife, and you've been a perfect rabbi for us. We've really found our way. We're a success story!" Carey and Bill smiled at each other and then at their son.

Oy.

There was a long moment of silence. Carey and Bill looked at Rabbi London and wondered what was wrong.

"When Andrew was born, what did you do about a Bris?" asked the rabbi.

"We had him circumcised in the hospital so that there would be no question about looking Jewish later," Bill said proudly, winking at his pre-teenager.

Oy.

Rabbi London turned to Andrew, who had wondered when it would be his turn, but the boy was surprised when the rabbi suggested he leave. "The hour is getting late, and we have a few weeks yet until the event. Go back to class, but before our next meeting, review your Bar Mitzvah Torah portion and see if there's an idea in it you would like to explore in your speech."

Watching the pre-teen leave gave Avi a minute to collect his thoughts. He had a lot of ground to cover and a lot of diplomatic language to use. When the door closed, he turned to Bill and Carey, who couldn't wait for the rabbi to begin.

"In biblical times," started Avi, who needed a few millennia to get some traction for this leap, "the identity of the children derived from the father's house. Joseph, for example, had an Egyptian wife, but his children and their families became known to us as the equals of Joseph's brothers, and together made up the famous Twelve Tribes that became the Jewish people."

Carey and Bill stared at him. Yes, it was interesting, but what did that have to do with what they were talking about?

"That changed, but you remember that we still use the identity of the father to establish what role men take today in religious life. Descendants of the Temple priests are Kohanim and get called to the Torah first, etc."

Yes, the Fernbergs knew that and could tell the rabbi that no one on their Bar Mitzvah list was a Kohen. They seemed relieved to have caught on to his line of reasoning.

No, that wasn't what he was getting at, Rabbi London said.

The rabbi paused. "For the past two thousand years, Jews have been ruled by Talmudic law that was derived from the Torah and was interpreted to meet needs as we encountered them. One of the rules that became firm was that a child of a Jewish mother was a Jew. The reason given, funny or not, was that you always knew who the mother was." His audience chuckled. Good, they're relaxed, he thought.

"An adoption becomes complicated when we don't know who the birth mother is, so halachic authorities require a conversion to erase any doubt."

Carey got it first. "In other words, when I was adopted, there should have been a conversion," she said. "I may not be Jewish."

Bill began to catch on. "Without a conversion, you're not Jewish."

Then Bill really got it. "If you're not Jewish, then neither are our kids."

"But last week in Shul," protested Carey to the rabbi, "you talked about us all coming from Adam!"

"Yes, that makes us all humans. It does not make us all Jewish," the rabbi answered.

"But I *feel* Jewish! I observe the holidays and keep kosher. My kid goes to Hebrew School. We go to Shul," Carey said, her voice rising and her bewilderment mounting with every sentence. "This seems like a small detail. We must be able to fix it. Wait a minute: Does not converting mean my son will be labeled a bastard?" she asked.

"No, of course not," said Avi, trying to calm her down. He knew that the common concept – a baby born of an unwed mother – was not the same as the Jewish legal status of a bastard, so he took a moment to explain. "The halachic definition of a 'mamzer,' which is translated as 'bastard,' has to do with the product of a forbidden union like adultery or incest, and that does not apply here at all," he assured them. "No, there's no problem on that score."

"So we can we fix this, right?" Carey asked.

"A conversion for you wouldn't be difficult," he explained. "It would be a simple thing for you to attend a few classes and add to what you already know because you have spent your entire adult life studying and learning tradition. What would complete it is a trip to the mikveh for a ritual immersion, and we're finished. Easy, and it can be done soon."

"So?" she asked.

That's where it gets complicated, thought Rabbi London.

Bill suspected what was coming, and he involuntarily sat up a little straighter.

"For a male conversion, however, there is one additional step," said the rabbi.

"Circumcision," mumbled Bill.

His wife looked at him.

"What? Andrew?" Carey's voice rose. "But he *was* circumcised! When he was *born!*" The mother hen jumped to protect her young.

Bill held her back until she got hold of her emotions.

"When the male has already been circumcised," explained the rabbi gently, "all that is needed is a Tipat Dahm, the drawing of a drop of blood. It's done by a mohel who performs a baby's Bris. Bris, in fact, is the nickname for a Brit Milah, which is the covenant between God and the Jewish people that we were told to seal in our flesh this way."

As he let the image sink in, he wondered how to tell a pre-teen boy that he had to undergo the procedure. There was a long silence, but then Carey had one more question for her rabbi.

"I have a daughter, too. She distrusts religion and has no use for rabbis, but she thinks she's a Jew. She's in Israel because she has always believed she was a Jew. What should we do about her?"

Rabbi London's mind was reeling. It was his turn to be silent.

A knock on the door interrupted the pause, and Andrew poked his head in to say that Hebrew School was over and the custodian wanted to close up. The rabbi suggested to the parents that they digest the information this discussion revealed and that they talk again the next day.

After they left, Emma peeked her head into the office door. "What was that all about? Andrew said you never even got to talk about his Bar Mitzvah."

Besides knowing and liking the family, Emma would understand the Jewish legal issues involved and what was required to solve them, so he summarized the situation for her. "Where do we go from here?" he asked.

"Oy," she said.

They went home and ate the tuna casserole the kids had prepared for supper. It was good and it was hot – just what the parents needed – but Emma and Avi were thinking the same thing. Despite wanting to keep their rabbinic duties separate from their children's lives, they both felt this was one set of circumstances when their teens' perspective might help.

So Avi posed a question, as if it were hypothetical. "When parents are estranged from their young adult child, how can they reconcile?"

Ahuva rolled her eyes as if the answer were obvious, and she immediately sided with youth. "I don't care whose fault it is, it's the parents' job to give their kids what they need. The parents have to do whatever it takes to convince the kid to come home. It's like their responsibility!"

Then there was the other question, and Avi made sure it sounded like a separate case. "If a teenage boy has to have a circumcision, is he likely to find more support among other young boys or from older men he can assume he'll never see again?"

Josh hated these discussions of Jewish law. He always felt his father was testing him. But in this case, he thought his age and male identity gave him some credentials and pointed out how important peers are to adolescents. "Kids have got to be a better choice. But I don't know if the boy would feel better with friends. He might want kids there he doesn't know so he doesn't have to see them later."

Ahuva and Josh added one point they both agreed on. They hated being asked and wished their father did something else for a living. After driving that point home to both their parents on several volume levels, they stomped off to their rooms to do their homework, to watch TV and to wish they could be like everybody else.

"They're right on both counts, you know," said Emma.

"On all counts," said her husband.

Avi went to Shul and was surprised to see Dennis at the minyan. His mother was not doing well, and he figured some praying might help. "She perked up when I told her where I was going," he told the rabbi.

Avi remembered Emma's story from her trip and decided it would boost Dennis's mood to hear it.

"Regards from Rabbi Bavli in Ventnor," Avi said. "He remembered you were there five years ago to help the day school." Dennis didn't brag about his good deeds, but he did a lot of fundraising for worthy organizations and he kind of liked it when people knew about it.

Then Dennis noticed that Avi seemed to have something on his mind, too, and asked if he could help.

"A family I'm counseling has a few problems. One of them is an estranged child, and maybe there's a chance that the kid would reconcile with the parents, but the first complication is that the youngster is very far away," the rabbi explained.

"There, I can help," the infrequent davener said immediately. To the rabbi's astonishment, Dennis whipped out his checkbook and gave the Shul two thousand dollars for this family to use. "That should pay for at least a one-way plane ticket from wherever that kid is. Maybe it'll pay the fare for the parents, too, or for you and you can go get 'em."

The rabbi was amazed. Was this Dennis's way of fortifying his prayers? Maybe the Shines needed a tax deduction. Perhaps it satisfied Dennis's need for power. It's possible that lost children were a favorite cause of his. Or maybe underneath all of Dennis's bluster, there was a soul that truly cared.

"On behalf of the family, thank you very much," said Avi.

Maybe Dennis had a good idea there, thought the rabbi as he walked home. Maybe Laura would come home to see her parents, convert, celebrate her brother's Bar Mitzvah, and everyone would live happily ever after.

Yeah, right.

Regardless, Dennis had done a mitzvah. He did God's work without knowing the people who would benefit and without getting credit for it. Dennis was a real mentsch.

At six thirty the next morning, the Londons' phone rang.

"The two of us were up all night," said Bill. "We cried together. We screamed at each other. We shared." Bill had to review the experience in detail before he could get to a bottom line.

"Then we talked it over frankly with our son. Our conclusion is that we have to do this right, make it right, like Carey said. We voted and agreed. Carey and Andrew will go through a conversion if Laura will come home and do it, too, and then we can be a family. A kosher family, so to speak."

This was better news than the rabbi had hoped for and so fast that it allowed time to attend to these extra details and still have the February Bar Mitzvah. The Fernbergs even put in a few calls to Israel to try to locate their daughter. They were expecting some e-mails or calls back over the next few days.

"When you find her, tell her that if she wants to come here to see you and to undergo the conversion, our Shul will pay the air fare," said the rabbi, grateful that Dennis had made the offer possible.

Chapter 6

There and Back

Avi got back from the Tuesday morning minyan less than two hours after the early morning phone call from the Fernbergs, and within ten minutes heard from them again. They had located Laura.

A mutual acquaintance had told them she left the commune and was staying at a youth hostel in Jerusalem. Laura was told there was some kind of family emergency, so she agreed to rendezvous for a phone call. Would the rabbi come over right away so he could be in on the conversation?

Absolutely not, he thought. What in heaven's name would I say to a twenty-two-year-old stranger, whose whole premise for being where she had spent half her life was now in question because of me, a stranger and a newcomer to the whole situation! And, I'm a member of a profession she doesn't respect! And, she would likely blame me for creating this entire mess!

Then again, he reflected, it's for the Fernbergs.

"Of course," Avi said aloud, dreading the conversation but managing to sound cheerful.

By nine o'clock, Andrew had left for school and the rabbi had arrived at the split-level house. Carey took the phone in the kitchen. Bill went up to the bedroom extension and Avi headed to the third phone downstairs in the family room. Bill dialed the hostel and Laura came to the phone.

"It's been years since I last heard your voice, and you were a child then. Now I hear a woman," he said. Carey was too choked up to talk. "Are you okay?" Bill asked.

"Yeah, I guess so," Laura replied, "but it's been kind of hard. A family from our kibbutz on a trip to Haifa was killed by a suicide bomber. Everybody was really depressed about it. I knew the kids." She paused, and then the words tumbled out. "I couldn't take being there any more, so I moved out." She was quiet again, and Avi wondered what more there was to the story.

"I came to Jerusalem two weeks ago to stay with friends," Laura continued. Then she remembered the reason for the call. "What's the emergency?"

Her father went slowly. First, Bill told her that her mother and their rabbi were on the phone, too. He also said that Andrew knew the whole story but wasn't home, so the adults could speak frankly. Then, he laid out the time line, the problems, and the conversion solution.

"You mean, after all that, I'm not even Jewish?!" she exclaimed at last.

Rabbi London had been quiet until now, not sure how Laura would react to him. But here's where he thought he might be helpful.

"That's a technicality, really," Avi explained gently, trying to keep the exchange civil.

"Oh sure," Laura said. "You can't think I really want to hear from you on this. This is a family problem, and there's stuff you don't understand. So why don't you just stay out of it."

Rabbi London persisted. "You may have been born Jewish to begin with, and in that case there would be no question, but we can't verify it because your mother's adoption records are sealed."

Laura was listening, surprised that the rabbi knew about her mother's adoption, but she remained on her guard.

"You've always behaved as a Jew," Avi continued, "so it's not something strange to you. And your identity would only be questioned under certain circumstances, such as when you were ready to get married, or to have a baby, or to claim citizenship in Israel, or to be buried. But it's easier to go through a conversion ceremony now and make your identity definite, don't you think?"

Avi wasn't sure Laura was still listening, but he took the plunge anyway. "I suggest you come here, where we understand the situation and you can go through the process with your family. Our Shul is traditional but Conservative, so we are more worldly than the rabbinate in Israel is. In any case, I will follow Jewish law to make it acceptable to the Orthodox both here, if you want to stay, and there in Israel, if you decide to go back. And," he was happy to add, "our congregation will pay for your air fare."

Wow, thought Carey and Bill. Surely she can't turn down the offer of a free trip.

"Oh, sure," Laura said again, "and let everyone there know that I have no money. What are they going to say when my parents suddenly claim they have another child they haven't seen in years? That we hate each other! Won't they wonder why? And what are they going to think when they find out the whole family's not even Jewish?"

Avi was ready. "The funds have been given anonymously by someone who doesn't know who the family is that needs help or why. The whole thing can be kept confidential. Nobody has to know about your relationship with your parents or about this conversion problem." Rabbi London paused and softened. "Please realize that this is a great opportunity for you to make your Jewishness official so there's never any question about it." He took a breath.

"In addition," he said, "coming here now would be a kindness to your brother that he would never forget. And, possibly, it could be a new beginning for you and your parents. Plus it's paid for. It would cost you nothing, but what could come out of it would be priceless. My advice is this: Take advantage of the opportunity and come home."

Carey and Bill held their breath.

Laura was skeptical. "How do I know you're not lying to me to get me to come to the States for some other reason?" Remembering vaguely some friction in the distant past and falling into an old mental set, she said to her parents, "It would be just like you to want to show that you can control me even if I'm on the other side of the world!"

"Laura, you always used to think we lied to you," said her mother meekly, "but this time you have to believe us. Maybe you don't trust me or your Dad, but you can believe this rabbi. He really wants to help us, and we need you here in order to make everything right."

"Look," Laura said to her mother, "I've seen a lot of rabbis in Israel who live in a different world than I do, and they couldn't possibly understand me or what I've been through or what I want in life. Why should I trust your guy when this whole situation is so complicated and unreal? I'm sorry you're going through this, but if your rabbi really cared, he would come here and talk to me. Maybe if I saw him for myself and talked to him face to face I could trust him, but otherwise forget it."

There was a long silence. Once again, thought Carey and Bill, our daughter is putting us in an impossible situation. How could Laura get to know Rabbi London when she is so far away? She won't come here, and we can't afford to pay for him to go there. Besides, we wouldn't dream of asking him to leave his responsibilities behind. And, the Middle East is dangerous and we wouldn't want to be responsible if anything happened to him. And, even if he were willing to go, the cost of a hotel would break our budget for the Bar Mitzvah! And, even if he were able to go and we could afford it, flying to Israel is a big trip and it would probably be impossible to get tickets any time soon. The time it would take to arrange a trip certainly would rule out getting this problem resolved before the Bar Mitzvah. It's all too much to ask. How could Laura do this to us now, when ...

"Okay."

Was that the rabbi speaking? Bill and Carey could hardly believe it.

"I'll come," Avi was saying to Laura. "I can be there in a day or two and we can talk. But promise me that there is at least a chance you'll come back with me."

Another silence, a long one. This time, everybody on the American side of the conversation held their breath. And then Laura said, "Okay."

The Fernbergs were stunned. Avi left them shaking their heads and went home to get ready for his emergency trip. On the way, he again mentally thanked Dennis for giving generously enough to enable him to go.

As soon as Avi got home, he called El Al Israel Airlines and told them there was an emergency, and they got him one seat on the next plane going from New York and two on Thursday night's flight back to Newark. When Emma got home from her morning job, she found Avi's passport and spare tallit and tfillin and packed his suitcase. She promised to call the yeshiva that afternoon to explain why he wouldn't be able to teach his Wednesday morning class. The London kids would be surprised by the sudden trip, but they knew the unexpected was in the nature of the job.

Avi explained to Cantor Goldberg which congregants to call to help make the minyan. The rabbi also told chairman of the Shul Board Harold Harrison that he had alerted Rabbi Melamed of the Orthodox shul, so that if a religious problem arose, the congregation would not be without guidance.

Of course, Avi's parents were thrilled when he called to tell them he was coming, even though they would hardly see him. They had retired to Israel five years earlier, leaving Avi in the States but joining two older sons who struck modern roots in the ancient homeland. Now, the senior Londons lived in Aliyat Esser, a small town near Jerusalem, and their youngest son would be able to stay with them. Avi hadn't seen his parents or brothers in a long time, and he was looking forward to it.

His near-midnight Tuesday departure got him to Israel in a quick nine hours nonstop, but because of the seven hour time difference, it was the middle of Wednesday afternoon when Avi landed in Tel Aviv. After clearing security and customs, he called Emma to let her know he had arrived safely. Then he waited at a Sherut stop for a shared taxi to Jerusalem and arrived at his parents' flat an hour later, tired and hungry.

While his mother set up a light supper, Avi made quick calls to his brothers and then phoned Laura, agreeing to meet for lunch the next day. Finally, the American and his parents sat down at the dining table and caught up on family news over shakshuka (eggs poached in tomato sauce) and Italian-style rolls. Mrs. London put the ubiquitous sliced tomatoes and cucumbers in the center of the table and a cup of hot decaffeinated coffee with milk near her son. When he finished, Avi staggered to the study/guest bedroom and fell into a deep, jet-lagged sleep.

At noon local time on Thursday (his body insisted it was only five in the morning even though he had enjoyed an eight-hour night), Rabbi London arrived at the Great Grill. The restaurant was a popular student spot at the intersection of King David and George Washington streets, a cultural collision in downtown Jerusalem. He was warm, so he put his light jacket into his backpack.

Waiting for her on a busy city street corner, Rabbi London wasn't sure how he would identify Laura, but she found him. She deduced who he was by the knitted kippah he wore with the baseball team design on it.

"I knew you were a Conservative rabbi, so I thought you'd have something on your head. But since you're not Orthodox, I figured you wouldn't be wearing a black fedora or big velvet yarmulke," she explained. "A Mets fan had to be from New York or thereabouts. I guessed you were you."

She has a logical mind, noted Avi, and a certain worldliness. And aside from being rather thin, she looked normal enough. There was no strange body piercing, spiked green mane or drug-slurred speech. Her light brown, straight hair was simply pulled back from her unmade-up face and fastened at the neck with a wooden clip. She wore jeans and a beige buttoned shirt, with the long sleeves rolled up to her elbow, and carried a large brown handbag. And as she looked away, he realized her narrow nose was just like her mother's.

They sat down inside the restaurant and considered the menu.

A meat meal was not the American rabbi's first choice, certainly not when his stomach was sure it was even too early for breakfast, but lunch was the big meal for Israelis and he wanted to be sure that Laura was glad to see him.

Kashrut was another reason he avoided certain foods mid day. Avi waited several hours after eating meat or poultry before he would have dairy products. Having meat would preclude the coffee with milk he enjoyed so much at lunch and again later in the afternoon.

Furthermore, noon was even a bit early for lunch in Israel, but these two people had a lot of ground to cover in a short period of time. So when Laura suggested the kosher Great Grill at noon, the rabbi was not going to argue.

They sat near one of the Great Grill's large open windows, from which they could see other diners who opted for outdoor tables. Either indoors or out, patrons could breathe the fumes from congested traffic on the street and see Montefiore's Windmill down the block.

The rabbi reiterated that the meal would be his treat, so Laura reviewed the choices carefully.

Using his Hebrew, Avi was happy to order what he thought of as a fast food choice: a hamburger with fries and a Coke. Such a common State-side meal was a real treat for a kosher Jew from suburban New Jersey who could never eat at McDonald's. He was a bit taken aback, though, when the waiter responded in English, recognizing the menu choice and accent as being American.

Laura's Hebrew went unchallenged. The server assumed she was a native. Living in Israel, she had the right pronunciation and always had easy access to kosher food even at McDonald's. She ordered a large meal because the food was excellent and she was hungry.

The waiter served assorted vegetable strips, tomato wedges and cucumber spears with chummus and techina first, accompanied by Iraqi-style pita, and Laura explained to the American that the appetizer was for both of them. Her squash soup came next and was quickly followed by steak with potato burekas. Her meal came with lemonade. The rabbi watched her eat, thinking it had probably been a long time since her last good meal.

Avi ate slowly, so the size of her dinner was not obvious. Between their English chit-chat, he overheard snippets of conversation from others in Hebrew, French, German, Russian, Japanese and several unfamiliar languages. He tracked the voices to find young adults who had come from around the world to study at the nearby Hebrew University.

About a hundred diners – from Africa, India and Asia as well as from the Americas and Israel – sat, as Avi and Laura did, on plastic chairs around tables covered with paper.

At long counters sat two dozen military personnel, all of them in uniform but off duty, and each with an unloaded Uzi slung casually over one shoulder. Two soldiers were black-skinned and probably arrived in Israel during the airlift of Jews from Ethiopia in the '90s. Half of the group were women, reminding Avi that equality between the sexes had a longer history in this young country than it did in the United States. A few men wore knitted kippot, signifying a commitment to religious life that included serving in the country's military. A small number were Christian or Muslim citizens of the Jewish State. They were all, including the officers, under twenty years of age.

Of the students, the native Israelis were older, having already served in the army and even traveled abroad for a few months afterward. Both groups noticed when a couple of Arab women in head scarves and modest dresses walked in, and there was a temporary hush as the ladies eased past a security guard. One of the undergraduates, who had almost finished her meal, recognized the Arabs as fellow students from Jordan and Egypt and gave them a warm greeting.

The noise picked up again, and Avi noticed that the off-white painted walls and the stone tile floor, typical of Israeli interiors, combined with the absence of acoustical ceiling tiles or window curtains to make the decibel level almost painful.

A series of five beeps and the room was nearly silent again. On the hour, the radio signaled a one-minute news break in Hebrew, and one of the waiters turned up the volume so all could hear. Out of habit, Laura stopped eating to listen to the headlines and the name of a soldier killed near Gaza that day. No one in the room seemed to recognize the casualty, so the outdated American music started again, discussions picked up where they left off and Laura resumed chewing.

By the time they got to dessert, she and the rabbi felt full and comfortable enough with each other to go beyond perfunctory conversation about weather, sports and international news. They shared a sliced afarsimon – a sweet local persimmon that looked like a seedless, orange-colored tomato and tasted like a peach – to top off their meal. As they bit into the juicy fruit, Avi explained how, in the course of planning a celebration, the Fernberg family learned of an earlier oversight that threw all their lives into turmoil.

"Your parents deserve a lot of credit," the rabbi began. "Here they are, finding themselves at the edge of a cliff, and they are not panicking. They are determined to do what is necessary to shore up support for everyone they love, regardless of the embarrassment it might bring them or the questions they'll have to face in the future. They're showing great courage."

"What do they need me for?" Laura asked, feeling somewhat more receptive to what he had to say now that she had eaten.

"Nothing. If you *never* came back, no one would ever know. They assumed you wouldn't want to come just to attend the Bar Mitzvah, and your brother said he didn't want you there. They all had made peace with letting you go your own way. But when there was a question of a family history that might affect you and your brother and those who will love you in the future, they did a one-eighty and their love for you took over. They want to make things right for your future, Laura, even if things haven't been right in the past."

"I owe them nothing, you know."

"Yes you do," Avi said. "There's a reason that 'Honor your parents' is one of the Ten Commandments. It's as fundamental and vital as 'Do not murder' and as difficult and visceral as 'Do not covet.' But it's just as critical a building block of society as the rest, and we are obligated to abide by that Commandment regardless of whether or not it feels right. You may not see from a balance sheet that you owe them anything, but you do."

Laura mulled over what he said, thinking that she had finally met a rabbi who made some sense. Maybe she would tell him her story. Maybe he would understand.

By the time they walked out of the restaurant, it was mid afternoon and they were chatting comfortably. The weather was balmy and they strolled from there along King David Street, past several of the city's finest hotels and lots of traffic.

They stole glimpses down side streets, where apartment buildings on stilts had residents' cars parked on the ground floor, and screenless balconies and windows let cool breezes flow through the residents' flats. Small stores and offices were flush with the sidewalk on the main road, and pedestrians could hear conversations through doors that were open for business and fresh air.

As pleasant as the weather was, every passing conversation contained the hope that it would rain soon. Meager precipitation in this region turned everything on the ground a light brown for most of the year, especially after a long, dry summer. The grass, bushes or trees that lined the roads were kept alive half the year by drip irrigation, a system invented in Israel to feed water directly to roots through black hoses that snaked along the ground. The only trees native to the area that survived the rainless summer were thick, stubby palm trees that could retain whatever moisture came their way.

With little lumber, the builders had to look elsewhere for construction material. The result was that almost all the buildings in this monochromatic city and in much of the country, including government locations and religious gathering places, were made of the one natural resource the country had in abundance: beige-pink Jerusalem stone.

As the Americans walked past facades that varied in style but not in color or texture, Avi brought Laura up to date about her family. Carey and Bill were known to be kind and intelligent pillars of both the Shul and the town, he told her. Andrew was generally well-behaved, loved baseball and was amenable to spending afternoons at the Hebrew School. Avi described Congregation Tefillah as drawing a diverse crowd to its Jewishly traditional style. And East Belleridge, only a half hour from New York City, he noted, was quietly residential and had a great public pool.

Laura was feeling relaxed as they turned down an old cobblestone street behind the perimeter gate of the sprawling YMCA building's grounds, so she started telling him a bit about herself.

As a little girl, she wasn't able to do what adults thought all girls her age could do – like reading for her own pleasure or ballet dancing for theirs – and became sure her parents wanted to control her for their own purposes. When Laura turned twelve, she convinced them to let her go to Israel with a youth group, but she was already rebellious and determined to break free. She finagled permission from the group and from her parents to stay in Israel instead of returning to the States. "Maybe they were relieved that, since I was in a Jewish place, they wouldn't have to worry about me for a while," she said.

Her parents had never been to Israel and thought the commune she wanted to go to was a kibbutz like any other. But it wasn't. The poor community was deep in the Negev desert and subsisted on charity. Founded by fundamentalist Christians, the commune drew a wide sampling of misfits – Jewish, Christian, Muslim and others – who couldn't find a place for themselves in modern Israeli society. The Jews for Jesus and Black Hebrews were mostly Americans, and Laura found it comforting to be able to speak English with them even when they discussed the apocalypse and the importance of being saved as Christians. But the commune also attracted druggies and sexual deviants, and Laura was frightened to be near them.

Avi stopped walking when he realized Laura had stopped talking and was hanging back. He looked over his shoulder and realized her practiced veneer had finally cracked. She was crying and fishing in her bag for a hankie. Avi went back the few paces to her and offered a packet of tissues from his pocket. She took the tissues and used them, and made him promise not to tell anyone what she was about to tell him, especially not her parents. Then she talked as if no one had listened before, saying things she never expected to tell anyone, ever.

"I lived in that commune for almost two years and thought I was real smart for being on my own, and then it happened. Some guys blindfolded me and hauled me into a hut in one of the fields. They kept me there and kept me drugged for three days straight. I was raped by who knows how many people or how many times or in how many ways," Laura whispered slowly.

"My whole body hurt for a long time, and I was only fourteen!" she said to Avi. "I wanted to go home to my parents, but I couldn't, knowing I had made such a mess of everything. I never told them about it, and they never asked. The only good thing that happened was that I didn't get pregnant."

Leaning her head into Avi's chest, she sobbed with the memory of the attack and again when she remembered how alone and stupid she felt.

"When the leaders of the commune found out," Laura continued when she could, "they went out of their way to be nice to me, letting me have a room to myself and offering me extra food between meals. I stayed for a while longer, but then I realized they were keeping me there only because they wanted to convert me."

What a misuse of religion, thought Avi.

Laura sighed unevenly and deeply, and the two started to walk again.

"I knew I had to get out of there, and then I got lucky. I was fifteen when I got a job at a mostly-Jewish kibbutz in the desert near Beersheva. It was a cooperative, so for the work I did, they let me live in the teenagers' house and eat in the community dining room. I helped take care of little kids in the children's center while their parents were working in the hothouses growing flowers or at the kibbutz guest house, where they fixed up rooms for paying visitors."

Laura smiled at the recollection. "The kibbutzniks were really kind to me. They treated me like an adult and included me in group sing-alongs and trips. It was great. I went to school there and made a lot of friends, but when we all finished high school, my classmates went off to the army. I was chicken, and I knew if I didn't ask for Israeli citizenship, I wouldn't have to serve. My friends didn't like that very much."

While her friends were in the army, Laura took classes in emergency training. She learned how to dress wounds, apply tourniquets, give CPR, ready patients with broken necks for transport and determine if casualties were still alive. One of her courses addressed how to talk to the survivors. Another taught her how to use hand guns and automatic rifles.

But most of her contemporaries were in the army, she continued, and there they formed new relationships. When they were finished with their tours of duty, they seemed to have direction for their lives and plans toward a career. "I, on the other hand, had to start all over again," she said.

Laura was in Haifa on a spring vacation with a kibbutz family when they were killed. The group had stopped for lunch at a cafe overlooking the Mediterranean, and she left them to get a newspaper, when a suicide bomber blew up the restaurant and everyone in it. Laura realized at that moment that none of the emergency training she had received – either on shooting a gun, medically treating a victim or counseling a survivor – could have helped them. For her, the feeling of helplessness was devastating.

"As Israelis, we always felt vulnerable, but then, on top of that everyday stress, the bombing tragedy made people take sides against each other. They either said that what was going on politically was breeding violence or that violence was encouraging political decisions. The kibbutzniks argued constantly, but it's impossible to know which way it works! The tension kept building, and it was awful." After that, she never quite found her footing.

Laura and the rabbi turned onto a main street.

"During the summer, we found out that the kibbutz was disintegrating financially – its plan was to cash in on the desert tourism boom, but that never happened because the tourists didn't come – so the settlement is disbanding, and because I wasn't a member, I get nothing," she said.

That was what finally pushed Laura out the cooperative's door. She went from there to the hostel in Jerusalem, but after a week, the manager said she had to leave. She moved into her friend Valerie's place, but because Laura could no longer afford a cellphone, she arranged with the hostel's manager to receive pre-arranged phone calls there. That's why her parents were able to reach her.

Laura and Avi meandered silently toward Jerusalem's municipal center and passed a corner travel agency with a sign in front for El Al. This kid deserves a break, thought Avi. More than Laura realizes, she needs some time in a quiet suburb where she can get away from violence and death. East Belleridge would be good for her.

"Our flight to the States leaves just after midnight tonight," the rabbi said. He hadn't yet asked if she would return with him. He thought it would be easier for her to just go along than to verbalize the decision to leave. "Why don't you come with me and eat supper at my parents' place in Aliyat Esser? We can leave for the airport from there." This plan also meant Avi would know where she was between now and then in case she bolted.

Laura considered the offer. "Do you think my parents would really want me back?" she asked.

She loved Israel, but felt she was leaving nothing behind. And her experience at the kibbutz made her wonder if maybe she had been too ready to reject her parents' well intentioned role in her life. Gee, it would be nice to have someone to lean on for a change, she thought.

"Valerie's place is near here," Laura said. "We'll have to pick up my stuff."

When Avi realized she was saying yes, he wasn't going to let any logistics get in the way. He said making that stop would be easy because it was in Jerusalem, but he had not realized that Valerie lived in the Arab Quarter of the Old City. The ancient town on the whole had very few streets that could handle motor vehicles, and from the Arab Quarter they would certainly have to carry her bags to a taxi outside the Old City walls.

But even more intimidating was the prevailing tension that made it dangerous for a Jew to visit the Arab Quarter in particular.

Avi decided to minimize the exposure and pulled a baseball hat out of his backpack to put on top of his kippah. He hoped that way they would look like two generic American tourists.

Laura and Avi turned east, away from the modern hotels and bustling capital. They headed down the wide walkway toward the Jaffa Gate, named that because it faced west, from the Old City of Jerusalem in the mountains toward the ancient Mediterranean port at Jaffa.

The downhill path followed the tall, stone, outer walls that encircled the Old City. The high wall on the left promised the silence of antiquity, but on the right, horns sounded to signal modern traffic. Vehicles inched by on the street, with several air conditioned tour buses jockeying for parking spaces. The coaches were there to disgorge or await their passengers, who undertook the emotional pilgrimage to the biblical city.

Signs on the vehicles detailed the itinerary for each group. Boarding one coach was a group of Spanish-speaking pilgrims from South America, flush with the excitement of having carried a cross past its holy stations and visiting the site of the Last Supper.

Getting on another bus was an English-speaking Jewish group that had visited the Tomb of King David before celebrating a Bar Mitzvah at the Western Wall. Their next stop was a fancy reception at one of the modern hotels of the new city.

A van awaited German-speaking visitors, who had started their day at the Yad Vashem Holocaust Memorial in a western neighborhood and ended it in the Old City. They would stop at the cone-roofed Dormition Church adjoining the ancient walls. At the church's cemetery, they would pay their respects at the grave of Oskar Schindler, whose real-life effort saved hundreds of Jews from the Nazis and whose list became the subject of a Hollywood movie.

Laura seemed less fascinated by the scene than Avi was (he assumed she had seen it all before and very recently) but he absorbed every detail. He saw one man in a keffiyah standing beside his camel awaiting visitors interested in being photographed atop a "ship of the desert." Two men in jeans rode past on horseback, enjoying the view and the fine weather. An Arab woman in a long robe and headscarf squatted next to a tub of prickly cactus sabras, which she offered to peel for any purchaser of the sweet fruit. A young teenage Arab walked past, balancing on his head a huge tray of freshly baked pita and sesame-covered Arab breads. Another youngster followed him, leading a donkey laden with crates and whose tail became a toy for the boy's younger brother.

Ahead of the two Americans was a family of four fashiona-
bly-dressed, well-groomed Israelis who were Jewish, but not religious.
Wearing T-shirts, jeans, sandals and sunhats, they were intent on
exploring some of the three-thousand-year-old archaeological finds
that digs have unearthed in the Old City.

A modestly covered, ultra-Orthodox family passed them,
heading to their home in the Jewish Quarter. The bearded father in a
black wide-brimmed hat, long black coat, white shirt and knee socks
carried groceries ahead of the wigged mother, wearing a loose-fitting,
long-sleeved dress. She was struggling with twins in a baby carriage
while trying to keep track of the rest of their seven children.

Groups of Eastern Orthodox Christian priests and Roman
Catholic nuns, both in flowing black robes and distinctive head
coverings, had already reached the Jaffa Gate and were heading to
their respective churches.

Avi and Laura walked the zigzag path under the arch of the
Jaffa Gate and entered the Old City. They stopped to buy bottled
water at a stand on their left, while on their right, visitors queued up
for the Citadel Museum, located in massive walls that were built two
millennia ago by King Herod. Beyond the museum, the one-lane
street led to the Armenian Quarter, which could be entered by car,
but carefully.

But for the two of them, progress would be strictly on foot.
They took a drink and then followed the crowd straight ahead onto
the narrow alleyway called David Street to walk through the Arab
market.

Along with other visitors, Laura and Avi meandered down
narrow steps, constructed centuries ago with ramps on each side for
the wheels of delivery carts. The smells of cardamom, saffron and
coriander filled the air. Clothing for sale hung from wires above
customers' heads and blotted out any sunlight that penetrated the
open spaces between stretches of arched ceilings. Boxes filled with
produce were piled up on the floor outside the tiny shops, which
stood flush against each other. Glass cases displayed religious
souvenirs, mostly olivewood crosses, for pilgrims from around the
world who had come to pray in the Garden Tomb or to tread the
Via Dolorosa to the Church of the Holy Sepulchre. Christian and
Muslim Arabs hawked their wares and loudly tried to get visitors'
attention, and potential customers barked questions and haggled
prices in several languages. Israeli soldiers watched from the roofs
three stories above and tried not to be noticed.

The American pair made a few left turns past the Christian Quarter and walked until they reached the end of the Arab section. There, in a quiet courtyard, sat a young woman on a plastic chair.

"Hi, Laura!" said Valerie in British-accented English. She was happy to see her friend but disappointed that the young woman was moving out. Once she understood there was an emergency at home, Valerie urged the two visitors to enter her dwelling and take what was Laura's.

Avi followed Laura through a drape of hanging beads into what could only be called a cave. The natural rock of the terrain at the far end was covered with cushions as a sitting area, and a small low table provided an eating surface. A couple of pads on the floor were arranged as a bed. Most of Laura's belongings were still in her bags; there was no place to unpack them.

This was home? Avi thought as he looked around. He had heard that the whole Old City had been modernized after Israel won it from Jordan in 1967, but apparently not this corner of the Arab Quarter.

A curtain hid the bathroom area, but there was neither indoor plumbing nor any signs of electricity or phone. Maybe Valerie had a cellphone, Avi thought. A goat wandered in and looked like he lived there. Hmm, Avi reconsidered, maybe Valerie didn't have a cellphone.

Laura quickly closed her bags and, as the Americans left, Avi had the feeling that Valerie was relieved to have her small abode to herself once again.

Laura adjusted her backpack on both shoulders and hung her pocketbook around her neck. The rabbi put on his backpack and then balanced Laura's large duffle on one shoulder while they considered their route. The way there had been all downhill, which made going back up that way difficult, especially carrying luggage, so he suggested they continue down. The two went through the narrow lanes of the Arab meat market, past slaughtered chickens and hanging sides of lamb, and down a long flight of stairs. They finally came to the end of the crowded Quarter to emerge at the northwest corner of the vast Western Wall plaza.

Avi deposited Laura and the bags at the center of the large open space and continued on to the sacred place to daven.

Laura looked around at the stone facades that were glowing golden and pink in the low afternoon sun. Opposite the Wall, workmen were testing the large electric menorah that would be turned on in a few weeks for Chanukah. Next to it were a half-dozen large electric lamps, a permanent memorial to the six million Jews murdered in the Holocaust.

In the plaza near Laura, a woman in a wheelchair joined the rest of her group, a dozen American reporters on a press trip to the Holy Land, to listen to their guide. A cat rubbed against the legs of one journalist, who started petting the animal until Laura told him that the felines all over the city were strays, allowed to run free because they kept the rodent population under control. He left the animal alone and turned his attention back to the group's escort.

Laura took another drink from her water bottle as she listened in and heard the Israeli explain the location's importance to several religions. Church bells began their hourly chorus as he talked, and she watched Rabbi London approach the Wall looking for a group with which to say the short afternoon Mincha service.

Avi found a minyan several feet away from one that was already finished and added a special prayer for Dennis, who had made this trip possible, and for his ailing mother. A young soldier with a kippah, who had davened with the earlier group, kissed the stones and went back to his post. In the women's area, a girl in a modest blouse and skirt put a small note between the stones before she backed away. At the Wall, the hum of praying – by the devout and the secular, the men and the women, the old and the young, the Jews and the visitors – was constant.

The people praying there looked like dolls because the Wall was so massive, thought Laura. The neatly stacked blocks of stone varied in size, getting smaller as the structure got higher, but they each were at least many feet wide and tall, and clumps of grass grew wild and long in the crevices between them.

From where she was standing, Laura could look up to the plateau atop the Wall and see the gleaming gold surface of Islam's Dome of the Rock. Just then, a muezzin called the Muslim faithful to prayer.

Laura had spent all these years in Israel and realized she knew very little about what she was seeing. When Avi returned to where she was standing, she explained her ignorance to him.

"Our kibbutz was in the Negev between the homes and farms of two of Israel's Prime Ministers, David Ben Gurion and Ariel Sharon, and they both loved the desert. So, we thought the Negev was the heart of the country.

"But you've been in Israel for so many years," said Avi, "and it's such a small country! You must have taken trips to see what the rest of the place was like."

"Sure," she said, "but we never came here. If we wanted to act rich, we would go south to Eilat. We'd sleep on the beach and watch the vacationers from Europe or America sail or swim in the Red Sea near their chic hotels. If we wanted something really cheap, we visited the Bedouin Arabs and slept under the desert stars. We went to Tel Aviv about once a year so we could see what was 'in' and go drinking and dancing. I only went north to Haifa once." She stopped talking for a minute, remembering the horror of that trip.

"Our kibbutz wasn't religious," she continued, "so it never occurred to us to visit Jerusalem. I knew it was the capital but thought the only people here were Arabs, ultra-religious Jews and politicians. I came here only because a family leaving the kibbutz offered me a ride, and when I got out of the car, I was surprised that Jerusalem was so modern. Then, just when I thought I had seen it all, I met Valerie and she showed me how quaint the Old City was."

Quaint, thought Avi. "The Old City isn't quaint. It's real history," he said, keeping the exasperation out of his voice. "That Wall where I was davening is more than twenty-one hundred years old."

"Is that what makes it holy?" she asked.

"No, lots of things here are that old and even older. The Wall wasn't meant to be holy. It was simply built by Herod as a strong retaining wall for the man-made plateau above it, where the Temple had already stood for a millennium. That's why the platform is called the Temple Mount. Herod wanted more room to expand the Temple so he could make it a structure Rome would be proud to have in its empire."

"So why do Jews go to the Wall to pray?" she asked.

"It's as close as we can get to the physical core of our faith," the rabbi explained. "The ancient Temple complex was on that hill for a thousand years, and Jews from all over the country used to come to it to mark Jewish holidays. But the Romans destroyed the Temple about two thousand years ago, and the Muslims claimed the Temple Mount about fifteen-hundred years ago."

"I saw signs for the Kotel, but where is the Wailing Wall?" she asked.

"It's the same thing," he said. "It was always called the Kotel Maaravi, the Western Wall, and it was the only thing left standing after the Roman destruction. Since then, most of the powers that occupied the Holy Land did not allow us anywhere near it. In the rare instances that Jews could approach the Wall, our prayers included a lot of weeping and wailing about the Temple's destruction and Jews' dispersion from the Land of Israel. Now that Israel has been reborn and Jews no longer wail, it is known by its classic name, the Western Wall."

Laura looked at the Kotel, and somehow it looked different.

"Why was the Temple built here to begin with?" she asked.

"Because this is Mount Moriah. This is where Abraham bound his son Isaac and was ready to sacrifice him. He didn't kill his son because, at the last minute, God told him not to. God doesn't want human sacrifices. But Abraham was ready to do what God asked of him, and in that way he showed he was ready to be the first Jew. Seven hundred years later, King David bought the land around Jerusalem from the people who lived on Mount Moriah, and his son King Solomon built the Temple on it."

Avi knew this was a lot of history for anyone to keep straight, so he put it in a nutshell for Laura. "Abraham lived about thirty-seven centuries ago. The Temple was originally built about thirty centuries ago. Jesus arrived on the scene twenty centuries ago. Mohammed was here fourteen centuries ago." To put it in perspective, he added, "Electricity and the telephone were developed only in the last century. There. The history of western civilization in five sentences," he said, pleased with himself.

The information was a lot to grasp, and Laura didn't think she followed it all, but for some reason, she felt more Jewish than she had ever felt before.

Laura followed Avi's finger as he pointed out other major landmarks. "East of the Temple Mount and to the north you can see Mount Scopus. Joshua first saw Jerusalem from there after the Exodus, and now that hill holds the main campus of the Hebrew University and Hadassah Hospital. Just south of there, to the right as we look at it but still east of here, is the cemetery on the Mount of Olives, which you might pass on the way south to Bethlehem and Hebron or east to the Dead Sea via Jericho. They're all outside the Old City walls."

Then he looked at Laura. "The whole Old City of Jerusalem is only about two miles square. We walked through the Christian and Arab Quarters to get to Valerie 's place and then came here. If we were to leave the plaza from the southwestern corner, we could walk back through the Jewish Quarter. The Armenian section is between there and the Jaffa Gate.

"And until the late 19th Century, there were no buildings outside the Old City walls at all. That was when Montefiore built the windmill we saw from the restaurant and tried to start a new neighborhood there."

Laura and Avi carried the bags a short distance from the Wall to the security checkpoint at the Old City's exit and then got into a 21st Century taxi. The car drove them on modern highways to new Jerusalem's suburb of Aliyat Esser.

Avi's brothers were already there, ready to catch up over blintzes and ruggelach. Laura ate and then walked to the balcony door, which was open to let in the cool air. The twilight view from the fourth floor was over similar, Jerusalem stone apartment buildings, nestled into the area's barren rolling hills. Drying laundry fluttered from lines on flat roofs and children played in the courtyards between buildings.

She turned back to the room and took a close look at the family that sat around the table. Mrs. London, with her gray hair pulled back into a bun, was beaming with the joy of seeing her sons together. The brothers looked very much alike, with age taking its toll on the hairlines of each man and in that way indicating the birth order. The youngest looked the most like his father, except that he still had brown-though-thinning hair, peppered with gray, whereas his father had only gray hair and very little of it. Neither had a beard, but the two Israeli brothers did.

As Laura listened to them laugh together, she realized for the first time what it felt like to be with a family and how much she longed for that closeness. Gee, she wondered, is my father bald? I better see my brother before he gets old! For the first time, she smiled at the prospect of seeing them and her mother.

After supper, there was just enough time for Laura to say a quick telephone goodbye to a few friends and for Avi to call some cousins. The relatives lived in what were technically called "settlements in the West Bank" and there was no time to visit them on this quick mission. Neither was there time to visit the Petach Tikvah cemetery near the Tel Aviv airport, the final resting place for several generations of Avi's family who spent their lives in the Holy Land.

Within an hour of leaving Aliyat Esser, the two travelers were at the airport checking in for their midnight El Al flight. They cleared security, and Laura waited while Avi joined some male passengers for a pre-boarding Maariv minyan.

When he was finished, the rabbi and the young woman walked down the corridor to the plane behind some business travelers, who frequented the Jewish state to renew old contacts and discover new innovations. Religious Jewish families with lots of kids, who accounted for at least a third of the boarding passes and most of the noise, passed them in a hurry to get there first.

Laura and Avi presented their documents at the bulkhead and squirmed down the narrow aisles to their seats, overhearing conversations from a variety of other travelers as they buckled up.

Nonreligious Jews, who liked to visit Israel because it touched their souls the way prayer never could, jockeyed to get to their seats before other passengers filled the overhead compartments. A variety of pilgrims with reinvigorated faith in their religions sat in groups reviewing what they saw and talking about how eager they were to impart their impressions to their co-worshipers. Tourists, feeling alive from what they saw, filled several sections of the plane and fell asleep almost immediately, drained from the demands of their itinerary. Israelis, many of them just out of the army, were sharing tips, planning fun and scheduling sightseeing for their adventure abroad.

Laura, who had barely survived a decade of adventure, simply wanted to go home.

Chapter 7

Priorities

With everything on her mind – from the suddenness of her departure to the prospect of reuniting with her family – Laura didn't think she would sleep at all during the ten-hour trip. She ate the airline supper and started to watch a movie, and suddenly the flight attendants were serving breakfast. She looked for her traveling companion in the next seat, but he wasn't there. Before he could eat, he had to daven.

Avi had joined a morning minyan at the bulkhead, from where he could see the dawning sky through a small porthole. As he put on his tallit and tfillin and recited the Shacharit service, he paused at certain prayers to insert his thanks for what had been a wonderful, worthwhile, safe and amazingly quick trip. In just four days, he had been to Israel and back. He had visited with his family and enjoyed balmy days under cloudless skies in a peaceful and relaxed Jewish State. But most of all, he had accomplished his mission. He had Laura.

By the time they both finished breakfast and the U.S. re-entry paperwork, the plane had completed its Atlantic crossing and was on an approach path down the east coast of North America. The flight was over Boston when Laura felt the start of its descent.

Avi always enjoyed the view when he made this trip, but for her, the sights were spectacular and new. She stared out the tiny windows to the right and watched the early morning light play off the forested mountains, fertile farms and flourishing cities of Connecticut and New York State. Towns, with buildings of many hues and sizes, clustered along the rolling terrain and glistened with the dawn. Leaves of different shades, turning with the season, decorated the hills with bouquets of color.

Out the left windows, she began to see the tall buildings of New York City, profiled by the rising sun's rays. Soon the light spread across the sprawling suburbs and heavy industry of the northern Garden State. Laura was amazed at how large and colorful everything seemed compared to the Middle East world she grew up in.

The flight landed at New Jersey's Newark Liberty Airport shortly after dawn on Friday. The two travelers identified their bags and cleared customs quickly, then found Emma waiting with jackets.

"I thought you would need them," Emma said. "It's about twenty degrees cooler here than in Israel." The coats were a welcome sight, but the warmth of the Londons' hug was the big surprise to Laura, who thought all rabbis lacked affection, even if they had a dozen children.

Walking to the car, the rebbetzin said she had called Carey and Bill and told them their daughter was on her way. The excited parents said the Londons should call when they got back from the airport. By then, Andrew would have left for school and the adults could come right over. What would happen next was up to Laura and her parents, Rabbi London said. If they wanted to try getting along under one roof or if they thought they'd do better at a distance, it would be their decision to make. Emma assured Laura, however, that whatever the future held in store, the Londons would always be available to her for help and guidance.

The London kids had gotten themselves ready early enough to catch the school bus, so the initial Fernberg meeting took place with some privacy. Carey and Bill came to the Londons' home and they met Laura as adult strangers – which they really were – with curiosity and courtesy. There was some initially stiff conversation, but then the three sat down in the living room and had an overdue heart-to-heart talk. The rabbi left them there while he walked the rebbetzin to her car, where the husband and wife caught up a bit before she had to leave for work.

In the living room, Laura's mind echoed with the loneliness she had felt for so long, so far away from her family and the love she yearned for. She envied the warmth and caring she saw when she visited the older Londons in Aliyat Esser and now sensed in the younger ones, too. And, thanks to this rabbi, she finally had some insight into what it meant to be a Jew.

By the time Rabbi London walked back into the house, the Fernbergs had established a starting point. Bill explained that he and Carey had prepared a room for Laura that was hers as long as she wanted to stay in their house. Laura agreed to try it, and promised to do what she could to make the arrangement work.

Laura left with her parents, looking forward to the chance to get to know them and her brother. The door closed behind them and the jet-lagged clergyman staggered toward his bed. He was fifteen minutes into a much-needed morning nap when the phone rang.

"I'm so glad you're there, Rabbi." It was Dennis. How could Avi be mad? "Dr. Frank called about my mother. She's been running a fever and he doesn't know why, and so today he put her back into East Belleridge General. I'm worried."

Through the fog of sleep deprivation, Avi knew what he had to say. "I'll meet you there in half an hour." Again, Avi reflected between yawns. Poor guy.

Dennis's mother was looking thin and gray, a sharp contrast to how she had been when the rabbi last saw her nearly two weeks ago. Although Dr. Frank had assured Avi then that Hannah had not broken her hip, it was clear that something was sapping her strength. Perhaps it was a recurrence of a long-ago cancer that the doctors thought she beat, the nurse said. Hannah hadn't been interested in eating for several days, and she was rarely lucid anymore. She was failing.

The doctor wanted to run some tests, but was afraid to drain Hannah further in her weakened state. She was too frail for Dr. Frank to request her permission to insert a feeding tube, so he asked her son, and Dennis gave his approval. By feeding her this way, the doctor hoped to build up her strength so he could go ahead with the tests.

Dennis didn't ask his rabbi what he thought of a feeding tube. If he had, Avi might have told him how he had witnessed the stress of a woozy patient being restrained so the tube could be inserted through the nose and threaded into the stomach. Avi had seen liquid nourishment poured into a funnel at the open end of the tube to give sustenance without satisfaction to the body on its other end. There was no kindness or even dignity to the procedure. Worse, he knew that to remove the apparatus once it was in place was to invite death, so the fear of guilt kept the tube in position.

Rabbi London had learned that modern medicine and mechanical implements could keep a body alive long after the patient's time had expired. He had been consulted when a young woman from the area was being kept alive in a vegetative state, and he knew all too well the ethical, legal and halachic ramifications of discontinuing life support. Even though the woman had very little brain activity, to remove the tubes was to starve her, dehydrate her and let her die, and some authorities equated "pulling the plug" with killing the patient. They pointed to the extremely rare case of a patient showing a glimmer of intelligence, even though proof of cognition was elusive. Ultimately, it was a question of whether or not an unending state of complete helplessness was indeed considered living.

Hannah Shine was ninety-two, and the rabbi knew her age made it unlikely that this would be a long, drawn-out ordeal even if she recovered from this particular episode, but the stress of inserting the tube would be at least as great for her. Would medical science extend her life or prolong her dying? the clergyman wondered. But Dennis didn't ask. Perhaps that's just as well, thought Avi.

The two somber men walked out of the hospital together. Dennis would come back in a few hours, but he had to attend to some details at his office. He owned Cleaner Shine, which developed, manufactured and distributed cleaning products around the country. The factory that produced the merchandise and housed company offices was in a remote corner of an industrial zone in the Steelbound section of Newark, a neighborhood that seemed to get more dangerous every year. The Beretta .22 handgun he carried – and the guns several employees kept with them during business and commuting hours – offered a feeling of security.

Dennis's commercial environment was far removed from Avi's world of philosophical discussions, existential dilemmas and ethical issues, but maybe being in business was better. It certainly seemed to have less of an impact on the emotional atmosphere at home. In addition, Dennis made a very good living and would have no trouble paying for college for his kids or making major donations to worthy causes, whereas the Londons struggled on the incomes of two wage earners and could not even think about retirement.

"Thank you for underwriting a mitzvah," Rabbi London said to Dennis. The rabbi was grateful personally for the chance to see his family when he could not otherwise afford a visit to Israel, but more than that, he knew what the trip was all about and that he had to keep the details confidential. "The family I told you about has been reunited, and it was all made possible because you were so generous."

"Well," said Dennis as he got into his car, "I hope it earned me some mitzvah points. I sure could use 'em."

As Avi drove home, he thought about that concept. A Jew is supposed to do a mitzvah whether or not anyone knows it was done or who did it. A mitzvah is the right thing to do because it is derived from God-given rules of behavior. That's what Bar or Bat Mitzvah is all about, that an individual at the threshold of maturity takes on the responsibility of fulfilling the commandments, which can mean anything from observing Jewish holidays to visiting the sick. There are no "points," Avi reflected, and as much as people would like to think that doing a mitzvah ensures the answers to prayers, it's not a quid pro quo arrangement.

Avi had just finished lunch at home and was considering a nap before Emma got back, when the phone rang again. "I don't understand why this is happening," stammered Dennis, who was calling from his office. The doctor said Hannah was getting worse fast, even with the feeding tube. "I've done all the right things. I've been generous with the needy, I've been active in my Shul, I prayed, and still my mother drifts farther and farther away!"

"Dennis," Rabbi London said into the phone, "we don't know why these things happen. She doesn't deserve to suffer, we know that. The truth is that she is over ninety and has led a full life. The doctors are doing what they can and so are we. She has not given up the fight, and neither must we."

As Friday afternoon wore on, Avi reflected on the events of the week and on the sermon he had to give the next day. And on how tired he was.

Days were short, and sunset, which determined the starting time for Shabbat, was growing near. At four thirty, Emma lit candles and said the appropriate prayer, and the family began to relax. Josh and Ahuva each had a friend staying over that night who brought flowers, which made the house look festive, and the kids were all off in different parts of the house chatting.

That gave Avi a chance to talk to Emma about the week, the trip, the Fernberg success and the Shine crisis. He tried not to yawn while she told him about the broken washing machine, flat tire and missed school bus she had to deal with while he was away. He described his hamburger in Jerusalem, the goat in the Arab Quarter and the loud children on the plane. The couple shared thoughts on colleges, too, and reminded each other that they would have to attend an evening session on that topic at Josh's yeshiva Monday night.

Shabbat's restrictions created the isolation and peace that made these conversations possible and gave relief to an overburdened psyche. As the 23rd Psalm said, referring to God guiding us to peaceful waters, "He restoreth my soul."

After a good night's sleep, Rabbi London thought through some ideas for his sermon later that morning. Since he could not write on Shabbat, he put bookmarks in the texts he wanted to use. Luckily, the week's Torah portion, full of applicable themes, focused on the early part of Abraham's life. Avi had a special affinity for that character because the name Avi was a short form of his Hebrew name, which was the same as the Patriarch's. And so, the preacher was delighted to review the scene of Abraham being told to leave the place of his birth and to go to a promised land.

"Lech l'cha, God tells him," said the rabbi to his flock during services. "Take yourself and leave the place you called home and go to a land that I'll show you, and I'll make you numerous and bless you, and everyone who blesses you will be blessed and everyone who curses you will be cursed."

Avi told his congregation that he was in Israel that week for a professional emergency, and was happy to report that everything worked out all right. Then he noted the coincidence, that during this week's portion he went to the very land that was Abraham's destination.

"It was as if God were telling me to go right away," the preacher said. "God told Abraham to go, and Abraham went because he believed in God, not because he understood where he was going or how long it would take or why it was important. The lesson we all must learn is that we don't always know what God has in mind because it's over the horizon of human understanding, but we have to remember that following God's word inevitably means that our future will be blessed."

He added that his trip and its positive outcome was made possible by the generosity of one member of the Shul in particular, and that this gesture set an important standard of righteousness for the rest of the congregation to try to match. "Like Maimonides said, the highest form of charity is to anonymously do the right thing for people in need so that they can help themselves."

As Avi finished speaking, he noticed that the usual number of worshippers were joined by others he did not expect. Sol and Sylvia Cohen, happy at last to have a larger family unit, came with their glowing newlywed daughter Sophie and new son-in-law Cliff Rosen. Ida Stein came as if her husband Harvey (may his memory be a source of blessing, Avi thought) were still there. But he had died just two weeks earlier, and Ida stood when it came time to say the Mourner's Kaddish. Ray Fisch sat with Dave Smith and Sig Fleishhocker, and the three sang out congregational responses with gusto.

The Fernbergs were there, too, and Carey and Bill introduced Laura as a relative from Israel. They did not mention to anyone that their family was the subject of the rabbi's sermon.

Dennis assumed he was the generous donor praised by the rabbi but did not identify himself to anyone as such. He could have made the connection between Laura's sudden arrival from Israel and the rabbi's emergency trip there to bring back an estranged child, but his mind was elsewhere. Dennis was in Shul with his son Brendan that day so they could pray for the well-being of both their mothers.

Saturday night, Avi found Dennis in his mother's hospital room, and the middle-age son told his rabbi what Dr. Frank had said, that the decline was continuing and she would not last much longer. Rabbi London went home but got the call right after he walked in the door that Hannah Shine was gone.

Dennis was an only child, so Rabbi London met him at midnight at the Jewish Funeral Home, where they could shop in the basement for a casket. The selection ranged from a plain pine box to a mahogany-looking, polished, rounded-lid presentation piece. The rabbi explained to the mourner that all the choices met halachic standards – having neither metal in its construction nor a split cover for viewing – but that the simpler was the more traditional. Dennis didn't understand why, and he chose the most costly one for his mother. After all, he said, she deserved the best, and he would make the decisions.

The funeral was at one o'clock on Sunday, so nearly everyone was available to be at the Jewish Funeral Home for the service. Emma was finished teaching at the Hebrew School at noon and got a ride with Florence Fischman. The entire Board was there with their spouses except Harold Harrison, who arrived alone because his wife Jane was home recovering from surgery. About half the members of Congregation Tefillah came as well as many of the leaders of philanthropic organizations headquartered in New Jersey and New York. Several Cleaner Shine employees and a smattering of people who attended Emek Emet and Temple Tikvah occupied some seats, too.

Some of the older folks who sat in the front knew Hannah from the assisted living apartments, but only a handful of individuals in the room knew her at all. Most people came because they felt obligated to Dennis.

As the crowd walked in, they formed a long line waiting to sign a visitors' book and then to express condolences to the family. Reeva, well-sedated and made presentable by carefully applied makeup and a fresh bun-like hairdo, sat between her children in the receiving room.

For the funeral service, Dennis directed Reeva to sit between their children again, while he sat next to Brendan, in the first row of the chapel. In front of the room on a gurney was the closed, well-polished, mahogany-finished casket, covered with flowers.

The ceremony began with Cantor Goldberg chanting several appropriate Psalms. Rabbi London spoke about the span of her life, which included two world wars, the founding of the State of Israel and the attacks of September 11, 2001.

"Life is a story," he told the crowd, "and every story has a beginning and an end. Although we are here to mark her story's end, we should recall how it started, too." The rabbi recounted that Hannah had been born in Germany, and through her horrifying experiences, earned her name – made famous in the Chanukah story – that of a woman who kept her faith even as she watched her children being tortured and killed.

Dennis continued the thought in his lengthy eulogy, describing in detail his father (may he rest in peace) and the relatives he and Hannah lost in the Holocaust. Dennis then introduced his children and, at his insistence, they shared some of their memories of her.

This was a *real* funeral, everyone agreed.

By the time the long service was over, the weather had turned bitterly cold and rainy, and that convinced most of those who attended the funeral not to go on to the cemetery. Emma left with Florence, who took the opportunity to consult with her about decorations for the brotherhood gathering and to complain that food had been banned by "Rabbi." Some members liked to call him "Rabbi," as if that were his name, and Emma hated it.

Her husband's car was one of just a few that arrived for the burial. Rabbi London, bundled up with his black fedora and gray scarf, stayed with the family and made sure that the details conformed to Jewish law.

The section of the Beit Chayim Cemetery where they were standing was crowded with tombstones, suggesting that Hannah was one of the last to arrive at her spot. Dennis now had both his parents in the same place, and he began to sob. Brendan supported his father then, surprised to see so much emotion, and didn't let go until the rabbi finished helping the mourner say Kaddish.

An icy drizzle pelted Dennis as he put a shovelful of damp dirt into the grave, and the heavy soil landed with a thud on the beautiful box and flowers. He told Brendan to go next, and the young man turned white and resisted before he finally complied. Pamela watched the scene from her seat in Brendan's car, relieved that she was told to stay there with her mother.

For Dennis's week of sitting Shiva, which he insisted be shared by his children even though they were not official mourners, the Shul provided what was needed. The ladies from the Sisterhood covered the mirrors and brought food for the family to eat. And although the residence was far from East Belleridge, the men made sure there was a minyan morning and night at which Dennis could say Kaddish.

Donations were made in Hannah's memory to the Shul, the day school in Atlantic City and other philanthropies in which Dennis was prominent. Visitors who could make the trip came from near and far to offer their condolences. Those who couldn't come sent cards, plants or fruit baskets. The rabbi and others from the Shul came every day.

For everybody else, the same week was routine. Its familiar pattern – plus the extra duties that accompanied the Shine loss – eventually helped the rabbi return to his schedule, readjust to the time zone and, in general, recover from the jet lag of his intense trip of the week before.

But when the week of mourning had first started, Avi was still groggy and time felt warped. The day after the funeral, he was driving back from the Shiva at Dennis's Northwood home to be at Shul for the start of that day's Hebrew School session when it occurred to him that he was not sure what day it was. As soon as classes started, the rabbi checked his appointment calendar and was startled to find it was already mid November! He realized he'd better check arrangements for the brotherhood service because the date was coming up fast.

"Did anyone ask you to set up extra chairs for the Thanksgiving event?" he asked the custodian.

"No, Rabbi," the dependable, respectful and reticent worker answered.

Joe Kripski lived in a tiny red house next to the gas station two blocks away and had been taking care of the Shul building for years. As a Polish post-war immigrant, he was happy to have a house at all and grateful that a job enabled him, his young wife and little daughter to live in America. The Kripskis were in the Our Mother of Mercy Church parish, and Joe was looking forward to being a guest at Congregation Tefillah's interfaith gathering. He hadn't expected to have to work that day.

"We need you to set up, but it could be done the night before because there's no food involved, and cleanup can wait until Friday morning. On Thursday, you can be here with your family as guests," said the rabbi, trying to be sensitive to the employee's own needs.

Avi thought the suggestion was taken well, but you never knew with Kripski. The rabbi often tried to ferret out Joe's feelings about his job at the synagogue, or about the congregants he had to work with, or about Jews in general. Avi knew that the employee had been in Poland during the war, but didn't know what his contact with the Nazis had been. Did he have an opinion about the millions of Jews who were worked to death in concentration camps or murdered in the death factories there? Was he on the side of the Nazis who incinerated Jews by the thousands in crematoria every hour, or had he helped some victims survive? Was his work in a Jewish institution a form of Polish reparations, or was it just a convenient income for an old man with a young family?

One thing for sure was that he never spoke Polish to the Holocaust survivors who belonged to the Shul. Maybe he was afraid how Jews might react if they heard a language that had been used by anti-Semites during the war, or perhaps it was because Jews tended to use Yiddish instead. It was also possible that his terse manner reflected limited intelligence rather than unwelcome opinions. Who knew?

"Okay," Joe said.

Avi was leaving with Emma after Hebrew school and longing for his bed when she reminded him about college night. By eight, they were expected to go with Josh to his yeshiva to find out about the best post-high school options for an observant Jew.

"That's tonight?" Avi couldn't believe how tired he was, that his son was old enough to start planning a career, how fast time went, and, yes, how tired he was.

"As parents of juniors," droned the high school guidance counselor that evening, "I'm sure your child's post-high school plans are uppermost in your thoughts."

Well, thought Avi, it may be one of the most important issues on our minds, but I'm not sure it occupies the top slot in all of the parents' deliberations. Right now I, for one, would rather be home sleeping.

"All your children certainly are going to college, but not necessarily right out of high school. And what schools are worthy of consideration is the assessment we are here tonight to make," she went on. And on. And on.

The evening turned out to be fairly informative, although Avi had trouble focusing on the details. On the short ride home, Emma drove the minivan and Josh sat in the front while Avi in the back tried to stay awake to discuss different schools. They also talked about the virtues of starting college right away as opposed to going to Israel to study or work there for a year.

"The Boston-New York-Washington area has lots of colleges and offers the best access to kosher food," Josh said, always considering his stomach first, "but California is a pretty sweet place to be and it's packed with Jews, so there must be plenty of kosher pizza there, too."

Send you so far away? To the land of earthquakes, forest fires, floods and mudslides? Where drugs are *de rigueur*? Where we wouldn't know what you were doing and who you were doing it with? Not a chance, kid, thought Avi. "It's something to consider," he said aloud, forcing the words out his mouth while his eyes were closing and his body yearned to stretch out on the back seat.

"But most of the kids are going to a yeshiva in Jerusalem for a year," Josh continued, "and that would be a lot of fun!" Then he thought better of what he was saying to his parents. The truth was that he was eager to go anywhere that was far from home. He was sick of being the rabbi's son, of people watching whatever he did and voicing surprise if he made any mistake at all. But Josh tried not to say it, and instead added what he thought his parents would like to hear. "And I would learn a lot, too."

Send you so far away when you're only sixteen? thought his mother as she changed lanes. To where kids die riding public buses that are targeted by Arab terrorists? Put off for a year the long road to establishing higher education credentials? Never! "We'll have to give it serious thought," Emma said audibly.

And so the ride home went, with lots of conversations, some of them vocalized but most of them not. What the young man and his parents would conclude about college would not be decided this night.

Avi was glad to get to his bed at last, and was very surprised that Tuesday morning came so quickly. Avi went to the morning minyan, got the kids off to school, and had an uninterrupted breakfast before the first call came.

Omar Shukran, as imam of the local mosque, called to say that his group would not be able to come to the Thanksgiving observance on the twenty-seventh. He said something about the prevailing attitude that Muslims were not welcome in America, but Avi wondered if their decision had more to do with the Israel-Arab issue. Although most members of the imam's group were born in America, he himself and several others were immigrants from Saudi Arabia and were very conscious of the suspicions aimed at them after 9/11.

But whether misgivings were warranted or not, their absence from this event was a disappointment to the unity of the community but a relief regarding some of the planning involved, Avi admitted. He would mention Islam respectfully at the event, but in terms of planning, there would be a need for fewer chairs and less security.

That call motivated the rabbi to outline a brotherhood program that would encourage mutual respect. It should start with an official welcome by someone on behalf of the Shul, he reasoned. Then each of the participating denominations would need a representative clergyman on the program. Father Dehaney and Minister Thorn could recite Psalms, but it was logical that blessings in a synagogue would be led only by Jews. Church music would not be appropriate, but singing together would be a good idea. There should be English readings so everyone would feel they participated, perhaps led by a Congregation Tefillah officer. Zev Wolfson was a printer and could be in charge of making up a program. I would be the main speaker, Rabbi London decided.

Wednesday, the rabbi made calls to the clergy and discussed what Psalms they would use. Then, to represent the Shul, he lined up Chairman of the Board Harrison to lead a responsive reading.

Avi asked Cantor Goldberg to lead "Maoz Tsur," which had an English version called "Rock of Ages." The words could be printed in the program so that everyone could sing along to the same tune used for the Hebrew on Chanukah. It was appropriate because the holiday was only a month away, the Jewish leaders agreed. The chazzan would conclude the program with everyone singing "America the Beautiful."

When Avi visited the Shine Shiva house on Thursday, he asked Dennis if he thought he would be up to speaking briefly to a large Thanksgiving audience, considering his personal situation. Dennis said he was looking forward to it, so that was settled, too.

It was good that Dennis was willing to speak at the Thanksgiving program, considered Avi. *He'll need something to occupy his mind when Shiva is over and the reality of his loss begins to sink in.*

By Thursday, however, Dennis had already given his loss a lot of thought. He felt good about the choices he had made for the funeral, opting for the fanciest casket, a big gathering and the largest sign-in book, for example. His mother (may she rest in peace) deserved nothing but the best, and he was able to give that to her as a final send-off. He would order a beautiful headstone for her grave and maybe replace his father's so that they matched. In a year, he would hold an unveiling of the monuments to which he would invite a lot of his friends and business associates. A tribute to his parents in the Shul was necessary, too, and Dennis was considering stained-glass windows on which their names would be prominent.

And Kaddish. He'd have to do a better job for her than he had done for his father. Dennis had been a young man when his father died and his religious efforts had been half-hearted. For his mother, he'd have to do it right. Yup, he'd get to the Shul twice every day and say the prayer for her, Dennis decided. And he'd say Yizkor on holidays. He knew that much for sure, but he'd have to ask the rabbi what else he should do. *It's nice to have a holy man at your beck and call who's not busy with important stuff,* Dennis decided.

And before the mourner could quite believe it, the intense week of Shiva was over.

For Rabbi London, seeing the Shines through Shiva, planning the brotherhood program and supervising the Hebrew School – plus, incidentally, attending to family responsibilities that might determine his son's future – added up to making it a hectic week. By Friday, the preacher was busy studying Vayera, the Torah portion famous for its story of the Binding of Isaac.

In the Shabbat sermon, Avi would not emphasize the obedience that Abraham displayed when God asked him to sacrifice his only son. Instead, the rabbi would focus on the fact that, in the end, God didn't want Abraham to actually do it. Unlike societies that value death for a holy cause, the religion Abraham was to establish would urge its followers to choose life.

The teacher decided it was important to give his congregation some historical background. In Abraham's time, he would explain, human sacrifice was widely practiced, so the demand to bind Isaac and ready him for slaughter was not as odd as it might seem to the modern mind. On the other hand, even today there are societies where martyrdom is more highly valued than survival.

Avi always wondered about the other characters in the story. He pictured Sarah, watching her only child going off with her husband to make the usual religious sacrifice of livestock or produce, but seeing that they took along nothing as an offering. She might have feared that the child-sacrifice common in other cultures was being adopted by their new faith, as well. Was she worried about what her husband might do? To kill their only child made no sense, she would reason. Abraham and Sarah both knew that the death of their son Isaac, who was born of their old age, would mean the end of a line that God promised would grow into a numerous nation.

And what was going through Isaac's mind as he went with his father? Abraham said an offering would become apparent, so what was the son thinking when Abraham bound him up and held a knife to his throat? Did he fight, or beg, or pray, or acquiesce?

And, what about the warped message of religious zeal that some people throughout history deduced from the story that drove followers to kill, or to subjugate, or to mutilate because they thought it was what their god wanted? Faith can make people willing to do anything, Avi observed, but we have to stop when what we're ready to do defies the basic defining principle, that nothing is worth choosing over life.

Maybe God expected Abraham to refuse to do what would have been wrong and waited until the last minute for the man to figure it out. God stopped the slaughter only when he saw that Abraham might not. Or maybe Abraham would have stopped himself a split-second later, knowing that to sacrifice his son was wrong.

Rabbi London would have to teach that binding children to blind faith has no place in Judaism. Living life well in this world – not death or an afterlife – life in this world is Judaism's highest priority.

He didn't realize that the lesson would be vital to certain members of his congregation who might not even be listening.

Chapter 8

Matters of Interpretation

Rabbi London finished delivering his Shabbat morning sermon about the Binding of Isaac and, as he returned to his seat, looked around to see who might have been listening. He hoped the theme of "choosing life" had not been too hard on the mourners in the group, but that was one of the main lessons of this week's portion, and he was obliged to teach it to his entire congregation.

Several people in their first year of loss, who were not accustomed to attending regularly but had been coming recently, were sitting in the congregation that day. This change in routine was common, Avi knew, because mourners found it comforting to say Kaddish and convenient to attend Saturday mornings.

Now added to the roster of new mourners was Dennis Shine. For the last couple of years, he attended Saturday mornings because he was Shul president. Now that he was finished with Shiva, he had the additional motivation of wanting to say Kaddish for his mother. Dennis had come to services the night before, too, and Avi thought he was likely to show up again Saturday evening. He would probably become a regular at all the services on Shabbat and might even become part of the daily minyan, at least during the year of saying Kaddish.

Avi was surprised, however, to see some other people. One was Laura, who felt comfortable enough to come again even though synagogue attendance was not part of her habit in the Jewish State. She became known as "the relative from Israel" and was warmly greeted as that by her parents' friends in Shul. At the Fernberg home, things were going well, too. Andrew thought it was cool to have a sister who fed chickens at a desert kibbutz and played with a goat in the Old City of Jerusalem. Next week, the rabbi would get specific with them about the conversions.

Suzette Z. Siegel, whose family membership in Congregation Tefillah was still fairly new, wanted to become better acquainted with the dynamics of this Shul. She was trying to decide if her children's Jewish education would be in the hands of its Hebrew School or the local yeshiva.

Suzette and her husband were partners in a large New Jersey law firm, she a specialist in criminal rulings and Jon the house expert on immigration issues. They saw each other all the time at work, and at home they were Jewishly observant. On Saturdays, though, they went their separate ways. She considered the Conservative philosophy more modern, and Jon preferred the traditional tone of the Orthodox service. He became a regular at Congregation Emek Emet on Shabbat morning and didn't mind that he and his wife were in different synagogues because he knew that, even if Suzette went with him, they couldn't sit together. Orthodox men and women were in different sections of the room during services.

A nanny stayed home with their two-year-old and an eight-month-old baby, and Suzette gleefully confided to her rabbi that she had just found out she was expecting again.

Morty (Fenstermacher) Fenn was there, too. Always ready with criticism of the Shul and the rabbi, Morty had been an infrequent sight on Shabbat mornings in the past but had begun coming more regularly in the last few months. Recently, he started attending the daily evening service, too, and Avi assumed a religious reawakening was taking place. Then Ray Fisch set the rabbi straight and told him it was a political maneuver. Because the new officers would be elected to their one-year terms in the spring, Morty decided now was the time to start being more visible. Morty wanted to be the next president of the Shul.

Dennis had already served two terms, however, and he showed no signs of quitting. His mother's death only reinforced his commitment to the leadership position in the Shul, and his increased participation was going to be noticed because he planned to say Kaddish at every opportunity.

As much as he was dedicated to the Shul, however, Dennis didn't like the rabbi's attitude. Rabbi London had argued with him about the important features of a funeral and the quality of a casket when those judgments clearly were Dennis's to make as the deceased's son. Now, the rabbi tried to convince him that Kaddish was not really a prayer for the dead. Dennis knew from personal experience that what the rabbi said couldn't possibly be right. And he told him so.

"How can you say that when everyone knows differently," Dennis argued. "The mourner has to stand up when he says it but everyone else can sit. He says the prayer out loud but everyone else just listens and says 'Amen.' If a mourner can't say Kaddish, someone else gets paid to do it. It's obviously a very moving experience for everybody, and it's important to ensure the deceased gets into heaven."

Rabbi London took on a teaching stance and tried to explain. "The scenario of saying Kaddish presents a public opportunity for a mourner, who in private is likely to feel depressed by the recent loss of a close relative, to regain some dignity. It gives someone who is grieving a chance to proclaim his faith in front of an official gathering. Doing so honors the memory of the deceased by demonstrating that important values had been transmitted. Only when people can't say Kaddish themselves should they consider paying someone else to do it. And because Kaddish cannot be said unless there is an official assembly, defined by a ten-men minimum, the responsibility of saying Kaddish gives the mourner an important public role."

"But," Dennis protested, "the Hebrew text obviously talks about the love the person had for the dead parent, otherwise it would not be as emotional as it is."

"The passage doesn't mention the deceased, or the mourner, or the loss, or the limits of life, or the afterlife, or even the emotions we feel toward those we love," answered the teacher. "Kaddish is a rallying cry for the praise of God. And, by the way, it is mostly in Aramaic, the language used for everyday conversation in the days of the Temple two millennia ago. Aramaic, which is as close to Hebrew as Yiddish is, is written with Hebrew letters, as Yiddish is, so it looks like, reflects and includes holy text."

Avi saw Dennis's eyes glaze over and realized that this was more than he wanted to know, so the rabbi shifted his weight and tried a different approach.

"Look at the English translation and you'll see that it tells us to recognize how great God is and that it expresses our hope that we be granted peace. Also, notice that Kaddish is repeated, but in slightly shorter form than the Mourner's version, between each section of a service, no matter whether that service takes place on weekdays or on holidays, in the daytime or at night. It always requires a minyan, so when there isn't one and we pray alone, we skip it altogether. And when we have a minyan but there is no mourner in the room at all, somebody says the Mourner's Kaddish anyway at the customary spot in the service."

Avi thought he explained it well and that Dennis's silence was a sign he understood and agreed. But Dennis was brooding. He was convinced that the rabbi was wrong, or lying. How could the translation not even mention the dead? The loss has got to be implied by certain words, maybe with mystical meanings, or the prayer wouldn't be called the Mourner's Kaddish! Why wasn't the rabbi admitting it and telling him the truth?

Dennis stopped arguing because he saw he couldn't win, but he never forgot.

Regardless of the disagreement, Dennis was grateful that the rabbi was one of the men he could depend on for the minyan so he could say Kaddish for his mother. But including the two of them, the group was never more than a dozen men, and he wondered what would happen if some of them couldn't be there.

As the days of the week wore on, Dennis began mentally taking attendance. By Thursday, he had observed certain patterns. Mr. Day was always at the minyan, but with Harvey Stein's passing, his buddies included only Sol Cohen (whose new son-in-law Cliff Rosen never came), Isaac Iskilovetzky, and Greg Greene. Cantor Goldberg could usually be counted on. Dave Smith and Sig Fleishhocker put on tfillin and davened at home every morning anyway and they felt guilty after their experience at the board meeting, so they tried to get to the morning minyan at Shul fairly often. Zev Wolfson and Ray Fisch didn't usually show up on their own but were at the top of the list to call if the group was short because although they weren't at all religiously observant, they always came if they were needed.

Dennis noted that Morty sometimes came to the minyan in the evenings even before he was called because of his political interests. Dennis encouraged the attendance by mentioning its importance to a leader's image, but he was careful not to encourage Morty's campaign to take over.

Matt and Phil Schwartz were usually at services in the evening to say Kaddish for their father. Dennis knew that Phil was on his company's staff of accountants, so the president/employer called him to make sure he and his brother would show up at Shul during Thanksgiving week.

Dennis knew he couldn't broach the subject of supporting the minyan with former president Stu Eisen. And although Stu had two sons, and the numbers would really help, teenage boys can't be persuaded to do anything they don't want to do. Teenagers can be really obstinate, Dennis reflected. Brendan is impossible. No, he concluded, getting a minyan on weekdays would continue to be difficult. The day of rest, thank goodness, was easy and the weekend was coming up again.

But, like Emma said about the day of rest seeming easy to men when the women did most of the work, Shabbat looked simple to laymen but it required a lot of effort by the rabbi. Avi had to prepare a sermon, for instance. Of course, the weekly Torah portion always gave him something interesting to talk about. The insight it contained was usually applicable to current events, too. This week, Rabbi London would speak about Jews' obligations in a new land.

The portion was called Chayei Sarah, meaning the Life of Sarah, but the text actually dealt with a burial plot for her that Abraham purchased in Hebron, just south of Jerusalem.

"They were newcomers in the area, and in order to avoid any future disputes over ownership of that property," the preacher said to his flock, "Abraham insisted on paying for it rather than just claiming it as an inheritance from God. Such was the foresight and greatness of the Jewish Patriarchs and Matriarchs. They understood that later skeptics could deny descendents' claims, but a purchase would have validity as a matter of record. Paying for it was part of their obligation as newly arrived residents."

At the end of the sermon, Rabbi London added the announcement of another new arrival, a baby born to a member family, the Millers, late Thursday night. The parents wanted to name her after the mother's Grandma Sadie, who had died two years earlier. At the rabbi's suggestion, they decided to link the baby to Jewish history by drawing on the week's portion. The father had been called up during the Torah reading and, as part of that honor, named the baby Sarena. Everyone now said "Mazal tov" and looked forward to the Kiddush after services that would be sponsored by the Miller family in her honor.

When Avi was included in the joyous events of members' lives and made a significant contribution to their future, he was glad he chose the rabbinate. Tragedies were hard, but the sad times were part of life, as well, and he was proud to be in a unique position to really help with both.

But one of his toughest ongoing chores – maintaining a minyan – was always a problem for one reason or another. The first week after the Shine Shiva, for example, the congregation easily had a minyan at the Shul, but for the second week getting the minimum required some calls. A few of the families were beginning to scatter for a Thanksgiving weekend trip or were busy at home preparing for a deluge of company. Others were working on their roles in the brotherhood service, which they saw as being more important.

Dennis was one who considered preparing his remarks to be God's work and decided the project was a good substitute for regular prayer. The rabbi and chazzan did not share that view and were somewhat surprised that Dennis acted on it, opting out of Shacharit on Thanksgiving morning. Phil, who had made a special effort to attend early on a vacation day for his boss's sake, was especially annoyed. Chairman of the Board Harold Harrison, on the other hand, who didn't come that morning and never saw any need to ever support the daily service, understood Dennis's logic and backed the decision completely.

They all, however, arrived on time at eleven for the Thanksgiving Interfaith Brotherhood Service. Rabbi London was delighted that nearly every seat was taken, even the folding chairs they borrowed from the funeral parlor next door. Predictions made by the Christian clergy about how many would come from the two churches were accurate. A handful of members of the Orthodox shul and about a dozen from the Reform Temple were there, too, and Avi hoped that someone from his synagogue would remember to acknowledge them. The rest of the seats were taken by members of the host congregation.

Florence Fischman did a commendable job with decorations. Fall colors predominated, with multicolored leaves and dried flowers placed along the aisles of patterned, blue cushioned seats. Pumpkins and gourds lined the navy carpet in front of the speakers' lecterns. Florence felt she deserved the credit she got when she saw her name listed among the organizers of the event. She felt, though, that her name should have appeared higher on the list in the program Zev had printed and was giving out at the door.

The proceedings began with greetings by Dennis as president of the hosting house of worship. "It's a pleasure to welcome everyone to Congregation Tefillah, East Belleridge's Conservative Jewish synagogue," he said. "I was happy to spearhead this project. An experience like this is important for bringing us and Christians together because that is what this country is made of."

Avi tried not to let the surprise show on his face while Dennis returned to his seat, but several things the president said in his short speech were simply not accurate. First, Dennis was not solely responsible for the success of the event, and others should get the credit they deserve. Second, saying the program ... no, the country ... is made of Christians and Jews makes it sound like there's no place in American life for Muslims, Buddhists, Hindus or the followers of any other religions. Or for non-Conservative Jews, for that matter. Well, the rabbi reconsidered, Dennis's heart is in the right place and he's been through a lot in the past few weeks. Maybe people didn't notice. I shouldn't be so critical.

Y. M. Pines, the Organization of Jewish Organizations representative who requested to be part of the lineup, spoke next. He explained briefly that the OJO was an umbrella organization that coordinated the efforts of several nonsectarian charities and non-profit efforts in the area, such as the assisted-living apartments and the Jewish Senior Home and Rehabilitation Center. He said his agency was delighted to extend greetings from the OJO at this uniquely American celebration. He was warm, brief and to the point, and a lot of the listeners, including Avi, liked him for that.

Then Father Dehaney said he had prayed that the ecumenical service at his church last year wouldn't be the last one, and so he was "delighted that God chose to open the doors and hearts of Congregation Tefillah in the spirit of brotherhood this year." He read the 23rd Psalm because he thought that one was the best known by all, but when he came to "Yea though I walk through the valley of the shadow of death I will fear no evil," Rabbi London started thinking it might have been a strange choice. Dennis, Harold and Morty, among others, admired the comments because the men found them very thought provoking. They all, however, cringed and felt it was inappropriate when the priest crossed himself at the end of his remarks.

Minister Thorn praised America's history of tolerance, omitting the issues of black slavery and restricted clubs that rejected blacks, Catholics and Jews. "This the closest mankind has ever come to perfection, and the effort brings us closer to God," the pastor said. Then he read part of the 100th Psalm, saying, "Enter His gates with thanksgiving; come into His courts with praise."

Rabbi London knew the Psalms were part of the Hebrew Bible, composed by King David a thousand years before Jesus came to Jerusalem. He knew they were appropriate to all three monotheistic religions, but he wasn't sure that fact was widely understood.

He also had no doubt that the Christians in the crowd were sure the word "God" referred to Jesus and that Catholics especially felt some comfort seeing the priest genuflect. Jews squirmed because they detected the Christian undercurrent to the remarks, but mostly they viewed the words as an example of how the faithful of every religion could address the Almighty. Anyway, the program indicated that Jews would dominate the rest of the event, so Avi's coreligionists got more comfortable.

Harold, as Congregation Tefillah's Chairman of the Board, led a responsive English reading, the text of which had been printed in the program. It began, he explained, with "Proclaim liberty throughout the land," which appears on the American Liberty Bell but was first a quote from the Hebrew Bible.

Cantor Goldberg introduced a hymn most people knew, and explained it was appropriate to the upcoming holiday season. The audience followed the transliteration or Hebrew words for "Maoz Tzur" in the tune used at the lighting of Chanukah candles. Then everybody sang the English lyrics to the same tune, "Rock of Ages let our song praise Thy saving power. Thou amidst the raging foes was our sheltering tower. ..."

By the time Rabbi London was introduced as the main speaker, time for the hour-long ceremony was running out. He would keep it short.

The rabbi started with the Shehecheyanu blessing, said at every momentous occasion, acknowledging that it is a precious gift to have lived long enough to see this day. Avi acknowledged the participation in this brotherhood service of the members of Our Mother of Mercy Church and the East Belleridge Community Church. Then he welcomed Jews from the other two synagogues in town, Emek Emet Orthodox Congregation and Temple Tikvah, Reform. Taking a certain degree of liberty in the spirit of brotherly love, he added that the Muslim group in town had expressed regrets that they were unable to attend.

"Here we are together. We started together as one form, when God created our common ancestors Adam and Eve. We grew together as a family as the children of Abraham, the founder of monotheism. Our future is together in the world community, and we will flourish together in this great nation called the United States. As I look around the room and see people of every color, from all around the world, following different faiths and foreseeing different futures, I know that we are all Americans, free to live and grow together. I know you all join me in praying for the success of our great nation and peace for all mankind."

Rabbi London finished with a shortened English version of the Hebrew closing line of several prayers, including the Kaddish, saying, "May the One Who ordains harmony in the universe grant peace to us all."

After everyone stood to face the Stars and Stripes and to sing "America the Beautiful," they reached for their coats and made for the door. The two Christian clergymen were the first to bid the rabbi farewell.

"I'm so glad we could do this again," said the Catholic priest as he vigorously shook Rabbi London's hand. "I hope it works as well next year."

"This is what it's all about," chimed in the Protestant minister, as he gently squeezed the rabbi's other hand and flashed his clerical smile.

Avi thought the event went well and he looked forward to overhearing comments from the audience as the building emptied.

"That was great!" said Florence to her friends as they walked down the center aisle. "Did you see the printed program?"

"I never realized that the Psalms were important to Christians," said Jon to his wife Suzette. They agreed that the program was a good community gesture, but because he usually davened with the Orthodox, the part they enjoyed most was being able to sit together and hold hands in Shul.

"Jews take credit for everything, even the Liberty Bell," said one disgruntled Catholic attendee to another, loudly enough to be heard by anyone at the door. The two had seen a few movies and passion plays about the Crucifixion that made them feel well-informed on religious issues, and they were quite convinced about their conclusion. They added the Liberty Bell claim to a long list of complaints they had against what they thought of as Christ killers, despite papal decrees encouraging tolerance. They saw themselves as extremely devout and were not about to forgive the descendants of Jerusalem's inhabitants, who, they were convinced, crucified their savior.

"It's not permissible to say Shehecheyanu if it's not one of the occasions approved by the Talmudic rabbis," said one member of the Orthodox shul to another as they put their hats on over their yarmulkes and walked out the door. The men came hoping to witness some juicy transgression to describe to their fellow congregants and they were sure they had one to report.

"Wasn't it wonderful that Christians and Jews could pray together," raved an enthusiastic woman from the Community Church to her husband on the outside steps. The couple had just come back from a group pilgrimage to Jerusalem and the Holy Land. He nodded somberly and said, "It gives you hope that the world might soon have peace."

"I wonder why the Muslims didn't come," said a Reform Jewish woman to her friends as they got to the sidewalk. She thought their participation would have been an important step toward uniting Americans and bringing an end to distrust in the Middle East.

"Your words were very welcome," Rabbi London said to OJO rep Pines in front of the building. Avi lauded the man's brevity and again apologized for not inquiring about the schedule in advance.

"Gotta run," Dennis barked as he ran past them. Avi was pretty sure Dennis heard the words of praise he shouted after him, but he wasn't certain. Dennis seemed to have something else on his mind.

He did. During the Thanksgiving service, when Father Dehaney talked about "the shadow of death," Dennis remembered Rebecca Iskilovetzky at the Jewish Senior Home. Whenever he would visit his own recovering mother or wife there, he, as Shul president, would stop to see Isaac's wife, even though she seemed unaware of the company. Once Dennis's mother died, he forgot about Rebecca. On his way to the Shine family turkey dinner, he would have just enough time to visit her.

Dennis found Mrs. Iskilovetzky alone in her wheelchair. Her roommate preferred to sit with other residents in the TV room, but Rebecca had little interest in watching any program that was on. The nurses sometimes put her in the same room, but she couldn't follow the details of any story, and her occasional involuntary shriek interfered with others who had their own problems hearing the broadcast.

In her room, the old woman's major occupation was to supervise the parking lot. She would look out the window and observe guests and employees coming and going or watch dead leaves being whipped by the wind. She hardly noticed Dennis was in the room and wouldn't remember the visit afterward, but enjoyed the hard candy he gave her every time he visited. On his way back to the car, Dennis remembered how alert his mother always was and how unexpected her death had been, and he wept. It was a while before he could drive on.

He headed straight to his mother's cousin's house, where the family usually went for Thanksgiving dinner. The main course was always a kosher turkey, and it didn't bother Dennis one bit that it was cooked in a nonkosher kitchen. It was his mother's family, after all, and the ice-cream dessert was always fabulous.

The holiday was only two weeks after Hannah's passing, and Dennis was certainly not up to making other plans, so he decided to carry on as usual. Still, it seemed odd to go without her. The Shine kids were especially resistant. Dennis convinced Pamela to escort Reeva to the dinner, but Brendan put up a real fight. In the end, he yielded in order to honor his grandmother's memory, but he resented his father's insistence on it. Brendan brought his mother and sister in his car and made it clear to them that he wasn't going because of anything his father had said.

The kids in the London house looked forward to the American celebration and were glad that, this time, no Shul emergency called their father away. Avi liked Thanksgiving because it was the one holiday he could participate in like every other proud American. Also, because it was not a Jewish religious holiday and never fell on a Saturday, relatives could drive and visit for the day. Avi's cousins arrived from Long Island early, as usual. Emma's brother and sister arrived late, after a brief stop to feed the deer at the mountain reserve, and they were hungry for a good kosher meal. Emma was famous for her stuffed turkey and always made a big one. Visitors brought sweet potato casserole with marshmallows, cranberry sauce, salad and pumpkin-raisin cake. Avi made a point of toasting America and expressing gratitude that the family was lucky enough to be living in such a great democracy.

The rabbi expected to see his regular group, picking their teeth and looking full, at the minyan that evening. Phil and the cantor were already there, but to their surprise, the president of the Shul didn't come. By going to the brotherhood event and visiting Rebecca Iskilovetzky, Dennis felt he had earned his "mitzvah points" for the day. His absence made getting a minyan that much harder a task for Avi.

Yes, the rabbinate had its highs and its lows, but concern over getting ten men for a minyan paled when, after Maariv, he got a call for a Sunday funeral.

Celia Dubinsky's grandson Randy, a junior at a state university in Florida and a good engineering student, had tried some drugs at a party. He thought the pills gave a relatively harmless kick, but the hallucinogenic drug put him out of his right mind. Randy left the party to take what he believed to be an evening stroll in the country, but he wandered instead onto a local highway. He was hit by a truck and died instantly.

Randy's grandmother had a cantankerous relationship with Rabbi London, who had not seen the dead boy or his parents since his Bar Mitzvah, but Avi was the only rabbi the family knew, so he would have to be the one to comfort them and see them through this crisis.

One repercussion from his calling that Avi did not expect was the toll these emotional ups and downs would take on his own children.

He waited until late that evening, after everything was cleaned up from a long Thanksgiving visit filled with laughter and loved ones and before the kids might get busy with their friends. He sat Emma down with the kids in the kitchen and told them about Randy Dubinsky. There was a long pause, and then an eruption.

"Just because one kid went berserk when he tried a drug doesn't mean it will happen to everybody," Josh screamed at his mother after she urged him to learn a lesson from a sad story. "Not every kid does drugs when he's away from home! And absolutely everybody tries something, even in yeshiva high school! But I never have. I would never do that. You trust me, don't you? Don't you?" he yelled, wondering if his parents would believe him. He looked at them, ignored his sister and stomped outside to wait for his friend in the dark, slamming the door behind him.

Ahuva – who had tried keeping to herself emotions that haunted her from the Shine visit, when she witnessed a wife accusing her own husband of trying to murder her – finally lost control.

"I can't stand this. Living here is just too weird," Ahuva complained to her father in the vacuum created by Josh's departure. "Some woman comes to our door saying her father will kill her and we're supposed to eat supper as if nothing's wrong. We set up a wedding in our own house that we're, like, not even invited to. You totally disappear to Israel and come back with a lady we never even *heard* of before. We're supposed to be happy over a new baby in a family we don't even know but don't talk about a dead kid we actually *remember*," she said, her voice getting shriller with every statement.

"You go to funerals and Shivas all the time. You're constantly running to the minyan at Shul or to old people at the hospital, so you're *never* here for us. And if we do *anything* – like if we smoke or curse or fail a test — absolutely *everybody* in the Shul knows about it and talks about it!" She took a breath.

"Why can't you be like all the other kids' dads?" Ahuva demanded of her father. "Why couldn't you be a lawyer or own a business like they do? *They* don't go to funerals all the time. *They* don't have to totally cancel vacations because somebody they don't even know got sick. *They* don't, like, have strangers bringing problems to their house every day. *Their* kids aren't, y'know, watched by everybody to see if they make a mistake!" Her eyes went to her mother and back to her father, and then filled with tears. She turned quickly and flew up the stairs and slammed the door to her room behind her.

Emma and Avi looked at each other. They understood that a certain portion of their children's theatrics was a reflection of teenagers' high-strung emotions, but the kids were right to complain. As much as their parents tried to shield them from rabbinical business, the kids invariably felt the impact, either from an incident itself or from the heightened tension it introduced to the rabbi's home. It was a tough life for them.

And it would only get worse.

Chapter 9

Lives and Deaths

Maybe it was the blow-up with the kids the night of Thanksgiving or maybe it was the sad news that prompted it, but Avi was fighting to come out of an unrelenting gloom.

It didn't help that a lot of familiar faces were missing from Shabbat services. People must be away for the Thanksgiving weekend, he reasoned. Or, perhaps they felt that, by supporting the brotherhood observance, they had fulfilled their quota of religious services for the week. Or maybe it was downright depressing to know a member had to bury a grandson the next day and they didn't want to come face to face with the reality of the loss or the people suffering it.

As it turned out, the reduced attendance was just as well. The sanctuary was filling up with Fisch Bar Mitzvah guests for a poignant counterpoint to the loss of a teen, and Avi reasoned that his own melancholy surely would yield to the joy of the morning's simcha.

Ray beamed with pleasure as he and his wife Dafna greeted guests. Then Eli made both his parents and two younger brothers proud when he not only read his entire Torah portion but was in charge of the rest of the morning's ceremonies, as well. Eli is a real achiever, Avi thought, and like his father, a really good person.

Eli walked to the podium and took a deep breath. Without looking up from the notes he clutched tightly in his hands, he recited his speech, which focused on the renewal of the promises God made to Isaac's father. "Abraham's descendants would become a great nation and inherit the land that was promised," he concluded.

The rabbi stood to preach his sermon, but on a day that was difficult for Avi for other reasons, the Torah portion presented an additional challenge. Toldot described the legacy Isaac planned for his two sons, and it was always hard to explain the circumstances that gave Jacob the birthright when it rightfully belonged to his older twin Esau. The ruse was a very logical maneuver by a mother who knew her sons' fortes and foibles, but the lesson of shaping history through deception was not easy to rationalize.

At the beginning of his talk, Rabbi London confessed that Rebecca's deception of her dying husband Isaac was a difficult story, but very understandable. "The Torah portrays our predecessors as real people. They had human failings. They sometimes made mistakes, and even lied or murdered. It is important to remember that they lived at the beginning of our people's history and lacked the insight we gain from studying their stories. Given that, we must recognize that these people also possessed the strengths required by the founders of a new nation."

Avi focused on the son who would be a Patriarch. "Rebecca knew that the younger son Jacob had greatness in him and that he had the potential to build the nation his father and grandfather had founded. Jacob, for his part, learned that the birthright meant little to his brother Esau when the older twin willingly traded it for one good meal. Jacob also understood that sustaining the family's role in the future of our People was critical. Isaac blessed both his sons, but knew – as his wife did – that history would be made by Jacob's line."

Rabbi London turned to the Bar Mitzvah boy. "We at the Shul have had the privilege of knowing your parents and seeing how hard they work for worthy causes. They are valuable assets to our community and have established a wonderful path for you to follow.

"Your parents, who know you well and love you deeply, see the seeds of strength in you. Right now, the greatness is only potential. It's up to you to live your life in such a way that what is special in you grows to be a resource for your fellow Jews and for all mankind."

The Bar Mitzvah boy was much more relaxed when he repeated the speech at his party the next day between courses of the catered dinner and group dancing, but the rabbi and his wife weren't there to hear it. Most people were off from work on Sundays and could celebrate at a party, but Rabbi London was working.

Hebrew School was off for Thanksgiving weekend, so Emma stayed home with her husband as he got ready. Avi studied several halachic texts for his mid-day duties, and his wife put his black fedora and gray scarf into the car in case he needed them later at the cemetery. She would go to the funeral in her own car, but Rabbi London left earlier to attend to an inconsolable family.

The Dubinsky family must be suffering badly, Emma thought. It was a terrible tragedy for parents to outlive a child, and it was unthinkable for anyone to have to bury a grandchild. She knew her husband would do what he could to bring the family solace, and she hoped Celia's difficult nature wouldn't make it harder than it had to be.

The funeral chapel was filled with the wailing of the teenage boy's school buddies, the parents' relatives, Celia's neighbors and the three generations' lifelong friends. After a eulogy by the boy's heartbroken father, Rabbi London spoke about the fragile nature of life, emphasizing that nothing should be taken for granted.

He told a story about the Talmudic character Bruriah, who was regarded as a scholar in her own right and who was married to a famous rabbi. Her husband was away studying at a yeshiva when a plague killed their two sons, and it was up to her to break the news to him. When the rabbi returned home, his wife prefaced the bad tidings with a question. Someone had left two jewels with her for safekeeping and now the owner wants them back. What should she do? Give them back immediately, was the rabbi's answer. The owner is God and the jewels are your sons, Bruriah told her husband, and God has come for them.

Randy Dubinsky was a jewel, Rabbi London told the grieving audience, and his family was lucky to have him as long as they did. They would always have the memory of the joy and light he brought into their lives, but their time with him was over. Now they had to give him back to his Maker.

Emma went home after the funeral, but Rabbi London accompanied the family to the cemetery, where an emotional crowd attended the burial. Celia and her former husband found comfort from the rabbi's words, and finalized the decision that the family's Shiva would be at the house in East Belleridge. Once there, Rabbi London launched into his usual explanation of the customs and, with the help of the Sisterhood ladies, set the family up for Shiva.

Avi left them then and devoted the rest of the day to congregants with health issues. He stopped in to see Jane Harrison, who was at her house still recovering from surgery, and Stu Eisen, who was home but awaiting test results. The rabbi also visited the Jewish Senior Home to see Rebecca Iskilovetzky. But he ended the work day with a moment of joy at the home of the Millers and their new baby, Sarena, who had been named in Shul.

That evening, Emma, who was still feeling the sadness of the Dubinsky funeral, told her husband that he had handled a terrible situation very well. "It was the right approach to take with such a terrible loss," she told him, admiring his talent for saying the right thing at such a difficult time.

Dennis had been at the funeral, too. He always found death sad, especially since his own loss, but wondered about the death of a child. It's different from the passing of a parent. After all, he thought, you know your parents your whole life and they set the standard for your future. A child is a hit-or-miss proposition. It spends the first few years just becoming civilized and then hates you for expecting respect. Brendan, for example.

The joys and heartbreaks of parenthood weighed heavily on everyone's mind, so it didn't surprise Avi that Dennis would want to talk about it. That night at the Shul, while they were waiting for a tenth for the minyan, Dennis asked the rabbi who would say Kaddish for a person who was too young to have children.

"There are several levels of mourners," Rabbi London explained, wondering if Dennis really treasured the gift of parenthood the way he did. Whether Dennis did or not, however, the question did not surprise Avi. A fresh loss can befuddle the thinking of anyone recovering from such a trauma, and an ordeal like the Dubinsky funeral can rekindle many concerns that people want to discuss.

"After the funeral, close blood relatives – siblings or a spouse – are expected to say Kaddish for a month. The custom is to say it an eleven-month year for a parent," the rabbi said, knowing that the obligation is not always met. Then he added, "There's also the Yizkor memorial service. It's combined with the synagogue service on major holidays and can be said by all the relatives, and unlike Kaddish, there is a place in the text where they name the deceased. In fact, that service includes a prayer for all Jews who died during history's persecutions – without naming the dead, of course – so victims of the Inquisition of the Middle Ages or the 20th Century Holocaust are remembered then, too."

Again, Avi realized from Dennis's glazed expression that he was explaining more than Dennis wanted to know. The rabbi scaled back and simply answered the question.

"In this case, the boy's parents would say Kaddish."

Dennis thought about that, but calculated that even if the grieving Dubinsky parents decided to say Kaddish, they probably would not go beyond the initial month for a teenager. Even if they came to East Belleridge often, the father would be unlikely to go to the daily minyan. This situation would not help him, Dennis realized. Getting ten would continue to be a squeaker.

Luckily, a tenth walked in for that night's minyan. Bill Fernberg was early for his meeting with the rabbi, so he put on a kippah and followed the unfamiliar service as well as he could. Rabbi London's habit of periodically announcing page numbers helped.

After the service, Bill followed the rabbi into his office. Avi was happy to hear that Laura's adjustment was going fairly well. "She and Carey are trying real hard to be civil to each other despite a history of not getting along, but the best news is that Laura really likes her brother," Bill said. "That makes this whole conversion problem easier and we can start planning for it."

Rabbi London reviewed the details of the process the family faced. Making sure that the conversion met strict traditional standards would require convening a Beit Din, a court of three Orthodox rabbis, to verify the legal process. These men would be the official witnesses to both a Tipat Dahm (literally a "drop of blood," a pinprick by a mohel that would suffice as a Bris in the case of an already circumcised male) for the boy and a dip in the Mikveh ritual bath required for both males and females. If scheduled right, the procedures could be arranged in short order and accomplished in a day.

"In your family's case," Avi said, "I would start planning now for your son. Decide when you'll be ready and, on your behalf, I'll set a date for a Beit Din and make an appointment with the mohel. I'll also reserve a couple of hours at the Mikveh so we'll have some time there alone to complete the conversions. You should give some thought, too, as to whether you want to have a private bite to eat afterwards to mark the occasion or prefer to celebrate big with a party for friends. It's up to you, but it is traditional to have something to eat to honor the fulfillment of a mitzvah."

By the time Bill was finished meeting with Rabbi London, Dennis was home. He went to his desk and made a list on his computer in a file he called minyanlist.doc. In the file, he recorded the observations he had made on who came to the minyan and when. Day, Cohen, Iskilovetzky and Greene were the regulars. Smith and Fleishhocker usually came in the mornings and Phil and Matt Schwartz in the evenings, so together the four made two. That's a total of six. He, the rabbi and cantor made nine. Fenn, Wolfson and Fisch – with his son who recently celebrated his Bar Mitzvah – were occasionally available. Together, they might or might not total ten.

Monday morning, Dennis confirmed his calculations when Shacharit presented the same old challenge. They were nine for a long time, and finally Mr. Day made the same exit he had a few weeks earlier and headed to Emek Emet. Most of the rest went with him, and Dennis was faced with a dilemma. He needed to say Kaddish, but didn't want to go to an Orthodox minyan, where he would get lost in the service because no one announced pages. He was also sure the men who regularly go there in the mornings would judge him to be inadequate because he didn't put on tfillin or know the service well. The Reform probably didn't even have a weekday service. He decided to go to the Orthodox this once, but vowed to fix the problem so it wouldn't happen again.

Later, looking back on it, Dennis couldn't accurately read the reactions of the Emek Emet crowd, whether they had been glad he came because it made the minyan larger by one or if they had resented his presence because he came without being able to fully participate. Either way, it was stressful and Dennis was glad it was over.

He spent most of the next few hours in his office, but the rough morning start set the tone for the day, and he devoted breaks to exchanging glaring looks with Phil Schwartz, who had his own thoughts.

Why should I go out of my way for Dennis when he doesn't even show up? wondered Phil, who was still seething over getting up early to make the minyan Thanksgiving morning. Where was Phil when I needed him? thought Dennis, who had felt humiliated at the Orthodox service that very morning and blamed it on Phil for not showing up at the Conservative Shul.

On his way home, Dennis stopped again to see Rebecca Iskilovetzky. Her husband Isaac had already come and gone for the day by the time the Shul president got there, so Rebecca was alone in her room and in bed. It was late, and she had already been fed her unrecognizable chopped supper, so Dennis gave her the usual hard candy for dessert. As always, he had to unwrap it for her because her gnarled fingers were all but useless. Her sunken cheeks struggled to position the candy in her toothless mouth so her sucking could produce a flavor, and Dennis talked.

He complained that the rabbi rambled too long before making his point and was downright boring at the Thanksgiving service.

Dennis told her how his business was going and about the Dubinsky funeral. It looked like they were visiting together, but Rebecca was oblivious to him and he didn't really care.

"I wanted to say Kaddish for my mother, but we couldn't get ten men," Dennis told the blank face. "Can you imagine that? All the years and all the money I spent building a beautiful sanctuary and increasing the membership, and we couldn't get ten men when I needed them. I bet if more people had to say Kaddish, they would understand how important having a minyan really is."

Then he thought about his own loss and started crying. "My mother was such a guiding light to me," he said. "She was tough on me when I was younger, but I grew to be grateful and love her for it. She never trusted Reeva and her red hair and she was right about her, too. Now I'm stuck with a wife who's no good to me at all and kids I just don't understand."

He looked at the old woman, propped up on pillows and covered with a blanket. Her skin was as gray as her hair, and she looked terribly frail. She said nothing that made sense and she couldn't control her bodily functions any more. At random moments, she screamed. This was living? he wondered.

"My mother was vibrant," Dennis muttered to her. "My mother was active and generous and full of good advice to the very end! Why would God choose to give you these useless years and deprive her of good ones?"

Dennis's eyes were full of tears as he turned and left, so he didn't see her distressed expression. Rebecca was having trouble positioning the hard candy in her mouth and was having difficulty breathing around it. But Dennis didn't notice. Or maybe he didn't want to.

Within a few minutes of his departure, Rebecca Iskilovetzky, age eighty-seven, choked on the candy in her mouth. As a matter of policy, the Home's ambulance took her to the hospital, in case the hospital's hi-tech services could revive her. The Home immediately called Isaac, and when everyone agreed it was all over, he phoned the rabbi to say she was gone. The small funeral was graveside the next day. They had no children.

Dennis attended the funeral Tuesday, but he was painfully aware that during the time Isaac sat Shiva, getting a minyan at the Shul would be really difficult. He was right. The regulars went to the Dubinskys' or to the Iskilovetzkys'. Men who did not go to the mourners' houses headed for the Orthodox shul, where there was sure to be a minyan. Dennis faced his dilemma again, knowing it would not be much better after the two Shivas were over, because Celia's family would go home and Isaac would return to the minyan to say Kaddish without any other mourners to increase the numbers. This was an intolerable situation, Dennis decided, and he was determined to find a way to fix it.

As he was falling asleep that night, he started doing the math about some leading members of the Shul and what the rabbi said about who was obligated to say Kaddish. Mr. Day has children but I don't know where they live, Dennis said to himself. Sol Cohen has only a daughter. Zev Wolfson has three girls. Florence Fischman has an adult son, but he's in Los Angeles. Phil Schwartz has two sons, so it would be a net gain of one. I wonder if his brother Matt has more than two sons and how old they are. Ray Fisch has three kids, and one just celebrated his Bar Mitzvah. Stu Eisen has two teenage sons. So does Larry Lansken. I wonder what kids Morty Fenn has? or Harold Harrison? or Greg Greene? Cantor Goldberg comes to the minyan anyway and his son Eitan is too young. The rabbi? He has a son old enough, but Dennis might need a rabbi. The wives? That would be a different calculation. Let's see ...

That's all Dennis could think through before sleep overtook him. A dream carried him to Israel, where he had no trouble getting a minyan because everyone was Jewish and most were in mourning.

Israel was in Avi's dreams, too, happy ones that he would have been pleased to stay with, but it was morning and the alarm was insistent. It would be a long day, so he'd better get started.

After the morning minyan and breakfast, Rabbi London taught his regular Wednesday morning class at Yeshiva Gavoha. The kids had lots of questions about his emergency trip to Israel. He portrayed the mix of young people and languages at the restaurant in Jerusalem. He described the meager accommodations in the Old City of Jerusalem's Arab Quarter and the goat that lived there. He mentioned that he had davened at the Kotel but had to explain to an Israeli why the spot was important. He told them how he joined the minyan at the plane's bulkhead and watched through the plane's small windows as the sun came up. What the teens were most concerned about, though, was the overall situation between Israel and the Arabs of the area, which was always complicated and a subject the students had to be conversant with when they left high school.

From the yeshiva, Avi headed for a meeting with other Conservative rabbis about Kosher food sources in the region. A Jewish market had opened next to a senior-citizen housing project in New

Jersey, near its northern border with New York State, and the rabbinical supervision had to be checked. The Kashrut Clarification Committee met in different places each month, and today's site was nearly an hour's drive north and west.

On the way home, he stopped at the local AAA office to pick up maps of the Boston and Washington areas for a few colleges Josh was considering. Avi had a dentist appointment at two and had to be at the Shul for Hebrew School by four, so he wouldn't have time to shop for Chanukah presents at the mall, but he would have to do it soon.

It was a busy day, and in that way very typical.

Dennis was having a regular day, too, but the calculations of the previous night were churning in his mind. By the time he got to the evening minyan, he had some questions.

"Rabbi, I was wondering how many teenage boys we have in the Shul."

"It's not easy to attract kids to Shul events, you know," said the rabbi. "The focus of their lives is school, friends, movies, TV shows, sports – not our Shul."

"Yes, but who else is there?" Dennis wanted to know. Surely the rabbi was involved in their Bar Mitzvahs and would remember who had not yet left for college.

"Well," Avi said, "I remember hearing that Stu Eisen was president when his son Mark celebrated his Bar Mitzvah, so that was about four years ago. I was the rabbi for his younger son Jeff's last year. Larry Lansken's boys Eugene and Ron are about the same age as Stu's kids.

"Morty Fenn has four boys and a girl, and I think three of them are in high or junior high school. Last week, Ray Fisch's son Eli celebrated his Bar Mitzvah. Harold Harrison has a boy still in high school but his daughters are out of college already." The rabbi suspected Dennis had a plan to attract the Shul's teenagers, and Avi didn't want the girls to be left out, so he added, "Melissa Greene's Bat Mitzvah is this Shabbat, so maybe other names will come to me."

But Dennis didn't want the girls. He agreed with the Shul's decision to follow the traditional practice of requiring a quorum of men, so the girls would not make the minyan even if they came. He personally believed that only the men's prayers counted anyway. He remembered that his sainted mother, rest her soul, was happy to have a son who would say Kaddish for her husband and, eventually, for her.

But this time the rabbi was right, Dennis decided. Even though the occasion this weekend was for a girl, it would bring other boys' names to mind.

During Hebrew School Thursday, Rabbi London met with Greg Greene's granddaughter about her Bat Mitzvah one last time before the occasion. Her parents belonged to the Shul and attended the Shabbat morning service while she was in Junior Congregation, but beyond that, Melissa also came Friday nights with her grandfather. She enjoyed Hebrew School and drew inspiration from Greg, who was a regular at Shul. In previous meetings, Avi checked that she knew what to do in order to lead the Welcoming Shabbat part of the Friday night service. Now that he had reviewed her speech, he knew she was ready.

Rabbi London would speak about the portion on Shabbat morning, too, but his audience was different. He would look at the Fernbergs when he quoted the text that has God saying, "I am with you and will keep you wherever you go." He would glance at the Cohens and Rosens and remember the wedding in his house when he retold the story of Jacob being tricked by a veil that hid his bride's face.

But first it was Melissa's turn. Friday night, the Bat Mitzvah girl was nervous. She was not worried about her family, but she had invited many friends. Her public school classmates did not make it a habit to go to shul at all and might find it strange. Pre-teens buddies who knew her from Yeshiva Beinoni had never before seen a girl lead congregational prayer and might think she's strange.

She led the opening melodies of the service and then everyone settled down to listen to her speech. Melissa started, but immediately was interrupted by an old man yelling, "Louder! We can't hear you!"

Despite the acute embarrassment the call caused, she started again. Louder. Melissa reviewed that week's Torah portion, Vayetzeh, which starts with Jacob's vision of a ladder used by angels to climb between earth and heaven. The Patriarch awakes, she said, knowing that God has renewed His promise to keep the Israelites in their land and that, through them, all the families of the earth would be blessed.

"Jacob named the place where he had the vision Beit El, and my Israeli cousins live there now," she said. "I believe the story speaks to me personally, and that it is my destiny that through me others will be blessed. I hope that my future as a Jew in the medical field will make that possible." Melissa thanked her family for their guidance and her little brothers "for being brothers." She also thanked Rabbi London for his help in preparing her talk and her favorite Hebrew teacher, Mrs. London, for always being there for her.

Rabbi London then described how the idea of becoming a nation was made possible by Jacob's growing family, and that the clan's development gave hope that the promise would be fulfilled. "We all hope the promise of Melissa's future will be fulfilled, as well," he concluded.

As soon as the service was over, Melissa ran out of the sanctuary and into the bathroom and burst into tears. She only returned when her friends urged her back. It was typical pre-adolescent jitters, Emma told the parents later, resuming her role of teacher. Otherwise, Melissa did everything right and they should be proud of her. With that, the rabbi and rebbetzin tried to help turn the Greene's bewilderment into a celebration.

Melissa's parents – who thought she was extraordinary because she learned so much about being Jewish – and her grandparents – who saw her as a spiritual replacement for relatives murdered by the Nazis – could not have smiled wider.

Dennis also smiled during the Bat Mitzvah kiddush after the service, but it was just a mask. Through it, he could observe Melissa's friends, and he was disappointed that most of them were girls. Moreover, because she was celebrating at the age of twelve and her brothers were ten and seven, the occasion drew very few teenage boys. But Melissa's parents were there, and Dennis made a mental note of them.

The Shul president watched Morty, too. The would-be-usurper was almost transparent in his political maneuvering as he shook hands with individuals and greeted members of the congregation by name.

If Morty thinks he can beat me and become the next president of the Shul, he's badly mistaken, thought Dennis. He watched the contender work the room, and then realized Morty's daughter was one of Melissa's friends. What did the rabbi say? That Morty had four boys and a girl, and maybe three were in high school. Could it be that all three high schoolers were boys? That would be hitting pay dirt!

Then Dennis's eyes landed on Harold Harrison, who seemed quite somber. His wife Jane was there, too, so she must be recovering from her surgery. Or maybe not. She didn't look too good.

The truth was that Jane's hysterectomy was healing okay, but the cancer they found had spread to nearby organs. She was in more pain every day, and it was kept tolerable only by increasing doses of medication. She was scared, too, and came to Shul hoping to find in prayer the strength to go on. She needed spiritual guidance.

The next Monday afternoon, Rabbi London visited Jane in her home to give her encouragement. A cure, or at least a new treatment, could always be just around the corner, he told her. Where there's life, there's hope. In the meantime, she should follow the best medical advice she could find to beat or manage this thing. The odds were in her favor, so she had to be courageous, her spiritual leader insisted.

"Remember," he said, "you spent many years teaching your children how to live. You owe it to them to teach them how to be strong and optimistic under these circumstances, as well."

She smiled and thanked him. But Jane's mind was filled with the nightmare that surely lay ahead. If she followed her doctor's advice, there would be months of chemotherapy-induced vomiting, weakness and hair loss. The initial regimen would rob her of her looks and be followed by months of radiation that would sap whatever personality and strength she had left.

If there were a reason to believe she would emerge cured so she could return to her former level of activity, it might be worth it. But prospects were slim. Even if all went well, she might be pronounced in remission for a while, but it was likely that the illness would return. Then she would become a burden to her family as she endured a long, painful death. Which was better, a degrading hard fight capped by a long painful death or a quick end now?

Jane told the rabbi that she was in pain and asked him to reach for her pills before he left. Avi handed her the bottle and watched her take two. When she had swallowed them, he replaced the bottle on the dresser and went home.

An hour later, Jane asked her husband Harold to bring her water so she could take her pills, and she took two. She slept for an hour and Dennis didn't realize his arrival woke her.

Dennis often visited sick members, both because it was expected of him as president of the Shul and because he figured it would earn him a few mitzvah points. With the loss of his mother on his mind, Mrs. Iskilovetzky's recent passing and Jane before his eyes – looking weak as much from the pain pills as from the illness – he talked about how difficult life gets at the end. "Dying can be quick or it could take a long time," he reflected.

She told him about what the rabbi said and, through her haze, concluded the same thing Dennis did. "Dying could take a long time." Yes, Jane thought, she had spent her life teaching her children how to live. Now, she would spend this time showing them how to die.

Dennis saw that she was in pain and was glad to help when she asked for her pain medication. After Dennis left, she told her husband she was going to sleep. She probably could have survived the pills she had taken until then, but now she had the rest. By morning, she was dead.

The funeral was Wednesday morning, and there was a large turnout from the Shul. Jane's husband Harold was, after all, a pillar of the community. Rabbi London and Dennis both were shaken by the fact that they had just seen her and assured each other that they tried their best to help.

The rabbi focused on what to tell Harold and the three children. Even though the two girls were adults, it was still a terrible loss to them. "Life is a story," said Rabbi London again, as he officiated at yet another funeral. "If it has a beginning, it also has to have an end." And starting with that thought, he began guiding the family through their crisis.

Dennis didn't remember that the rabbi had started the same way at his mother's funeral. He was watching Harold's son, noting that he was a senior in high school. At the Shiva house, he talked to the boy.

"Your father doesn't come to the daily service, but I'm sure you will want to come to say Kaddish. I'd be happy to pick you up."

"That's a nice offer," replied the son, "but if my father doesn't think it's necessary, I won't go." And he didn't.

Dennis needed more Jewishly committed mourners.

Chapter 10

Impending Doom

"The bodies are really piling up," cracked Josh as he ran out for school the next day. He and Ahuva were on time to catch the bus – it was rare, but it did happen occasionally – and they were leaving just as Avi returned from the morning minyan. The father knew better than to get in the path of kids flying out the door, so he stood back and stayed out of the way, but he considered Josh's observation. The quip reflected the teenager's wry humor, and his parents discounted it as that, but like everything that makes people laugh, somewhere in it there was a kernel of truth.

Once the kids were on their way, Avi and Emma sat down over a cup of coffee to get a reality check. They agreed that, for the most part, an average variety of life cycle events had unfolded in the past few weeks. There had been a wedding, a baby naming and Bar and Bat Mitzvahs. A usual number of congregants were sick and required special visits. Some Jewish legal questions had come up. But, they noticed, the calendar for the last two months had been rather full of funerals.

Harvey Stein had died of a heart attack, Hannah Shine succumbed to old age, Celia Dubinsky's grandson walked into highway traffic during a drug-induced hallucination, Rebecca Iskilovetzky choked on a candy and Jane Harrison chose quick death over a difficult fight for life.

"Josh was right," Emma said to her husband. "There have been a lot of tragedies in the last few weeks. And the kids probably feel it more than they should – after all, they don't really know most of those people – but they feel it because they see what it does to us.

I wish there were a way to shield them better. Kids shouldn't have to grow up with so much bad news about people they don't even know. It's like living in a soap opera that you can't turn off."

Their five bonus minutes used up, the parents both rushed off to their duties. Emma left for her teaching job and Avi sat down at his desk to review his schedule. It was Thursday and not too early to plan a Shabbat sermon. This week's talk would have to be uplifting so that his flock would not get depressed over the recent rash of tragedies. Finding a source would not be hard, since Vayishlach describes Jacob's struggle with a stranger, frequently likened to the fight an individual wages against a sense of impending doom.

The feeling of helplessness was growing with Dennis, too, but for a different reason. Even Jane's death, which he considered to be for everyone's good, did not help fill the ten slots he needed in order to say Kaddish for his mother. He went from the morning minyan directly to his office, where he called in Phil Schwartz to find out more about him and his brother Matt.

"I see you often at the Shul's evening minyan, Phil, and I realize I know very little about you except that you're one of the company's accountants," Dennis said in his warmest manner. He made sure to smile. "Tell me about yourself."

Phil was suspicious about his boss's sudden interest, but started talking. Dennis smiled and nodded, but hardly listened to the details of his employee's childhood or education or his wife Marjorie's talent as a physical therapist. His ears perked up only when he learned that Phil's older brother Matt, a teacher, was married to Terri, also a teacher, and that they were the parents of an adult daughter and two teenage sons who were about the same ages as Phil's boys.

"And you're saying Kaddish for your father?" asked Dennis.

Phil explained that he and Matt had promised their father they would do it because the old man had been so disappointed that they didn't take on the responsibility when their mother passed on. The brothers decided, however, to go only to the minyan on weekday nights because "very few people paid attention to that service." Truth be told, their commitment to even that was waning, Phil admitted.

"Oh, no, don't give up on it! It's very important," insisted Dennis, "especially since you promised your father." The employer knew what a pledge was. Dennis had promised his mother she would not be forgotten and he intended to make good on that. He needed

Phil and his brother. "Kaddish does great things for the departed soul. And you have to do everything you can to make sure the dead become angels in heaven."

Funny, thought the employee as he left Dennis's office, "becoming angels in heaven" was not a concept Phil remembered hearing from the rabbi. I wonder if Dennis makes up his own rules, Phil thought wryly.

In the meantime, a former Shul boss was having trouble, and the rabbi heard about it on his cellphone just as he was leaving home for errands at the cleaners, florist and bakery.

"Dad was just taken back to the hospital," said Stu Eisen's son Mark. "Jeff and Mom went in the ambulance with him and she told me to call you before I left in the car."

When Rabbi London got to East Belleridge General, he asked Stu's wife for details. "Stu had been feeling better, and we had hoped that the test results would give us an encouraging report," Mona said. "but one test showed a large blockage in an artery from the heart. Stu is facing bypass surgery! Just hearing about it made him crazy, and the tension from that alone might have been what drove him back to the hospital. But on top of that, he's been worried all along that his business might fall apart in this economy if he got sick, and the added pressure was too much. Now an operation!"

Although Avi couldn't make any predictions about the success of the Eisen department store chain in the coming holiday season, he did speak to the doctor before visiting the patient and confirmed a reason for optimism about the surgery.

"Don't jump the gun, Stu," Rabbi London said when he got to the forty-five-year-old man who feared for his life. Avi liked Stu and felt a rapport with him that allowed for gentle teasing, even though they were not on the same page religiously. Stu was a major financial supporter of the congregation, but wasn't the backbone of its religious life. As his attitude toward the Thanksgiving Brotherhood Service demonstrated, he believed the privilege of being Americans trumped any identity as Jews, and on those types of subjects there was, and would be, much heated debate between the two men.

But four years ago, when Avi applied for the job of spiritual leader, Stu was Shul president and appreciated the worldliness and religious savvy he saw in the young rabbi. Avi cherished the support at that time and enjoyed the intellectual challenge he had gotten from Stu since then. Rabbi London was glad he could encourage his congregant through this medical crisis and felt sure he would be okay.

"I know it's scary," the clergyman told the patient, "but lots of folks have heart bypass surgery these days and come out of it feeling better than they've felt in a long time. You have a strong, positive outlook on life, a family that loves and supports you, and great medical expertise. God willing, you'll be fine."

Then Avi remembered a joke. "Did you hear that the Shul Board voted you a get well wish? The vote was eleven for, nine against and three abstentions." Stu thought it over for a moment, and then burst into laughter. His change of mood set off giggles of relief from his wife.

Avi was glad to see Mona's worry lines relax, and the change of tone soothed their sons' anxieties. At seventeen, Mark had enough on his mind just being a new driver and choosing the right college. Jeff was a year past Bar Mitzvah and certain religious issues were bothering him. He was even considering bringing some of his questions to the next Teen Dessert gathering at the rabbi's house.

Rabbi London made it a point to keep in touch with both Mark and Jeff, at least by e-mail, so that when they had questions on Jewish issues, they could feel comfortable asking.

Avi knew that a college campus was sure to pose even more challenges than their public school environment did, and that was no cakewalk. There was the problem these teens faced every year, for example, when they tried to take off time for all the Jewish holidays. In a year when Rosh Hashanah started on Sunday night, for example, observing them all meant a Monday and Tuesday absence for that holiday, Wednesday the following week for Yom Kippur, Monday and Tuesday the next week for Sukkot and Monday and Tuesday again the following week for Shmini Atzeret/Simchat Torah. In Israel, or here in the yeshiva or Orthodox world, celebrating all those days was expected, but in the atmospheres of American public schools and businesses, a seemingly endless stream of absences was hard to explain. Often the pressure placed on dedicated Jews made forgetting the holidays easier than observing them.

Questions and comments came from teachers, students, bosses and co-workers. "What, another holiday?" or, "Are you sure you're not making this up?" "How come your other Jewish friends aren't taking off but you have to?" "Didn't you just have a holiday?" "What's this one about?" "Can't you get special dispensation for this one?" "I wish I were Jewish and could take off all those days." "Sure you can take off, but you'll be responsible for all the work anyway." and "You'll have to make it up, but at our convenience, not yours."

Public school students, in particular, were put on the spot and sometimes they were asked to bring a note from their rabbi verifying the reason for the absence. Avi was willing to provide one any time, but two years ago, he tried doing what he heard colleagues in other communities had tried, often successfully, to take care of the situation in advance. He attended an East Belleridge school board meeting to request that public school students who wanted to take the time off for the holidays not be penalized. Some anti-Jewish feeling at that meeting prompted a phone call to the Shul Board, and Dennis, who was president by then, asked the rabbi to "butt out." So much for being pro-active.

Avi knew, too, that along with an eruption of anti-Semitism worldwide that's been the largest since World War II, Jew-baiting was growing on college campuses, sometimes in the guise of anti-Israel sentiment. Questions thrown at Jewish students – such as "Why does Israel have a right to exist as a Jewish state?" "Are the Jewish laws of male circumcision and kosher slaughter barbaric and outdated?" Why do Jews call themselves the Chosen People?" or Did the Jews really kill Jesus?" – were difficult even when tackled by educated adults. Avi's Wednesday morning yeshiva class grappled with many of those issues, but public school kids had less information and guidance and found these topics more awkward. Mark and other teens needed facts in advance.

But right now, Rabbi London had to help the Eisen boys wrestle with the more immediate question of why bad things happen to good people. There's really no answer, but doing something concrete might bring them comfort, so Avi suggested they give tzedakah.

"The English word 'charity' doesn't do justice to the Jewish concept," he explained to them. "Tzedakah is a gift for someone who really needs it, but giving it is considered a righteous act. The donation, usually in the form of money and often given anonymously to an unspecified recipient, is made without any expectation of a reward. But it is often given at a time of stress or celebration, and donors hope that God will notice and act favorably on outcomes that are out of human control."

Avi also promised Mark and Jeff that he would help them "make a Mi Sheberach" at Shul services Shabbat morning. He reminded the boys to be there early because the prayer, which asks publicly for the sick person's complete recovery, is said during the public Torah reading.

Having done what he could, the rabbi left the Eisens, knowing they would spend some time counting their blessings instead of focusing on life's frights.

That evening, Rabbi London reported on Stu's condition to the men who came to the evening minyan. Isaac Iskilovetzky, who led the service because he was a new mourner, made sure to recite a psalm in hope of Stu's speedy recovery.

The group finished their rituals and got ready to go home, but Phil lingered and approached Avi with a question.

"Do we say Kaddish so that the dead will be angels in heaven?"

Rabbi London was taken aback. He thought he had explained to Phil and his brother what the Kaddish was all about, and that they were intelligent and would remember. But the rabbi repeated, as if he were saying it for the first time, that Kaddish had nothing to do with the dead and everything to do with a public affirmation of faith at the low point of a mourner's life. "Why do you ask?"

"Oh, just something somebody said," said Phil. "I guess he didn't really know what he was talking about."

The conversation lingered in Avi's thoughts. It seemed as if no matter how many times he explained Jewish mourning practices, misconceptions remained. Sometimes he wondered if he was talking to himself.

This professional frustration, combined with the depressing events of the last two weeks, convinced him he needed a break. And just as some people jogged or got a massage when they needed to feel recharged, the rabbi studied.

He considered his local Talmud class, which he had missed for several weeks because of scheduling conflicts. The Friday morning session tapped Emek Emet's members who appreciated a teacher from their own ranks, many of whom worked in other fields but also had rabbinical degrees and were qualified to teach holy texts. This week's class would deal with the Talmud's rules of ownership and liability, and Avi decided to go.

"If an ox belongs to someone else and you are taking care of it when it gores another animal, who is responsible?" asked this week's teacher in the singsong voice typical of Talmud study. With that, he launched an analysis of one aspect of the legal page before them.

The text presented a famous discussion and was not as irrelevant as it seemed. Although housing an ox was not a typical concern in the 21st-Century suburbs of northern New Jersey, the logic of responsibility was eternal. The discussion covered several possible scenarios. Whether an individual is being paid to watch the animal or is doing it as a favor makes a big difference as to who should pay damages. Where it happened, whether on public property or within private boundaries, also matters. Whether the animal is untamed or domesticated is important. The extent of liability depends on whether or not the incident could have been avoided. The calculation of damages should factor in the relative values of both the guilty animal and the victim.

Talmudic discussions like these guided Jewish ethics and behavior and set a standard on which American law is based. For Avi, though, the sheer mental exercise of following the logic was revitalizing. Discussions like these helped him see situations from different perspectives, and he needed to hone that skill.

On Shabbat morning, a re-energized Rabbi London made sure the chazzan recited a Mi Sheberach for Stu Eisen's recovery during the Torah reading. For that part of the service, the scroll was on the large, blue-velvet-covered table. The reader faced the congregation and lifted his silver pointer when he was finished reciting each segment, rolled the posts toward each other and covered the Torah with another blue velvet cloth.

When the recitation and appropriate blessings were finished, Mark and Jeff got the honor of putting the holy manuscript away, following the traditional sequence.

Mark lifted the Torah by the ends of the two wood posts, between which the scroll stretched, and held it high so the congregation could see the hand-written text on the parchment and sing "V'zot haTorah …," "This is the Torah that God told Moses to put before us …." When Mark sat down, he held the Torah vertically while his younger brother rolled the posts toward each other so the slack parchment was drawn taut. Then Jeff tied a ribbon of cloth around the middle to secure the package, slipped a gold-colored velvet cover over the top end of the posts so it hung down to cover the scroll, added the chain attached to the pointer used by the reader and topped it all with a silver crown, which was decorative. Then Mark returned the regally outfitted Torah to the Holy Ark to join five similarly clad holy scrolls, and the Eternal Light above marked the center point as Jeff closed the curtains.

Rabbi London, now at the podium, began his sermon with a review of Vayishlach, which had just been read from the Torah. Avi knew that his talk must include ideas that would boost his congregation's spirits the way his Talmud class had invigorated him.

"Jacob must have been afraid the end might be near when he found himself in hand-to-hand combat with a stranger in the middle of the night. Only when Jacob realized that he had been wrestling with an angel, and that he had won, did he understand that God had sent this opponent and this struggle. As a victor, Jacob demanded a blessing, so God blessed him and changed his name to Israel. By emerging victorious, the man's very identity had changed," the preacher said, "and from then on, Jacob's descendents were known as the People of Israel." He paused.

"Life's challenges can be like that. They can seem life threatening but, when we face them head on, we realize we are stronger than we thought we were. We grow and become better people," the preacher continued.

"That's also why the liturgy talks about problems but focuses on the help we get from the Almighty to deal with them. Even the mourner's Kaddish talks about how great God is and how we have an obligation to recognize the many ways in which we need Divine succor."

Avi concluded with "May the One Who ordains harmony in the universe bless us and all Israel with peace," again drawing on the frequently used phrase that ends several prayers, including Kaddish.

At the kiddush after services, the rabbi's talk received rave reviews, even though most people did not know what succor was. Mark and Jeff liked the part about becoming better people by facing problems. Ida said she was grateful for the many ways God has helped her deal with the loss of her husband (of blessed memory). Isaac hoped that wrestling with the angel and winning meant his wife Rebecca (may she rest in peace) was now in a better place. For Celia, the fear Jacob experienced in the middle of the night seemed very real. The fact that life's challenges can be so scary really spoke to the recently widowed Harold Harrison.

Morty Fenn also said the sermon was great, but that's all he said, and the rabbi wondered what part interested him and why.

Dennis didn't wonder. He knew. What appealed to Morty was that people saw him talking to the rabbi after services. Being visible, more than anything else, would ease his election to the position he sought as the next president of Congregation Tefillah. How contemptible, Dennis said to himself.

He took a long look at his challenger. The two were about the same age, but Morty was tall, trim and graying, whereas Dennis was short, fat and bald. Morty was a professional, Dennis a businessman. Morty had lively children, Dennis had Brendan and Pamela. Morty had a devoted wife, and Dennis had Reeva. One thing he had that Morty didn't was seniority in Shul politics, Dennis said to himself, and that was what really mattered.

While Dennis was watching, the Fenns went to the coat-room to get ready to leave. Their daughter was eleven and got there first, but then her brothers came into Dennis's view. Three of them were teenagers, but there was one more. The oldest of Morty's kids joined the group with his wife and baby. Dennis's eyes opened wide. Pay dirt, he said to himself, and he made new calculations during his drive home.

When the Londons got home for lunch, they talked about the favorable reaction of the congregation to the day's sermon, and even the kids said it was pretty good, although they didn't know what succor was either.

"You've got to stop doing that," Emma said to her husband while the family set the table. "Nobody knows that succor means help! If you want people to understand what you're saying, use words they know!" Avi argued that they should know a word like that, but admitted that she was probably right about using less obscure vocabulary in future homilies.

Ahuva and Josh changed out of their Shul clothes and arranged the Kiddush cups. Emma checked lunch, a slow-cooking cholent stew kept warm on a hot plate they used for Shabbat, and Avi relaxed and read the paper in his recliner chair until it was time to eat.

Lunch started, as usual, with blessings over wine, ritual hand washing and cutting the challah. Over hot cholent and cold salad, the family reviewed the past week, good and bad. They talked about test grades and teachers, friends and put downs, eating problems and drug abuse, fads and fantasies, births and deaths. They discussed the changing weather and their plans for Chanukah. Finally, they sang a few songs and the long Blessing After Meals, and bedded down for a short afternoon's quick nap.

The sun set early in the winter, and by six Avi was back from the evening minyan. He made Havdallah for the family over wine, with Ahuva holding the candle and Josh in charge of passing around the aromatic spices. The whole ceremony took just a minute, but for this busy family, it marked a big difference between Shabbat's peace and the pace of the rest of the week, between holy ideas and everyday duties. It was a magical moment that could only be appreciated by other Jews doing the same thing in homes and synagogues around the world. Within half a minute of the candle's flame being extinguished, the kids were on their phones with friends.

Saturday afternoons were not like that for most of the members of this Conservative congregation. After services, the consensus was that the religious part of Shabbat was over. Most members went shopping, watched sports or were off to the theater. When Dennis got home from morning services, he found Reeva resting and the kids out. He spent the afternoon at his desk, working on the minyanlist.doc file.

Phil has two sons and so does his brother Matt, the calculation began. Dennis saw Phil all the time, so there would be lots of opportunity, but a net gain of only one, and there is no evidence that even one would come.

Stu Eisen has two sons who like Jewish stuff, so they would probably come frequently. He was in the hospital facing life-threatening surgery, and a visit from Dennis would be expected. The score would be plus two. It would be the same if Mona Eisen were on the list because Stu is a zero.

Morty Fenn is healthy, which might make explaining it complicated. He has an adult son and three teenage boys, which might be a gain of three. He's an ambitious son of a bitch. A lawyer too, which means he has lots of enemies. He has been attending the evening minyan recently, but that's just for political reasons, I'm sure, thought Dennis. He wants my job.

Dennis returned to Shul for the late afternoon service. He had made a decision.

Chapter 11

Making Choices

It was decision time. Friday's Talmud class was one of several options Avi had considered that would give him the break he needed, and it was a good choice. Exercising his brain refreshed his thinking and raised his energy level.

Phil Schwartz, the probing intellectual skeptic, decided that going to Shul after work every day was giving his life a structure and rationale he had never experienced before. He began to appreciate prayer's perspective on existence and he was enchanted to find a spiritual leader who made sense. He elected to keep attending the minyan and would try to get there on Sunday mornings, too, especially after seeing that he was at least as astute as the president of the Shul.

Former president of the Shul Stu Eisen pondered his situation and decided to have the heart surgery he feared and to do it soon. He became convinced that facing the experience would make him a better husband, father and businessman. His family took strength from his courage and chose to be optimistic about this health crisis. The positive attitude of the patient and the encouragement of his family, the doctor predicted, could be a major factor toward a favorable outcome.

In order for the Shul to have good prospects, Morty Fenn thought, it needed his well-rooted expertise as an attorney. There were tough issues ahead, he reasoned. This congregation had to pick whether (a) to follow the popular movement toward gender equality in religious roles or (b) to align with traditional positions against female participation in public ceremonies. The choice would determine an official synagogue position for the future – regarding, for example, homosexual marriages – and that was no job for a rabbi. Only a lawyer could foresee the repercussions of such a decision. Rabbi London would require strong guidance, so Morty would do what was necessary to become Shul president.

Laura found the Shul and her parents to her liking and decided to give her new life a chance. That meant the Fernbergs could go ahead with their plans, so they told the rabbi to make arrangements for the conversions as well as for the Bar Mitzvah.

But before Avi could attend to the Fernbergs' details, he had to make some selections for his own family. Chanukah began in a week. Emma had already gotten the music and movies the kids wanted, but he still had to pick up some software for them. He also wanted a good book for his wife. The stores were already getting crowded with shoppers, so he'd better hurry.

As soon as the family was out the door Monday morning, Avi put on a warm jacket and drove to the mall. He finished his coffee in the car and parked in the vast lot's Section M between the large Christmas tree and the Santa Is Here sign. "Silent Night" was playing on loudspeakers as he entered the mall, but it took him until "Jingle Bells" to find the right store. At the beginning of "Hark the Herald Angels Sing," he found the part of the store where computer accessories were on display. He was still studying the array when he heard the "pa rum pum pum pum" of "Little Drummer Boy" and could no longer concentrate on what he was doing.

Carols like this are beautiful, often stirring, Avi admitted to himself. I just wish that the lyrics of the ones played in public places didn't have such strong religious sentiment. "Jingle Bells" is okay and "I Saw Mommy Kissing Santa Claus" is easy enough to tolerate. They're seasonal and cute, even if they are for a holiday that is not ours.

But phrases in the other songs, like "round yon virgin mother and child," "glory to the newborn king," and "I have no gift to bring that's fit to give our king" are unmistakably Christian. They venerate the basic premise of that religion – that Jesus's arrival offers his followers otherwise unattainable divine redemption and entry into heaven – and that very principle is incompatible with Muslim, Buddhist, Hindu, Shinto and Bahai as well as Jewish beliefs.

And although I am a Jew, the rabbi noted, I have learned all the words to all these carols just by going shopping!

Perhaps it's best not to think about what the words mean, Avi decided, sure that most people didn't.

The music changed to "Over the River and Through the Woods," and that was a song Avi's brain could sing along with, so he happily turned back to the hi-tech task at hand. He picked up a Hebrew word processing program for Ahuva that she could use for yeshiva assignments. He also chose a map-and-travel software package for the soon-to-be licensed driver and college student so Josh could find his way home from wherever his future took him. Rabbi London charged his selections and the Hispanic cashier wished him a Merry Christmas as "Feliz Navidad" played in the background. What was he supposed to reply? he speculated, and chose to stay silent.

Next, he waited for his turn at the ATM, wondering if Laura had been to the mall since she got to East Belleridge. Sure, there were ATMs in Israel, but the culture shock – from a Jewish state, where Christmas is hardly mentioned, to a Christian society, where it dominates the commercial year – must be enormous.

Avi took his restored cache of cash to a book store to get the newest publication on Israel for Emma during "I'll Be Home for Christmas." He was leaving the mall to the tune of "The First Noel" when he wondered about Bethlehem. How were the Christian Arabs there doing in an environment that is largely Muslim? he wondered. And, are my Israeli cousins on duty at roadblocks to keep the peace for Christian pilgrims on their way from Jerusalem to that little town?

He glanced down and saw an electric Chanukah menorah, fully lit even though the Jerusalem-centered holiday wouldn't begin for another week. Bethlehem and Jerusalem, geographically only a few miles from each other, represented philosophies that were worlds apart. Yet both were symbolized in the "seasonal" decorations that the mall set up every year to bring joy to the hearts of all American shoppers at this merry peak of the selling year.

Avi walked back to his car, admitting that American society does its best to be inclusive. If a minor holiday like Chanukah fell at any other time of year, he reflected, it would go unnoticed.

He considered the plight of Jewish kids in public schools, who had to sit through "holiday" assemblies that throw one old, bland Chanukah song in with majestic Christmas choir arrangements. Some of the adults in his congregation complained that, in their offices, a lit menorah was always part of the decorated Tannenbaum display.

On the air, TV stations mention the Jewish holiday but absolutely rave about the fabulous plots, acting, and emotionality of Christmas programming. Withstanding the all-encompassing deluge and enormous beauty of the larger society's celebration is a tough act, the rabbi concluded.

Avi unlocked the car door and got in the seat, closed the door and thought about his flock. In different ways, nearly all his congregants saw the pervasiveness of Christianity as a threat, but they had different views on the best way to act Jewish. One thing they were unanimous on, however, was their right to pick and choose the rules. Morty and Harold valued being Jewish but thought all religious behavior was divisive. Dennis and Mel saw Judaism as the best route to the divine, but expected religious obligations to bend to suit their needs. To Ida Stein, Jewishness was only lifestyle, and to the minyan regulars, it was just habit.

The rabbi glanced at the Season's Greetings sign on the walkway outside the mall and wondered why the symbol used for Chanukah was usually the menorah. Lighting a chanukiyah represents the "miracle of the oil" – that the fuel burning in the ransacked Temple's menorah was only expected to last one day and lasted eight – but that's small stuff, Avi noted. Maybe a better symbol would be a dreidel, whose letters stand for the real marvel, that the Maccabees, who were a small family, led a fight for religious freedom and won. It didn't matter that the victory was temporary. The later decline of the Maccabees' descendants is never even mentioned. The earlier decision to rebel took courage, like the courage of the American pilgrims to settle a new land that is honored at Thanksgiving, and we proudly proclaim that.

Honking snapped Avi back from his musings. Drivers needed parking spaces near the mall, and he was keeping one tied up. He started the motor, buckled up, backed out of the space, shifted into Drive and drove toward the exit. He did not notice that Dennis was behind the wheel of the honking car that pulled into the vacated spot.

Dennis didn't notice his rabbi, either. He was preoccupied with his mission. Next week he would phone in a purchase of Christmas fruit baskets for business associates and candy packages for Cleaner Shine employees. He had already ordered several Chanukah gifts for each member of the family through the Internet. But he wanted to pick up a specific quilt for his son that was on sale at the mall. He figured Brendan could use it this winter and then take it with him to college. He thought it might be useful in other ways, too.

As Dennis shopped, he absent-mindedly sang along with the beautiful music, which he thought of as generically seasonal, and was proud to see that Chanukah was part of the scene. It was good for Jews to be part of American life, he thought. Of course, he was sure that the rabbi saw it differently. Rabbi London always did.

As Avi drove over soggy fallen leaves in the sprawling parking lot and onto the adjoining highway, he returned to his daydreaming and recalled his visit to Jerusalem's Western Wall with Laura. If the Maccabees had not rededicated the Temple for Jewish use, he decided, Christians would not have the story of Jesus visiting there nearly two centuries later. By some logic, Christians could venerate Chanukah, but not the other way around. Christmas marks the divergence from Judaism that gave birth to Christianity, and it is that departure that makes its followers distinct from Jews.

Avi hung a right onto East Belleridge's main street and stopped at home, where he covered the loot in gift wrap and hid it in the basement. Then he hurried over to the Hebrew School, where kids would learn how to light the chanukiyah, play a game of dreidel and sing holiday songs in English, Hebrew and Yiddish. They had been studying the story of the Maccabean revolt and today would discuss living in a Christian society where they were free to be proud of being Jewish.

While the children were in class, Avi noticed that Joe Kripski was sweeping the floor in the all-purpose room and considered the Shul custodian's position. It must be difficult for a Catholic to go to work every day in a non-Christmas environment when the rest of his world was at full throttle in their holiday preparations, the rabbi thought.

Avi turned back to his educational duties. He believed it was healthy for people to maintain their own identities, and Avi saw the Hebrew School as an important way to teach the congregation's youngsters why they should value feeling Jewish and celebrate Chanukah, even when it seemed difficult.

In yeshiva, Ahuva and Josh were learning about Chanukah, too, but they had learned the basic stuff in the early grades. As more mature students, they studied the Talmudic disagreements of how many and in which direction the candles should be lit. They also compared Jewish suffering under the Syrian-Greek occupation of the Holy Land to religious oppression in western Europe during the Spanish Inquisition and deadly discrimination under Nazi domination. But there was not enough time to go into these subjects in the afternoon setting of a Hebrew School.

Avi would have to keep the differences in education in mind when, during Hebrew School the next day, the rabbi would meet in his office with the family of Aaron Klein, this week's Bar Mitzvah.

Avi was surprised when the boy arrived for the appointment early to speak on a private matter. Rabbi London wondered what could be on Aaron's mind that hadn't come up before. He already knew the convoluted family history. The boy's mother died and his father remarried but then divorced his new wife and disappeared. Aaron's stepmother got custody, so when she remarried, the new couple officially adopted him and then had two more children. In the end, Aaron had a family and, although he knew what the facts were, he remembered no other version of reality than the one he lived with.

"Can you speak to the caterer for me please?" Aaron asked the rabbi. He was eerily composed, as if he had thought deeply about the decision to ask the rabbi for help. "I want to send my birth father a package of food from the Bar Mitzvah party."

"Your biological father? You know where he is?" Avi was stunned.

"I always knew he was in prison but I just found out where," mumbled the young teen, wringing his hands. He looked up at his rabbi. "You probably don't know this, because when I was little I didn't want my parents to tell anybody. He killed my birth mother so he could marry my Mom, but it wasn't her idea and she tried to stop him. He was sentenced to life, and my Mom divorced him and married my Dad."

Almost pleading, Aaron continued. "I don't really know my birth father and I don't want to, Rabbi, but I just think he should know that I'm growing up right. I have the address of the prison, so can you arrange it for me?"

Oy.

Avi assured the boy that he would take care of this detail and that Aaron didn't have to have it on his mind at this important point in his life. Furthermore, the rabbi would not tell anyone, so it would only become common knowledge if Aaron wanted it that way.

This boy is terrific, Avi reflected after the Klein family Bar Mitzvah meeting. Even with the support of his relatives, Aaron's burden is tough enough to crush anyone's spirit, yet he's managing it beautifully. Life deals some folks a really tough hand, and it's amazing to see the inner strength certain people suddenly seem to have.

Like a Maccabee, the rabbi thought, Aaron recognized a righteous idea and bravely acted on it.

Avi had seen similar bravery with Stu Eisen, who confronted his fears with a store of courage that his children could draw on when they needed it. With or without him, his decision had laid a foundation Mark and Jeff could build on for a long time to come. With Stu's decision to go ahead with the surgery, his sons sent donations to their favorite charities and opted to go to that night's minyan at the Shul.

The Eisen boys showed up just after Mr. Day, Greg and Isaac arrived, but even with the two unexpected young men, getting ten was a cliffhanger. The rabbi, cantor and Dennis gasped when Phil told them his brother had other plans. The group was at nine for a long time before they called Morty, and were only able to begin once he arrived. This did not bode well for the coming Chanukah holiday, when families wanted to be home at supper time to light the candles together, or for the soon-to-follow Christmas week, when many Americans took vacation trips, or for the cold, snowy winter that was yet to come.

This holiday season would really aggravate Dennis's problem, and he knew it. When he got home, he walked past his wife and daughter, who were in the kitchen helping the housekeeper make supper, and headed to his home office, shut the door and began evaluating his options.

Dennis knew who, but he still had to decide where to start. The timing would have to be right to stagger the results over the long term and solve winter shortages. Location would need research, since he didn't know much about where people went after Saturday services, but one place on his list could certainly be the Shul.

He had a few ideas on how to go about it. A suggestive conversation was easy, he noted. It worked well with a receptive ear in the past and required no explanation at all. Then there was the Chanukah gift he had just bought. Its wrapper could work.

And, if things didn't go right and he got into any legal trouble, the right attorney could fix things. Lawyers will do anything for money, Dennis sneered. And now that Suzette and Jon Siegel were members of the Shul, they would surely help its president. To be certain, he'd better solidify his relationship with them. He might need them.

Dennis turned to the minyanlist.doc file. He printed it out and wrote some notes in its margins, but found he was having trouble netting the information out. He turned back to the computer to refine it the way a businessman would. He put the data in a chart and used abbreviations where the columns were too narrow. On the first row, he put titles: Name, Method, Level of Difficulty, Potential Change and Real Net Change.

Dennis started with an example. He wrote in Jane Harrison, who was susceptible to his suggestion but whose suicide did not net the result he had expected. Method, drug overdose. Difficulty, 2. Potential, +1. Net 0. He put this entry first because it was a painful lesson in poor returns on investments.

After that he listed future choices. Stu Eisen, Method ? Difficulty ? Potential, +2 (because the father never came but the boys might). Net ? That last column would be calculated after each event.

On the next line, he put Mona Eisen, although he knew the entries for her and Stu were identical. Next were Phil and Matt Schwartz and their wives. The men's numbers were the same, with the potential column showing an entry of -1 +2 = +1 (because the father did come and would have to be factored out), Net ?. In the case of their wives, however, the net gain could be 3 (because the men stay in the calculation).

With Ray Fisch (whose son is now of Bar Mitzvah age), the net was uncertain, but, as with the Schwartz brothers, the wife's line showed two more than his. Dennis was amazed. The numbers proved it: When the husband remains, the numbers are much better.

Then he got to the last name on the list, Morty Fenn. Method, blanket bag. Difficulty, 6. Potential, -1 +4 = +3. Net ? Dennis did not know the wife's name and, although he knew the numbers would be better if he listed her, he didn't care. The numbers were good enough.

He decided he would fill in the blanks or ?s in the file later, and he was sure he was finished with this starter list.

Then he thought of one more. He remembered his sainted mother, rest her soul. She wanted her son to say Kaddish for her, so his own son should to the same for his mother. Brendan came to Shul once to pray for Reeva, Dennis said to himself, and stood by me at my own mother's funeral. Brendan does what he's told, and I'll make sure he does his duty.

So Dennis added a name to the handwritten list. He transcribed that name and the relevant information onto the chart in the computer before printing it out. Reeva. Method, gun suicide (with the Berreta that was still registered to her). Difficulty, 4. (He would have to find a time when she would be home alone.) Potential, +1. (Dennis prayed for his mother and Brendan would pray for his.)

The file now looked like this:

NAME	METHOD	LEVEL OF DIFFICULTY	POTENTIAL CHANGE	REAL NET CHANGE
JANE HARRISON	DG OVDS	2	+1	0
STU EISEN	?	?	+2	?
MONA EISEN	?	?	+2	?
PHIL SCHWARTZ	?	?	-1 +2 = +1	?
MARJORIE SCHWARTZ	?	?	+1 +2 = +3	?
MATT SCHWARTZ	?	?	-1 +2 = +1	?
TERRI SCHWARTZ	?	?	+1 +2 = +3	?
RAY FISCH	?	?	-1 +1 = 0	?
DAFNA FISCH	?	?	+1 +1 = +2	?
MORTY F.	BL BAG	6	-1 +4 = +3	?
REEVA	GN SCD	4	+1 +1 = +1	?

Dennis printed out the chart and put the original hand-written pages in his pocket. The next day, he tore up the original and put it in the trash at his office. But he carried the carefully folded printout with him for the next two days to see if there should be any changes.

It was difficult, as Dennis expected, to get ten for the Shacharit minyan, but Dave Smith and Sig Fleishhocker eventually showed up both mornings, so the group was able to start just a few minutes late. (Dennis would have to remember them later when he added other names to the list.) In the evening, it was just as hard to get a minyan, but Morty came again and the group could proceed. Dennis was glad Morty had sons or he would have to recalculate the list.

Shacharit on Wednesday was late starting because they had to wait for a tenth. When it was over, Avi came home as quickly as he could and rushed through breakfast in order to get to his yeshiva class on time. They would discuss growing anti-Jewish feelings around the world and their connection to tensions in the Middle East in the context of next week's Chanukah celebration.

After class, the teacher returned to his home study to make several calls. First, he arranged a time to meet with the Fernbergs Sunday morning to make plans for the conversions. In preparation for that meeting, he turned to the Orthodox assets in the community to ensure that leading Jewish authorities would recognize the halachic legality of all the procedures. He called Rabbi Melamed to discuss convening a Beit Din, the mohel for the details of a Tipat Dahm Bris and the woman in charge of scheduling mikveh use to reserve a time slot.

Next, the rabbi called the caterer for Aaron Klein's Bar Mitzvah and asked them to send a package to the prisoner. A note that the boy had composed with guidance from his spiritual leader would accompany the food. The message explained that one of the Ten Commandments was to honor parents, and Aaron decided his Bar Mitzvah meant he was old enough to be responsible for a mitzvah like that, despite the circumstances. The gesture would not, however, be the start of any future relationship and should not become public knowledge. The communication was just between the two of them and just this once.

Then, Avi was off to Shul. The principal got there a half-hour before Hebrew School began in order to check supplies for Chanukah. It would not do for the Shul to run out of candles, and there was still time to get to the Judaica store for more. He also wanted to make sure the teachers were ready with small gifts for all the children.

The preacher spent much of the next day poring over the week's Torah portion, trying to tailor a sermon to Aaron's occasion, but he was having trouble. It was the story of Joseph, how he goes from being Jacob's favorite son and the recipient of a coat of many colors to being a reviled sibling and then a slave. He even becomes a prisoner in the Egyptian Pharaoh's jail, but then is released and becomes the second most-powerful man in Egypt.

Aside from the mention of prison in both Joseph's and Aaron Klein's lives – and Avi couldn't refer to that publicly anyway – the stories didn't fit. The boy's father was no hero; he was a murderer. He killed Aaron's mother and would spend the rest of his life in jail. Unlike what happened in the biblical narrative, there would be neither a release, as there had been for a wrongly accused Joseph, nor a joyous reunion between father and son, as there had been with Jacob. Yet, Avi wanted to say something appropriate from the Torah that would be meaningful at this occasion. How could the rabbi give this Bar Mitzvah a lesson he could use for the rest of his life?

Avi put that project aside for a while because he had to get to the Judaica store that afternoon for his Hebrew School order. He needed eight more boxes of Chanukah candles, sixty large plastic dreidels filled with chocolate coins, four copies of last year's Chanukah board game and the new movie spoof of a private investigator who saves the large Knesset Menorah, Israel's national symbol. Avi added six copies of the latest review of Israeli cultural offerings as a gift for the teachers and hoped they would find in them some innovative ideas for their classes.

Rabbi London, with the Bar Mitzvah sermon still on his mind, returned to Shul for minyan that night, but the group had to wait a long time for the tenth. At last, Phil walked in. Isaac Iskilovetzky launched into the opening line, "Vhu rachum yichaper avon vlo yashchis," and the process was under way.

"And God will be merciful and forgive sin and not destroy." Avi thought about Aaron Klein's father and that the son's kindness was a taste of God's mercy. But the rabbi also wondered how many times that sentence is said without anyone realizing what it's about.

As usual, the liturgy's relevance captured Avi's thoughts. On the practical level, he considered that the evening service portrayed the earth's seasons and hours as being determined by the movements of celestial bodies. It was remarkable that Jewish tradition understood the influence of the heavens long before planets could be seen by the human eye. Philosophically, he further contemplated, placing the description of the universe before the Shma statement of faith underscores our conviction that creation and all the evolution it involved was God's doing. The whole package puts us humans in our place by requiring us to acknowledge our small presence in the vast universe before we dare to address its Creator.

Rabbi London enjoyed discussing these ideas with people who were curious about them. Most of the questions were easily answered, but when Avi had to do some research to give his response depth, he liked it even more because he learned something. He was especially keen on the questions Phil posed because they showed he was thinking about religious concepts. Why, Phil wanted to know when he started his year of mourning, are the prayers said as if we were in a group when the same words are used when we're alone? Because we approach God as a part of the Jewish People, Avi answered. Why, Phil asked more recently, is a man's status as a Kohen, Levi or Yisrael derived from the father but his identity as a

Jew from the mother? The rabbi said he had to do research on that one and still had to get back to him with a response.

Avi had to admit, though, that very few daveners thought about the meaning of the verses and instead relied on rote repetition for divine inspiration. Dennis was one of those. That's okay, too, agreed the rabbi. Whatever achieves a closeness to God is a worthwhile effort.

He saw Dennis leave with Phil and hoped that coming to the minyan was building a friendship between them. They were still talking near Phil's car when the rabbi walked out of the back door of the building, but the discussion did not seem friendly, and Avi began to wonder what was going on. He heard Phil say the word "wrong," but then he heard Dennis say it, too. Avi didn't want to intrude on their conversation, so he walked on.

Rabbi London had already rounded the corner on his way home when he realized he had left a book in his Shul office that he wanted to consult for the sermon at Aaron's Bar Mitzvah, so he turned back to the building. He saw Dennis still standing next to Phil's car, but their conversation had escalated into an argument.

"Anything I can do for you?" asked the rabbi loudly, hoping the interruption would give them both a chance to cool off.

Phil gave Dennis a venomous look, but seemed to change his mind about saying what he was thinking. He glanced at the rabbi, then turned on his heels and got into his green Ford. He considered the semi-automatic that he knew was in its case under the seat next to him, kept handy for his commute to work, but decided to suspend his violent thoughts and sped away.

Avi stared at Dennis, as if to ask what that was all about, but the man seemed to be purposely maintaining a vacant demeanor. Dennis finally locked eyes with the rabbi, said good night, climbed into his white Lexus and left.

As he turned back to the Shul, Rabbi London looked at the Shul keys in his hand and wondered if what the two men had argued about was the end of their disagreement or just the beginning.

Chapter 12

A Woman's Role

Whatever the argument the night before was about, the encounter did not seem to affect the men's morning minyan habits. Dennis was there, as usual, and Phil wasn't, as always.

Luckily, numbers were not a problem that Friday. The Eisen boys came because they wanted to express gratitude to the Almighty and to share an optimistic report with the men at the minyan. Stu's surgery the day before had gone well and the family was optimistic that the Shul's past president would be back on his feet in no time. Dave Smith and Sig Fleishhocker were glad to be there to hear the happy tidings.

Ray Fisch and Mel Rubin were also present for the good news, although for Mel it was coincidental. He didn't like being at the minyan and was only there that morning because Ray insisted. Ray had told members of the Employment Review committee that seeing the minyan at work would help them understand the Shul's needs, and he started the process of orientation with Mel.

Dennis didn't really care why they came, but he knew all of them arriving on time meant the forty-minute service would be over sooner. He had been saying Kaddish for only a month and the regimen of coming to the minyan morning and evening, every day, was already wearing him out. On the other hand, he was glad to see new faces because it helped him consider additional options for his list.

Avi noticed Dennis hanging back after minyan. The rabbi wanted to ask delicately what the argument with Phil the night before had been about, but he saw Dennis making a few notes on a chart of some kind and assumed it was business related. Maybe now is not the right time, the rabbi said to himself.

Avi went home and spent most of that morning on the phone. He got a call from Larry ("ledger") Lansken, who wanted to know why there were extra expenses for Chanukah at the Hebrew School when most of the celebrating was done at home. The principal explained it was an important outlay so that Chanukah might counterbalance the prevailing Christmas-gift orientation in the minds of the students.

Rabbi London also conferred with Phyllis ("bang for the buck") Kimmel to get details he could announce in Shul on Shabbat about the Sisterhood's Chanukah party Sunday night. He wanted to make sure she was getting her money's worth.

That afternoon, Avi was determined to spend time on a sermon for Shabbat. Aaron was a kid who really understood what being a Bar Mitzvah was all about, and the rabbi wanted to do the right thing for him.

As the preacher got his facts together, mouth-watering smells from the kitchen diverted his attention. He followed his nose and found Emma dropping ice-cold matzah ball mixture into the boiling soup. Chicken was roasting in the oven and rice revolved in the microwave. Water for tea and instant coffee was boiled and ready. He calculated that Shabbat preparations were ahead of schedule, so Avi asked if Emma would have time for him.

"Sure, if you don't need clean underwear until Sunday," she said. Emma did not have any extra time on the shortest Friday of the year.

Avi said he had enough to wear and asked her to spend a few minutes on his dilemma. He didn't want to tell her the details of the complication, but if she could review some of the points of the Torah portion with him, he might get an idea how to use them.

She washed the cooking utensils, he dried them, and they talked.

"Well, in Vayeshev," she began, "we learn that Jacob liked Joseph best of all his sons. The sibling rivalry intensified when Joseph told his brothers about his dreams and that they meant he would rule over them someday."

"All this probably made relations very tense, both between Jacob and all his sons and between Joseph and his brothers," Avi chimed in.

"It makes you wonder about a few things," continued Emma. "Why did Jacob show his favoritism? Did Joseph's brothers hate their father for it? Is that why they lied to him and said Joseph was dead, as much to punish the father as the brother they sold into slavery?"

"You've got to wonder, too," said Avi, "how Joseph conducted himself when he was on his own in Egypt, far from familiar surroundings and the parents who would keep him in line."

"As a slave he didn't have much choice," she said, "although he did defy the wife of Potiphar, the head of the house, and maybe that was because he was acting on values he had been taught when he was a child."

She turned off the water. "But my biggest problem with the story is this: Did anyone deserve the anguish and heartache that misguided love caused? Jacob lived with grief for years thinking his son was dead. Joseph suffered in slavery because his brothers hated him. The brothers endured guilt over getting rid of one of their own. For what? Just because Jacob couldn't keep his affection in perspective!"

Emma wiped her hands on the dish towel, calmed down and looked at her husband. "Do any of these thoughts help you?"

"Not directly," he answered, as he put away what he had dried. There was so much he couldn't say in his sermon about Aaron's personal history. "But thanks for trying."

The sun set earlier that Friday than on any other during the year, so by four o'clock in the afternoon the kids were home for the day, the telephone answering machine was cleared, lights that would be left on for the duration were set, the food was cooked, the oven was turned off, the candles were lit, the table was set for supper and whatever didn't get done would have to wait twenty-five hours. With no TV, radio or phone, the silence was deafening and the break from the everyday world complete. When Avi got back from Friday evening services, he gave the children his regular Shabbat blessing. The family talked, ate, sang, laughed, restored themselves and then slept soundly.

The next morning, Aaron Klein was called to the Torah for the first time in his life, but his thorough training helped him act like he had lots of experience. As a Bar Mitzvah, he read the entire portion directly from the Torah. He also would lead the rest of the service, with his younger sister and brother joining him at the end, but first he would give his speech, which he had worked on with Avi. Then the rabbi would talk.

Aaron focused on how Jacob's son conducted himself in Egypt. "Joseph was far from home, abandoned by his brothers, young and on his own in a far-away land. No one was watching and he could have given in to Potiphar's wife, but he knew it wouldn't be right. Because he rejected her, he landed in prison. But Joseph learned to interpret dreams there, and that brought him to the Pharaoh's attention," the young teen explained.

"But I think that the real reason God put Joseph there," Aaron said, "was because, as the Pharaoh's right-hand man, he could prepare Egypt for the seven years of famine that were coming. During that famine, Joseph's family came from the neighboring Promised Land to Egypt looking for food, so Joseph was able to save the forefathers of the Jewish people," Aaron said.

"I would like to think that I can play an important role in the survival or success of our people, even if I don't know now what that role will be," the Bar Mitzvah boy concluded.

"Nobody knows what the future holds," Rabbi London said to Aaron in front of the congregation. "We can only hope that something we do now will bring about a positive result at the right moment. Maybe Jacob said one thing in particular to Joseph when he was young that prepared him for future challenges, that made him do the right thing when it mattered. It is for that reason that the mitzvah of honoring your parents is one of the Ten Commandments. Honoring them may or may not seem right at the time, so we may or may not be inclined to do it, but something they do or say will probably be important in the long run." He glanced at Laura, sitting in the congregation, and remembered making a similar point to her in Israel. He was gratified to see that she seemed to remember, too.

"Occasionally, people make mistakes," the rabbi continued, "and sometimes we make them when we're kids and sometimes we make them when we're adults. If we're lucky, the mistakes are small ones. Jacob made some pretty big mistakes. He cheated his own brother out of the firstborn's inheritance. He favored one of his children over the others. But Jacob must have said or done at least one thing right with Joseph because later, when it was vital, his son provided the leadership everyone needed." Rabbi London looked straight at the boy and felt sure Aaron got the private message.

"No one knows what will be, Aaron, but you have a keen understanding of what our tradition is all about. Moreover, your loving parents have given you excellent guidance all along. We are sure that your future will be filled with shining moments, just as Joseph's was. It is a privilege to know you now and it will be a joy to watch you grow into your destined role among our People," concluded the rabbi. "Mazal tov!"

Over chopped liver and crackers at the kiddush after services, the Kleins accepted congratulations from relatives and fellow congregants and beamed about their son. As they sipped their soda, they told the rabbi how much they appreciated the way private matters were kept out of public conversation. Aaron licked icing off a piece of cake and then quietly gave Avi personal thanks for the extra help with the caterer. The boy trusted his rabbi to keep their secret.

Emma didn't know why her husband had found the subject so difficult that she had to give up valuable laundry time to be a sounding board, but told him she was glad he was able to speak directly to the boy's needs. Josh and Ahuva, as enthusiastic as ever about Shul events and their father's prominence in them, shrugged and said, "It was okay."

Mark and Jeff Eisen found the sermon hopeful, but the same message evoked grief from others. Celia Dubinsky could only think of the future lost with the death of her grandson. Holocaust survivor Helen Levine broke down thinking of her parents and brothers who were denied a future because they were slaughtered by the Nazis. Harold Harrison and his three kids, still reeling from the choice Jane had made, wondered which of her words they could look to for guidance in the future.

Dennis had his own thoughts: The Bar Mitzvah boy might understand what our tradition is all about, but the rabbi sure doesn't. Talk about a destined role among our people! The rabbi saw me at the minyan all the time but didn't understand my destined role! Why couldn't he understand that I was guaranteeing heaven for my blessed mother by saying Kaddish all the time? That's honoring your parents, too. How can I do my mitzvah when I'm was faced with a rabbi who just doesn't get it? And, how can I say Kaddish when men won't even show up for the minyan? They don't get it either!

That night, after the Maariv Havdallah service, Dennis heard the rabbi remind everyone to light Chanukah candles Sunday night.

"This holiday marks the courage of a small band of men who decided to take action at a treacherous time," Rabbi London explained. "The Maccabees expected their effort to necessitate some suffering or sacrifice, but they knew standing up for their beliefs was important for the future. We are the future they fought for, so let's mark their victory appropriately by lighting the first candle of the chanukiyah tomorrow night. After we light at home, let's come back at nine to celebrate at the Sisterhood party in the downstairs hall."

The daveners who were not in mourning went home to get ready for a fun, pre-Chanukah Saturday-night party at the local Jewish Community Center. The mourners, who knew they weren't supposed to party during their period of saying Kaddish, just went home.

Dennis tossed and turned that night. The rabbi's words about Chanukah were tumbling around in the mourner's head. Courage. Important for the future. Take action.

He got out of bed early, careful not to disturb his wife. He turned his back to the expansive view, sat down at the kitchen table and had his coffee. Courage. Important for the future. Take action.

He walked quietly into the master bedroom, making sure not to wake his wife, and found the comforter he and Reeva planned to give Brendan for Chanukah. Dennis took it into the guest room, took the blanket out of the heavy-weight plastic bag that covered it and tossed it onto the bed. His attention remained with the bag, which he examined for holes and weak spots near the drawstring. Satisfied that it was strong and intact, he took the bag into the rec room and flattened it carefully on the sofa to make sure all the air came out. He folded the plastic compactly and put it in the right pocket of his sport jacket. Then he went into his home office, found the folded printout of the list he had been carrying around and put it into his left pocket.

Dennis reviewed the morning's schedule in the kitchen over a second cup of coffee and a buttered bagel. He would arrive at Shul by eight and the minyan would end by nine, when all the daveners would go home for breakfast. Hebrew School wouldn't start 'til ten. Now, it was seven fifteen. He decided not to wear an overcoat. He walked out the front door and took the elevator to the street level.

As he put his key into the ignition of his car, Reeva looked out the bedroom window. She had awakened when Dennis toasted his frozen bagel and, hearing a car start, she knew he was leaving for the Shul. If she had still cared, she would have told him to take a coat. Yes, the medicine was definitely helping her think more clearly. Reeva decided to dress before checking her e-mail. She looked at the clock and wondered when the kids would be up.

The rest of the neighborhood seemed to still be asleep, too. Very little traffic jockeyed for the roads' fast lanes early on a Sunday morning. Dennis drove east down the mountains past the deer reserves and then north on the parkways, so the eighteen-mile trip from Northwood to East Belleridge was quick. He arrived at the Shul ten minutes before the other daveners.

Dennis parked his car under the trees near the back entrance, in the spaces marked Reserved for the Shul's president and rabbi. He got out, leaned on the car and waited. Joe Kripski came on foot five minutes before eight, on time as usual, to open up the building.

Soon the others arrived and parked in their usual places, but Morty Fenn, who saw himself as heir-apparent to the presidential throne, pulled his black Porsche up right next to Dennis's white Lexus as if to practice parking in the regal position. He was bubbly and full of smiles and told Dennis he wanted to sound him out on something.

"Have you ever thought that the Shul has lagged behind the times on the subjects of gender equality in religious life?" asked Morty.

Dennis's jaw dropped. No, he said to himself. The movement to equalize the sexes undermines our holiest customs! It's bad enough to have a rabbi that doesn't understand tradition. This man wants to be president! To have a Shul leader pushing the wrong way would be terrible for the future!

Chanukah. Suffering. Sacrifice. Courage. Important for the future. Yes, the future. The Maccabees took action.

He toughened his resolve. Dennis's jaw clenched shut. It was all starting to come together, he realized.

Getting no audible response from the president, just a look that could kill, Morty thought he'd better drop the subject altogether. Instead, he suggested they go inside because they might soon be able to start, and he walked toward the door. Dennis watched him, then followed.

The rabbi and cantor were already entering the building. Mr. Day walked in next, followed quickly by Greg Greene and Sol Cohen. Dave Smith, Sig Fleishhocker, Morty and Dennis made nine, and then they waited. Most of the men chatted to pass the time, but Dennis sat in his seat, quiet.

Suddenly two more arrived and the group was in business. One was Bill Fernberg, who planned to participate in the Shacharit minyan and then to wait for the rest of his family to arrive for their happy meeting with the rabbi. Phil Schwartz, who had been thinking about becoming a regular davener at the morning service, was the other. He came despite, or maybe because of, his last exchange with Dennis.

At their last meeting, Phil had tried telling his boss he was wrong, that the rabbi said Kaddish had nothing to do with the deceased, but Dennis had responded angrily that the rabbi was often wrong and he was this time, too.

When Phil arrived at the Sunday morning service, he expected a dirty look from the man he had argued with, but Dennis was still.

Each of the daveners put a kippah on his head and a tallit on his shoulders. Some wound tfillin straps on their arms and heads. Others didn't. Phil abstained because he thought tfillin were strange. Morty didn't because he thought phylacteries looked as funny as the word sounded. Dennis, who had not touched his since his Bar Mitzvah, now refused to use them because he associated tfillin with the rabbi and his old-fashioned ways. Greg Greene, however, was fully outfitted and began the morning service for the whole group.

When they finished forty minutes later, each man who had brought his own tallit folded it neatly into its zippered velvet pouch. The rest of the men, including Dennis, tossed the tallit they had used onto a rack at the back of the room. Every man who had used tfillin wrapped their straps around the boxes in which their cubes were stored and packed up the whole package in a second velvet bag. Each man worked at his own pace, Dennis noticed, and he had to look busy until his quarry was ready.

He watched as most of the men left before nine, but saw that Morty was still there talking, sounding out Bill about a woman's role in the service. Dennis ran out of excuses and slipped out the back door to wait. He knew that Bill was waiting for a meeting with the rabbi in his office, and they would probably start soon and talk for an hour. The Hebrew School teachers would not arrive for another fifty minutes or so. He knew that Joe was busy cleaning the kitchen for tonight's Sisterhood Chanukah party.

Dennis looked around the parking lot. Aside from cars belonging to Bill, the rabbi, Morty and himself, the lot was empty. Finally, Morty came out the door and headed to his car. Perfect.

"Morty," called Dennis, who was outside between the door and the parking lot, "I've been thinking about the women's matter and I had a few questions." He looked around to make sure no one else was there.

As they walked together to their cars, Dennis checked his watch. He definitely had more than a half hour, but could do with even less.

"Do you think women should be given full participation and be counted to the minyan or that they should participate and not be counted?" Dennis asked Morty as they stopped walking near his car. Dennis didn't really care if the question made sense or if Morty could answer it. The stalker wanted to set his target off balance.

"It depends on what similar congregations are doing," answered Morty, who was shifting his weight from one foot to the other and trying hard to focus on what Dennis meant. If Morty could win the president's support, he thought, the whole coup would be easier. "In some cases, the women want leadership positions alongside the men. In other cases, women want to lead a group of other women and be separate from the men." Morty went on for a while, expounding on how he felt it was important to bring gender roles at the Shul into line with prevailing changes in American thinking, but Dennis wasn't listening. He was watching the clock and building up his nerve.

Courage.

"Well, thanks. That was very interesting," Dennis finally said. He opened the unlocked car door for Morty, who was puzzled at the abrupt end to their chat. Morty chalked up the curt conclusion to the other man's quirks, got into the driver's seat, closed the door and started to unlock the rod over the steering wheel.

Important for the future.

Dennis had started to walk away but suddenly turned back to Morty and signaled for him to open the car window. "I had one more question," Dennis said, pulling the plastic bag out of his right pocket and leaning into the opening.

Take action.

Morty watched, wondering what it was that Dennis had fished out of his jacket and seemed to be pushing into the car between the driver's seat and the locked steering wheel. Suddenly, Morty felt a layer of heavy-duty plastic being held taut across his face and he panicked. Dennis held the plastic in place with his left hand and used his right to flip the other side of the bag over the headrest. He pulled the bag down over the bucket seat's back and yanked the drawstring, and the plastic closed tight around Morty's chest. The tight closure pinned the tops of the victim's arms in place inside it and locked the air out. Dennis wedged himself between the steering wheel lock and the driver, knowing that the rod would prevent the horn from sounding. He applied pressure to Morty's face and stared into the usurper's eyes as the victim ran out of air.

Morty tried pushing his attacker away, but found his arms were free only below the elbow and the plastic of the bag dulled his sense of touch. He fought back as much as he could, but Dennis had downward weight's gravity on his side. With a silent plea for mercy, the man on the list stared wide-eyed at the one keeping score. Morty turned blue and stopped struggling.

When the thrashing stopped, Dennis knew the deed was done. The moment was so intense, he could not hear anything above the ringing in his ears. The motion was so forceful, his heart's pounding blocked any sense of movement around him. The experience was so completely engrossing, it filtered out any awareness of what was going on around him.

Dennis stood up straight next to the Porsche and took a breath. He felt a searing pain in his chest, which he assumed was due to the pounding of his heart. He knew he had to reach back into the car to get the bag, but found the movement difficult and wondered why. He looked down. He saw blood begin to saturate his shirt and couldn't figure out where it was coming from.

"Dennis," Reeva said as her hand loosened on the Berreta. He looked over his left shoulder and saw his redheaded wife standing next to their son's car. "I found the list."

Brendan and Pamela were in the front seat, their mouths gaping. Reeva studied Dennis for a moment, then let the gun fall to the ground. Beyond them, Carey Fernberg and her kids stopped climbing out of their SUV to stare in the direction of the blast. Bill and the rabbi had heard the shot and raced out of the Shul door, but stopped short when they saw the blood.

"But it was for the minyan. It was for my mother," Dennis said plaintively to them all. "I was a Maccabee!" He focused on Rabbi London and they locked eyes, but Dennis was dead before he hit the pavement.

Laura was the first one to react. She ran to Morty's car and immediately removed the plastic that covered the victim's head. Carey followed close behind and the nurse worked with her daughter to loosen his clothes. Together they followed the sequence Laura had learned from Israeli emergency drills and aligned Morty on the ground to start CPR. Andrew called 911 on a cellphone and reached into the back of the car for a bottle of water in case the victim needed it. Bill went toward Reeva and carefully kicked the gun into the bushes, then ran over to Dennis to check for any signs of life. Rabbi London took charge of Reeva and her kids until the police came. And Joe Kripski redirected arriving Hebrew School traffic so emergency vehicles could access the crime scene.

Chapter 13

Perspective

As if nothing had happened to turn the world upside down, Joe Kripski stood at the entrance to the parking lot. This time, though, the custodian directed cars to side streets where parking might be available because the lot was already full.

Nearly every place was taken inside, too, even though it was a Monday morning and despite the fact that Joe had borrowed extra chairs from the funeral home next door.

Suzette Siegel sat in a middle row near the Smiths and the Fleishhockers and her husband Jon stood at the end of that row. Seeing the crowd, Dave and Sig gave up their seats next to their wives so that Celia Dubinsky and Helen Levine could sit down. The grieving grandmother and the Holocaust survivor had both known unfathomable grief and understood each other's tears. Dave and Sig moved to the back and stood with some of the men who came from Emek Emet with Rabbi Melamed.

Set in motion, the Orthodox congregation followed procedure. It provided three male volunteers for the Chevra Kadisha, and one of them stayed with the deceased from the time the police released the body to the Jewish Funeral Home until the interment, thus fulfilling the religious requirement that the dead not be left unattended. Additional Emek Emet members arrived for the funeral because they deemed it a religious obligation, but they also felt indebted to the deceased for donations and support over the years. For the most part, only the men came, knowing that (by their own custom) they would not sit next to any women and therefore would have to stand through the entire mixed-seating ceremony.

Four women from the Orthodox shul went directly to the mourners' residence. There, they worked with five Congregation Tefillah and four Temple Tikvah Sisterhood members to cover the mirrors, fill the kitchen with food, tidy up and otherwise work with the housekeeper to make everything at home ready for the youngsters. Then, some of the workers went home to wait for family members returning from the distressing event and to give them solace. The rest went to the Conservative Shul for the service.

Even though it would be an ordeal, a few Congregation Tefillah adult members brought their older children. The Kleins came with their son Aaron, who understood what it means to grow up with a shameful family history. Aaron positioned himself near Eli Fisch, who was next to his father, Ray. This was the first funeral the boys had ever attended, but having recently "come of age" and celebrated their Bar Mitzvahs, they felt they should be there. The Eisen boys joined them, grateful their father was in the hospital recovering from surgery, not in that box at the front of the room.

Remembering how it felt to know what was in the casket, the newly widowed Ida Stein seemed more broken up than at her own loss. It was a cumulative effect. She hadn't fully grieved yet, and it finally got to her. The shock of this death on top of the enormity of losing her own life partner was almost too much to bear.

Just starting their life together, Cliff Rosen and his bride Sophie were there partly to accompany Sylvia Cohen. Her husband Sol had been pressed into service for the funeral and she needed an escort. The joy of the recent wedding would return after the sadness of this day lifted. The newlyweds, even at this wrenching occasion, were still buoyant from their recent simcha. They were glad they had a chance to share happiness with their rabbi before they had to see him in this context.

Mel Rubin and Zev Wolfson understood this was a tough situation for the Shul's spiritual leader. Not only was Rabbi London on the scene for the tragic event, but he would have to officiate at the murderous man's funeral. After that, he would have to see the family through Shiva as well as Reeva's medical treatment and trial. On the other hand, the two men couldn't help but criticize the rabbi for being so out of touch with his congregants that he didn't see this tragedy coming. He should have done something, they agreed. The men decided that the next meeting of the Employment Review committee should praise the rabbi for this weekend's work but also scrutinize the spiritual leader's prior performance.

Phyllis Kimmel was also making mental notes for the next evaluation. Was this whole tragedy the rabbi's fault because he gave a mitzvah the wrong interpretation? she wondered. Shouldn't he have known his congregants and foreseen that this might happen? Phyllis wanted to sit with the often-critical Florence Fischman during the funeral to compare notes, but Emma understood that dynamic. The rebbetzin escorted them both into the sanctuary and sat between them. Mrs. London used the opportunity to demonstrate warmly compassionate support for them and for others during this congregational crisis.

In this instance, Phil and Matt Schwartz felt they were part of the congregation and sat nearby with their wives. Driving through the icy rain in Matt's car, the four of them had ruminated about how short life is and how suddenly things can change. The women had agreed it might be time for them to add a religious component to their lives, and since Phil regarded this rabbi so highly, this synagogue might be a good place to start. Matt had been more reluctant but was willing to go along. He knew his name had been on the list, and that made living a subject close to his heart. Once the four entered the synagogue and saw how quiet the crowd was, however, they stopped talking and found places.

Off in a corner, Larry Lansken seemed to be reflective and by himself. He only understood numbers, and this scenario didn't add up at all. He also wondered if his wife harbored violent thoughts toward him the way Reeva did about Dennis. Communication wasn't what it should be at the accountant's home with her or with their kids, and Larry resolved to make that situation better before the sum came up negative.

Apparently, results were positive for the Fernbergs, who were huddled together in another corner. They knew that they had been deeply involved in Dennis's last moments but, like so many people there that day, didn't know how much they really owed him. They would never know it was Dennis's donation, given in the spirit of truly righteous Tzedakah, that brought Laura back to her parents.

As an old friend of the dearly departed, fellow philanthropist and chairman of the Shul Board, the still-grieving Harold Harrison felt obligated to be there. He sat in the second row on the right side of the center aisle, next to Temple Tikvah's Rabbi Lee and its officers. At his other side sat Y. M. Pines, representing the same agencies he had on Thanksgiving and knowing that the deceased had been a major supporter of many of the OJO's philanthropic projects.

The hall's spaces between familiar faces were filled by members of the three shuls plus a few folks from the churches, many of them recalling that they had participated in the ecumenical program here just three weeks earlier. Drs. Obes and Frank sat among them, sheepishly wondering if they could have done more for this tragic family.

Rows were filling up quickly. Reeva's relatives and friends found each other and sat toward the back on the left. Somewhat behind that group, and as far to the right as possible so as to be out of their line of vision, four members of Dennis's family found spaces together. Three Cleaner Shine employees settled near them. Friends of the Shines didn't know what to say to whom, and they sat quietly, scattered around the room.

Places were designated for Brendan and Pamela in the front row, and they had asked Josh and Ahuva to sit near them. Even though the Shines saw the rabbi's children as younger and having less life experience, the London kids' fluency with ritual and their understanding of Jewish traditions somehow bolstered them at this difficult time.

The rest of the mourners' friends took rows farther back. Most of them were schoolmates and came in order to be supportive, but even the Jews among the teens didn't know what to expect because they had never been to a funeral before. What they saw depicted on TV and in movies – with music, flowers and an open casket – did not match the quiet and simple scene and closed coffin they saw before them. The young people didn't actually know very much about what had transpired the day before, except that there was a shooting. The two Shine kids had said they simply did not want to discuss it.

Pamela and Brendan didn't want to talk about it, but they remembered the scene clearly. After the confrontation, they had stood, shaking, near Brendan's car with their mother, and Rabbi London came over to help get everyone's emotions under control. Bill attended to the weapon and then to the man it killed.

The police and three ambulances arrived quickly. One of the medical teams continued the CPR Laura had started, inserted an intravenous drip and took the victim to East Belleridge General. Another worked more slowly, taking the dead man to the morgue. The third put restraints on Reeva, even though she was very still, and took her to the hospital's secure wing. Brendan's car was towed to the police station.

Avi stayed with the kids. The three of them left the crime scene with the police, one officer riding with Avi in the clergyman's vehicle and the kids traveling together in the squad car. The Shine youngsters spent most of the day in separate interrogation rooms at the station, where they dictated their narratives and answered questions. Suzette Zuckerman (Siegel) Esq. was there as the children's attorney.

Yes, Brendan and Pamela both said in their own words, they were aware for many years that their parents had an unhappy marriage. Yes, they knew their mother had a long history of emotional problems. Yes, they knew she was using the computer that morning because she had been feeling better and wanted to check her e-mail. Yes, that morning after their father left for the minyan, they heard several loud noises, but they didn't know what they were.

Yes, they knew there was a gun and bullets in the locked drawers of the desk. Yes, they were aware that their father usually took the loaded gun to work with him, but he left it locked in the desk at all other times, and they respected him for being so careful. Yes, they knew they weren't supposed to touch it. No, their father didn't let their mother have access to it, either. Yes, they knew that it had originally belonged to their mother, that she had bought it when she was younger and enjoyed shooting as a hobby.

No, they didn't know their mother had broken into the desk to get the weapon. No, they didn't know she had the Berreta with her. No, they didn't know why she was so eager to get to the Shul. No, she didn't say anything about the gun or the reason for the trip or the list – or much of anything else, for that matter – in the car; she just insisted they both be with her. No, they didn't know what the numbers on the chart meant. Did their mother see the list? Probably. Did she understand the chart? Maybe.

Avi answered the questions posed by the police officers about that morning's events, too. Then he got his first look at the printed chart from Dennis's pocket. The rabbi agreed that what Reeva had concluded was probably correct: It was certainly a hit list. But he didn't understand the logic behind the numbers any more than the interrogators did.

Rabbi London thought about the math on the list. What could $+ 1 + 1 = + 1$ mean to Dennis? It looked simple, like the kind of figuring that Emma taught to kids. Then he remembered Dennis's grief at his mother's death and his obsession to say Kaddish, as if it had some mystical power. Suddenly Avi understood. The list used a kind of twisted arithmetic, and he knew he had to share his insight.

Oy.

"Jewish custom puts nearly all our prayers in the plural," the clergyman explained to the police. "Unlike other religions, which put a premium on individual devotion and let their spiritual leaders accomplish holy tasks, most of our religious duties are done by individual Jews, and it's even better when they do it as a group. In the absence of a critical mass, or when conditions demand that we pray alone, we say the same prayers, but some parts are shortened or omitted." He paused.

The teacher was concerned that the people listening might not follow him, so he made it more specific.

"Dennis lost his mother six weeks ago," Rabbi London said. "He was fixated on the Jewish custom of saying Kaddish in her memory. He believed that, above all else, it was his duty to say it for a year and that her soul would somehow benefit from it and thereby become an angel in heaven."

"Don't Jews believe in heaven?" one interrogator asked.

"Many do," the rabbi explained, "and our philosophers discuss it, but Jewish customs are meant for *this* life, to help us appreciate the world God has given us and to teach us the way we should deal with our fellow creations. Whether or not there is an after-life, or what its nature is, I have no way of knowing," Avi stopped to ponder.

"I tried every way I could think of to explain to Dennis that the Kaddish prayer is just a public expression of faith," the spiritual leader continued, "that the prayer is said anyway, at every group service, whether there's a mourner in the crowd or not. An individual who has suffered a loss and is thinking about the dead is given the honor of leading prayers in order to make that person feel needed by the living." The rabbi thought some background information was necessary, but the officers looked at each other and wondered how long the explanation would actually be.

"Kaddish can be said, however, only if there are at least ten *men* present," Rabbi London explained. "Our synagogue, like most others, tries to provide the minimum of ten men, aside from any women who might want to be there, for services two or three times every day, but we sometimes have difficulty getting the basic ten."

Avi was stunned by the conclusion he was reaching. He was reluctant to put it into words, but he had to say it aloud for the sake of the investigation. "I think Dennis believed that the problem would be solved if there were more male mourners. In this case, if Morty died, his family would come to say Kaddish because of their own loss, thereby guaranteeing that Dennis could say it because of his. He must have worked out the numbers on the chart and taken steps toward implementing his conclusions."

The interrogators understood the logic, but wanted to be sure it really covered everything.

"Why was Jane Harrison on the list?" challenged one policeman, who wasn't sure the rabbi was right. "Did Dennis Shine kill her, too, according to your theory?"

"No," said Avi, not at all as sure as he sounded. "She was very sick and took too many pills. You could check his computer to see if the list was composed before or after she died, but I doubt that he did anything wrong there. I don't know why her name is on the list." Avi didn't mention that Dennis had been the last to visit her. No one asked. And he saw no reason to introduce an idea that would only compound people's sadness.

"So why do you think he started with Morty Fenn?" another officer wanted to know. "His name was not the first on the list. If you're right about Dennis's motivation, why not start with Stu Eisen, who I understand is the first live person's name on the list? The entry in the 'potential change' column was almost the same."

Yes, two or three ... the numbers were close, the clergyman noted. So why Morty? Why indeed not start with Stu?

"Getting to a man whose health is being carefully monitored is harder than cornering someone likely to be alone in a deserted parking lot," Avi reasoned aloud. "But beyond that, eliminating Morty in particular would solve other perceived problems, as well. First of all, Morty wanted to be the next president of the congregation, so he was a threat to Dennis's standing in the community. Second, as president, Morty would have pushed hard for modern politically-correct ideas such as gender equality in the synagogue and alternate lifestyle choices in Jewish society.

"Most of our members prefer a more traditional approach to these issues, so I don't think he would have realized a change," Rabbi London noted, "but Dennis was vehemently against those ideas. He perceived the possibility of Morty being president as a danger to what he saw as time-honored values."

With that, the interrogations were finished. Rabbi London's next task was to attend to the body and make sure there would be no autopsy. From a halachic point of view, an autopsy constituted the mutilation of a dead body and it was to be avoided unless secular law demanded it. From the police perspective, the procedure would only be routine if the cause of death were in question, and here it was clear what had happened. Avi called the Jewish Funeral Home and made sure they would take care of the deceased properly.

Then Rabbi London vouched for the children's character and, after promising they would all be reachable, took them home. Pamela and Brendan were glad to get to the sprawling apartment, where they could settle in with relatives from Reeva's side who planned to stay with them.

Avi went back to East Belleridge to make funeral arrangements and to pick a coffin. The Reform congregation had offered to foot the bill, and Rabbi London made sure the casket would be simple, in keeping with Jewish custom.

From there, he went to the Shul, where Joe had finished cleaning up outside and had started arranging tables and chairs downstairs for the night's Chanukah program. The rabbi explained to Joe what would be needed for the next day, stayed for Maariv and then went home. The party was mostly for families with young children, and he didn't think he'd be missed. He needed time to grapple with the day's events.

Also trying to make sense out of what had happened were the Fernbergs. Right after the tragedy, Bill had taken Andrew home where they could talk, and Carey and Laura had followed Morty to East Belleridge General Hospital. The Fenn family arrived soon afterward, and they were all greatly relieved an hour later when the doctors reported the patient was again able to breathe on his own. Damage to Morty's trachea was expected to heal and there was no apparent brain damage from the loss of oxygen. Carey and Laura rose to leave but were stopped by the Fenns, who hugged them with a lot of gratitude and very few words.

Early the next morning, between Shacharit and the funeral, Avi put his black fedora, gray scarf and Rabbi's Manual into the car and drove over to the hospital.

Morty was still in a fog, but something was on his mind. In a low, rasping voice, he asked the rabbi, "Why shouldn't shuls have equal roles for men and women?" It seemed like a strange question considering what Morty had been through, but Avi had no way of knowing it was a natural next thought from the last conversation the patient remembered having. The rabbi decided to answer as if nothing were unusual.

"Women are different from men, and their roles are of equal importance, but different," he said. "They aren't counted to a minyan because their body's requirements or their families' needs might present an urgency that can't be ignored, and their sudden absence would impact the viability of a group that depended on them. Women's prayers and their role in the life of the Jewish People, though, are just as valuable as the men's."

Avi thought his philosophical answer had put the traumatized man to sleep, but with eyes closed, Morty hoarsely whispered through his drugged fog, "What about legal, uh, unions? You know, men-men or women-uh …"

A lawyer is a lawyer, even when half asleep, thought Rabbi London. "Such relationships are forbidden by the Torah, so we can't sanction them. It's like eating pork. American law decides it's okay for Americans, so it's legal, but halachah makes it illegal for Jews. Some people do it anyway, but that doesn't make it kosher." Like most good Jews, Morty dozed off while the rabbi was talking.

The doctors agreed that the patient should stay in the hospital for a few more days. The Fernbergs promised to visit later that afternoon, after they were finished at the Shul. Morty's family, of course, would be with him all day. They certainly had no intentions of going to the funeral.

When Avi left Morty, the rabbi went to visit Reeva. For that day and probably many more, she remained confined to the security wing of the hospital, where she seemed more at peace than she had been in many years. Maybe it was because she could finally envision a future for herself and her children that would be of their own choosing. Perhaps she finally felt released from her husband's emotional prison. Or maybe it was just the medication.

Avi didn't know the source of her peace, but he wanted to tell her the good news, that Suzette had promised her firm would represent Reeva at the upcoming sanity hearing and stand by her and her children at any subsequent trial. But Reeva was sleeping and the rabbi had a lot to do at Shul, so he left her a note and went on to his office.

Rabbi London found a stack of condolence messages on his desk that he had to sort through. Expressions of consolation came from Minister Thorn, Father Dehaney and Imam Shukran. Avi made a mental note to read them aloud or reference them during the service.

Other messages had been e-mailed from the leaders of a wide variety of charitable organizations that Dennis had supported. One came from the OJO, which had benefited in large measure from Dennis's generosity. Another was from Rabbi Bavli in Atlantic City, who said he had specific recollections of both Dennis and Reeva and that his prayers were with both of them. Avi made sure all the notes eventually would become the property of Dennis's children so that, someday, they could cherish the memory of their father's earlier accomplishments.

Dennis's devotion and charity drew a large assemblage to the funeral, and the crowd never would have fit into the Jewish Funeral Home. Furthermore, Pamela and Brendan decided it would be appropriate for the burial to be from the Shul, where their father had spent so much of his life and, finally, his death. They didn't want words of praise, however, regardless of his long list of good deeds.

"My father's death was his own fault," Pamela insisted. "My mother was always saying he was going to kill her, and we thought she was crazy! Especially me. Yesterday morning, I figured she finally snapped. Brendan and I were both glad she wanted to go for a ride to find him because we thought he'd know what to do. Later at the police station, when I saw the list in black and white, I finally believed her. She must have found the list on the computer yesterday morning when she went to check her e-mail and went ballistic when she realized her name was on it."

"Yeah, the list. Pamela's right. That's what he was doing all along," added Brendan. "First, Dad convinced all of us that Mom was nuts. Then, he bought me a car to make sure that the college I chose was in driving distance so he could watch me every minute. He made Pamela into Mom's watchdog and nursemaid so the kid couldn't have a life." Brendan paused. "Yeah. We didn't know Mom would shoot him, but I'm glad she did. I'm glad I drove my car to help her find him. And, even though I didn't understand what she planned to do, I'm glad she did it."

Rabbi London told them the same thing he had said to Laura Fernberg in Israel and Aaron Klein on Shabbat: that the Ten Commandments insists we honor our parents even when it's counter-intuitive, that there might have been just one thing they said or did that made their children better people.

Pamela and Brendan understood what he was saying, but they weren't ready to agree. They started arguing and only stopped when the rabbi told them it was Chanukah.

"So?" they asked.

"Jewish law does not permit a eulogy on Chanukah. Praise of the recently departed might, after all, make mourners cry, and sadness is contrary to the spirit of the festival," he told them.

They both said they wouldn't cry anyway, but knowing the service would be short made it easier to face. They calmed down and reluctantly followed the rabbi's instructions.

As tradition dictated and Rabbi London directed, Brendan and Pamela ripped a corner of their clothing as a sign of mourning, entered the sanctuary and sat down in the front row. Josh and Ahuva sat with them.

Standing nearby were Sol Cohen, Greg Greene, Isaac Iskilovetzky and Mr. Day. They had witnessed many of life's pleasures and tragedies, and pondered them as they waited to do their unhappy tasks. With all his illnesses, Sol knew he was lucky to have lived long enough to see his divorced daughter remarry. Greg was grateful, too, because – unlike his relatives in Nazi Germany – he had survived and lived to enjoy his granddaughter's Bat Mitzvah. Isaac realized how fortunate he was to have friends who saw him through the deterioration and recent loss of his life partner.

As usual, Mr. Day kept the facts of his sorrows to himself, but the day's tragedy was stirring up a distant memory. The old man remembered being young, watching a Nazi force his first wife to shoot their baby son, then witnessing the sadist shooting her. His wife's screams haunted him and, with the Shine calamity, raised the perpetual question: How can anyone believe there's a God when such terrible things happen? His features, however, did not betray his thoughts, and he remained his stone-faced self.

The four minyan regulars were ready to do their jobs as pallbearers along with two stunned remote relatives of Dennis Shine. Together, they would perform the mitzvah of accompanying the deceased to his final resting place.

The cause of the community's chaos was in his plain wood coffin, covered with a black velvet drape, at the front of the Shul, and Rabbi London would have to put the whole picture into perspective.

When Cantor Goldberg was finished chanting the appropriate Psalms, the spiritual leader rose and stood at the lectern. Avi looked at the upturned faces of his congregants, full of hope that he could lead them out of this spiritual morass.

"Today is the first day of Chanukah and so there will be no eulogy for Dennis, but it gives us no pleasure to have to deal with sadness when we should be focusing on joy," began the rabbi.

"On Chanukah, we are supposed to be grateful for the success of Jewish rebels who fought for religious freedom more than two millennia ago. We are joyous over the rededication of our

Temple in Jerusalem, and we mark the triumph with candles that represent a miracle. Like the oil in that menorah, our people have survived longer than anyone expected, and that is a cause for celebration. But today, when we should be radiant with the light of the first candle, happiness is hard to come by because grief has intruded.

"Was sorrow part of the Chanukah story, too? Let's place its events in time."

Laura recognized from their stop at Jerusalem's Western Wall her rabbi's way of reviewing the millennia.

"The record of our earliest history is contained in the weekly Torah portion. The incidents the Torah describes – about Abraham, Isaac, Jacob, Joseph, the Twelve Tribes and the subsequent Exodus from Egyptian bondage – all happened at least thirty centuries ago. The story of the Maccabees and the restored Temple in Jerusalem was more recent, about twenty-two centuries ago. The Temple was destroyed about twenty centuries ago.

"Since then, we often got our role in human history right and were a 'shining light unto the nations.' Sometimes, unfortunately, we made mistakes."

Rabbi London had said something similar to Eli Fisch and Aaron Klein at their Bar Mitzvahs, and hearing it again made them more comfortable about being at the funeral.

"The years gave us lots of time to practice, but we still have a lot to get right. Perhaps that's why we begin every Maariv service with 'Vhu rachum yichaper avon vlo yashchis,' hoping that God will be forgiving and not destroy us when we make a mistake.

"Our people made mistakes even long ago. The Chanukah story, for example, as great as it was, had a downside.

"Two centuries before the Temple's destruction, the Maccabee brothers led a rebellion against religious oppression and won, restoring Jewish worship in Jerusalem. They achieved much and we honor them, and their leadership has been a model for us through the ages.

"But their descendants succumbed to the lure of supremacy. Power itself became the end game, not serving God or leading our people or seeking loftier behavior. And it was this lust for supremacy that became the downfall of the Hasmonean family.

"The power that grows out of being sure you are right – of being convinced you are holier than the next person, of being certain that your cause is truer than any other – breeds arrogance. We see it happen globally, when the followers of one religion persecute another. We see it locally, when the members of one house of worship shun those of another. We see it privately, when one person dominates another. We are tempted to use power to accomplish our own goals, but history itself should convince us to weigh our wishes carefully.

"We have to view our actions in the context of the values our tradition teaches us: to love our fellow beings, to improve the world, and most of all, to choose life. And we must remember that, two centuries after the Maccabees, the Temple finally was destroyed. And the loss of our religious core was traditionally traced to one overwhelming problem: baseless hatred.

"Our tradition praises the success of the Maccabees in their former times and the important victory they achieved."

The rabbi paused to let the lump in his throat settle.

"Let's remember to rejoice in the light this holiday was meant to bring us and to be proud of the accomplishments of earlier years."

Rabbi London looked at his flock and hoped they understood. Then he addressed Brendan and Pamela in the traditional way, saying, "May God comfort you among the mourners of Zion and Jerusalem."

Avi signaled the mourners and their escorts, and the pall-bearers moved the casket down the center aisle to the waiting hearse.

Epilogue

The day had been draining, but that was not what made this episode so unusual in the life of a pulpit rabbi. Avi had officiated at trying funerals before and had been at the cemetery on other cold, snowy days. What made the difference was that this day had exhausted the whole London family and the entire community.

"The funeral went well," Emma reassured Avi while she arranged the food in disposable trays. Potato latkes and breaded turkey cutlets were ready but had to stay warm until the Chanukah candles were finished burning, so she loosely covered the pans with aluminum foil, put them in the oven and checked that the setting was on low. She did it all by rote, and the routine of making supper allowed her to utter the encouraging comment, but her mind was struggling with something else. She was trying to remember if there was anything in this world that she or her husband could have done to avoid the anguish and heartache the Shines all suffered.

Her husband was grilling himself along the same lines, but he responded to her remark. "Thanks, but there was so much I couldn't say," Avi explained as he set the table. He thought about Dennis's secret mitzvah that reunited Laura with her parents but that also brought her to his victim's aid. Avi considered the many children, like those in Atlantic City, who would get a superior Jewish education because of Dennis's efforts. So many people – Jews and Gentiles in America and around the world – would benefit from his generosity, and none of them would ever know.

Avi wondered, too, about who shared responsibility for the tragedy. He thought back to his Talmud class. If your ox gores another … If your gun kills … Who is liable if the situation could have been avoided?

"Brendan is amazing." Josh's comment interrupted his father's contemplation. The boy was spreading aluminum foil on the living room end table to protect the furniture from the soon-to-be-melting wax of the Chanukah candles. In another few minutes, the family would light the chanukiyah near the window so the flames could be seen by passersby. In that way, they would publicize the miracle, as was the custom.

"He's only a few months older than me," Josh continued, "but he has really taken over. Brendan says Suzette told him that his mother is going to get some psychiatric help, which she probably always needed. She might have to serve some time, too, but she'll be home pretty soon.

"Suzette also told him that he and Pamela would have a hearing, too, as accessories to a crime," Josh added. "But considering everything, they would probably not be in any big trouble. Brendan is trying to protect his sister from all the publicity, too. And, he decided to apply to colleges in New York so he can be home a lot to see her and their mother. Boy, I don't know how he does it."

"Pamela is having a hard time," Ahuva muttered as she put Chanukah candles in the first two places on the right and sealed them in with melted wax. "She tries to be a friend to her mother, but she, like, can't sleep. She keeps thinking about her own mother killing her own father. I don't know how anybody could deal with that, y'know? And she's worried about a temporary custody hearing while her Mom is recovering because she and her brother are both under eighteen. Brendan will leave for college soon, and Pamela doesn't know where to go."

Everything was ready and it was dark, so the Londons gathered around the chanukiyah. In Hebrew, they recited the blessings, lit the candles and sang some songs. One was about the miracle the candles represent and how God saved the Jewish People long ago at this time of year. Another was the same Maoz Tzur that was part of the Thanksgiving event.

Then they gave each other presents. Josh and Ahuva got some music they wanted that Emma had ordered and the software they needed that Avi had picked up at the mall. Emma received a book on Israel that had just been published because her husband found it on a pre-Christmas sale table while he was shopping. From his wife and children, Avi got a waterproof carrying bag for his tallit and tfillin that would protect their velvet bags when he had to go to a minyan in bad weather.

As they kissed each other, shared hugs and laughed together, each one was thinking the same thing. Next year, their lives would be different.

Josh would be finishing high school and visiting colleges to see which he wanted most of the choices his parents wouldn't veto.

Ahuva would be starting high school and would be increasingly focused on her social life and peer approval.

Emma wondered if the future could ever be happy again in East Belleridge for her and Avi, considering the tragedy that they went through with this congregation. Furthermore, being in this pulpit or in any other one was not easy. Congregants were always full of criticism, and friends and family felt very far away. She would have to talk to Avi about it, but not now, while the Chanukah candles were still burning.

Avi was depressed to think that something he had said, or failed to say, might have made a person in a teetering mental state fall in the wrong direction. It's possible he failed to explain some tradition or philosophy as well as he should have. Perhaps this was not the right profession for him at all.

A change would mean a new lifestyle in a different home, but maybe this was the right time to discuss it. He'd love to see the new day school in Atlantic City and find out if they needed an instructor. Teaching teens is something he'd really enjoy. A vacation was long overdue, too, and going to the oceanside resort just to get a whiff of sea air would be refreshing.

Or maybe they should consider Israel for a vacation or a new career. They have family there, too, and the Holy Land has beautiful beaches and several good choices for their children's education. Emma could teach math there, but Avi wasn't sure what job he could find in a country that already spoke Hebrew and breathed Jewish history and customs. He would have to talk to Emma about it, but not now, when they were almost ready to sit down to a Chanukah meal together.

After supper, the rabbi went to daven at the Shul. Several people came to the minyan because they were mourners, but others came, too. A few men who were there simply wanted to daven. Some women felt attending would make them feel more a part of the religious scene. Several kids came because they couldn't shake the trauma that they had witnessed people their own age go through. All of those who came were driven by the understanding that praying together was important for the community. The total in attendance was many times the ten that were needed.

What was left of the Shine family lit holiday candles at their Northwood apartment, where they were observing the week of Shiva. There was a minyan there, too, and Pamela and Brendan honored their father's memory by facing east toward Jerusalem and saying Kaddish, publicly proclaiming their faith.

GLOSSARY

Afarsimon – An Israeli winter fruit, also known as a Fuyu persimmon, looking like an orange tomato and tasting sweet like a peach.

Bar/Bat Mitzvah – The age at which a boy (thirteen) or a girl (twelve) becomes religiously responsible.

BCE – A Jewish way of counting the years using Before the Common Era instead of BC (which means before Christ) and CE for Common Era instead of AD (meaning year of our lord).

Beersheva – A city at the northern end of the Negev desert, mentioned in the Bible as a stop on Abraham's travels. Also spelled Beersheba.

Beit Din – A court of three rabbis convened to validate a Jewish legal matter.

Birkat Hamazon – The Hebrew prayer after meals.

Brit or Bris – A religious circumcision, usually done when a boy is eight days old. Also one of the requirements for male conversion. See: Tipat Dahm.

Burekas – Triangular flaky-dough pastry, usually filled with potato, vegetables or cheese, popular in Israel.

CE – Common Era. See BCE.

Challah – A braided bread, often with seeds on top or raisins within, customarily eaten at the main meals of a Shabbat or festival.

Chanukah – A minor Jewish holiday in December, lasting eight days, that commemorates the successful rebellion of the Maccabees against the ancient Syrian-Greeks in 165 BCE and the rededication of the Temple in Jerusalem.

Chanukiyah – Hebrew for Chanukah menorah.

Chazzan – Hebrew for cantor, the one who leads prayers.

Chevra Kadisha – A group of Jewish volunteers that would cleanse the body of the deceased and wrap it in a shroud for burial.

Cholent – Yiddish for a slow-cooking bean-and-beef stew, a dish that simmers all Friday night and is eaten hot on Shabbat, when cooking is prohibited.

Daven – Yiddish for pray.

Dreidel – Yiddish for a four-sided top with the Hebrew letters that stand for "a great miracle happened there;" in Israel, "here."

Goyim – Plural for "goy," a Hebrew word meaning nation that originally referred to the People of Israel. The plural became popularly used to mean non-Jews, or Gentiles, sometimes but not always in the derogatory sense of "others."

Halachah – Jewish law. Halachic: according to Jewish law.

Harei At – The first few words of the Hebrew formula said by a groom to his bride that makes a Jewish marriage binding.

Havdallah – A short ceremony, using a candle, wine and spices, that marks the end of Shabbat or a holiday.

High Holidays – Rosh Hashanah and Yom Kippur, which start the Jewish year, usually in September.

Kashrut – The laws of eating kosher.

Kaddish – The public proclamation of faith in God, said in Hebrew and Aramaic between sections of the regular Jewish services. Saying Kaddish: The obligation of a mourner, in memory of a deceased close relative, to proclaim faith publicly during group prayer.

Keffiyah – An Arab head scarf.

Ketubah – Jewish marriage contract.

Kibbutz – An Israeli cooperative settlement, usually agricultural. Kibbutzniks: Members of a kibbutz.

Kiddush – The blessing over wine. Also: Refreshments provided after a religious service.

Kippah – Hebrew for a skull cap worn by Jewish men for religious reasons. Plural: Kippot. Yiddish: Yarmulke.

Kohen, Levi or Yisrael – Status of a man being called up to the Torah, derived from the role of his direct biblical ancestors.

Kotel – Hebrew for the Western (Wailing) Wall in the Old City of Jerusalem.

Latkes – Yiddish for pancakes, usually made of potato and fried in oil, that are traditional on Chanukah.

Maariv – The evening service.

Maccabees – Members of the Jewish Hasmonean family that rebelled against religious tyranny. See: Chanukah.

Maoz Tsur – Hebrew for Rock of Ages, a song popular on Chanukah.

Mazal Tov – Hebrew for good luck, but often used as congratulations. Yiddish: Mazel tov.

Menorah – A seven-branched, oil-burning candelabra, used in the ancient Temple in Jerusalem, now the national symbol of the State of Israel. For Chanukah, adapted to eight branches and called a Chanukiyah, with an extra candle (or wick in a pot of oil) for the one that lights the rest.

Mentsch – Yiddish for a man, an accolade for a person who acts graciously.

Mi Sheberach – The Hebrew prayer said after reading parts of the Torah to honor a loved one or to ask for the recovery of a sick person.

Mikveh – A ritual bath.

Mincha – The afternoon service.

Minyan – A quorum of ten, traditionally only men, needed for Jewish group prayer and required for the mourner to say Kaddish. Also: Any service that requires the minimum.

Mitzvah – Hebrew for a commandment, but often meaning the right thing to do, as dictated by Jewish tradition and laws. Plural: Mitzvot.

Mohel – A rabbi who performs ritual circumcisions, thus sealing the Jewish covenant with God.

Motzi – The blessing over bread said at the beginning of a meal.

Rebbetzin – Yiddish for the rabbi's wife.

Rosh Hashanah – The Jewish New Year, a two-day holiday, usually in September. See: High Holidays.

Ruggelach – Small, sweet, rolled-up pastries filled with cheese, jam, cinnamon or chocolate.

Shabbat – The Jewish Sabbath, lasting from before sunset Friday to after sunset Saturday.

Sabra – A cactus prickly pear. Also: A nickname for native-born Israelis because they are considered to be prickly on the outside but sweet on the inside.

Shacharit – The morning service.

Shakshuka – Eggs poached in tomato sauce, an Israeli dish.

Shehecheyanu – The Hebrew prayer said at special occasions, giving thanks to have lived to see that day.

Shiva – A week of mourning following a burial.

Shma Yisrael – The beginning of the central Jewish declaration of monotheism.

Shmini Atzeret and Simchat Torah – Two adjoining holiday days, three weeks after Rosh Hashanah.

Shtender – Yiddish for lectern.

Shul – Yiddish for synagogue.

Simcha – Hebrew for happiness or a happy occasion.

Succor – Old English word meaning assistance in time of distress.

Sukkot – Feast of Tabernacles, a week-long festival for which the first two days are observed as holidays, two weeks after Rosh Hashanah.

Tallit – A rectangular shawl, having long fringes on the four corners, worn by men during morning prayers.

Tfillin – Accessories (traditionally a man's) for daily morning prayer: Scripture-filled boxes held in their positions by straps applied to the head and one arm. English: Phylacteries.

Talmud – The major compendium of Jewish law, compiled in post-biblical times, which still forms the basis of Jewish legal decisions and provides guidelines to modern legal systems.

Tipat Dahm – Hebrew for a drop of blood, usually achieved by a pin prick, required of a male convert who previously underwent a non-Jewish circumcision.

Torah – The Five Books of Moses, read in the synagogue from a parchment scroll. Sometimes, meaning all five books plus Prophets and Writings (which includes Psalms), together known as the Hebrew Bible, and even later books, such as the Talmud.

Tzedakah – Help for the needy, like charity, coming from the Hebrew word meaning righteous.

Tzitzit – A short poncho-like prayer garment with long fringes on the four corners, often worn all day by a man between his undershirt and shirt and used for prayer instead of a tallit.

V'zot haTorah – The first few words of the statement made by a congregation upon putting away a Torah scroll after reading it during a service in the synagogue.

Yahrtzeit – Yiddish for the anniversary of a death.

Yarmulke – Yiddish for a skull cap worn by Jewish men for religious reasons. Hebrew: Kippah.

Yeshiva – A day school of Jewish learning.

Yizkor – The memorial service said in the synagogue on major holidays.

Yom Kippur – The Day of Atonement, a 25-hour fast and holiday, ten days after Rosh Hashanah. See: High Holidays.

Printed in the United States
106400LV00001B/404/A